LEOPOLD WARNDORF

HENRY NEVILLE SUMMERSETT was baptised on June 23, 1774 at Hadleigh in the county of Suffolk. Nothing is known of Summersett's early life except that he was a self-taught man with a love of literature and the plays of Shakespeare. When Summersett's father, an innkeeper in Ipswich by profession, was declared bankrupt in 1792, the 17-year-old apparently set out for London to try his hand at writing in order to support his parents. His first novel, *The Offspring of Russell*, was published anonymously by the Minerva Press in 1794 and is an impressive debut written in the popular pseudo-historical Gothic vein. Two more novels followed, both published by the Minerva Press, *The Fate of Sedley* (1795) and *Probable Incidents; or, Scenes in Life* (1797); the latter was the first to feature his name on the title page. *Aberford* (1798) was something of a departure from the first three novels, being a short picaresque novella featuring a large amount of Summersett's poetry.

Three major Gothic novels followed, *Mad Man of the Mountain* (1799), *Jaqueline of Olzeburg; or Final Retribution* (1800), and *Martyn of Fenrose; or, The Wizard and the Sword* (1801), which boast some of Summersett's most memorable characters and gripping plots of damnation, revenge, murder and unspeakable horror. During this productive period, Summersett also wrote two novels of individuals struggling against adversity in a hostile world, *Leopold Warndorf* (1800) and *The Worst of Stains* (1804). Critics had always been dismissive of Summersett's novels, and it appears that he left London after 1804 to pursue other literary ventures, publishing volumes of poetry and penning plays that were performed in provincial theatres. Summersett's final novel, *All Sorts of Lovers; or, Indiscretion, Truth, and Perfidy* (1811), perhaps his best, was published by the Minerva Press and is a humorous and detailed study of life at the start of the nineteenth century.

Summersett's later life remains a mystery. Archival research reveals that a Henry Neville Summersett married at Spalding in Lincolnshire in 1813; however, his date of birth is listed as 1778. There are also no records to indicate Summersett's year of death and place of burial, although in 1818 he appears to be residing in Nottinghamshire and working at the Southwell theatre.

STEVE ORMAN is an Associate Lecturer in the Department of English & Language Studies at Canterbury Christ Church University. His research interests lie in the early modern period and the long eighteenth century.

By Henry Summersett

The Offspring of Russell (1794)
The Fate of Sedley (1795)*
Probable Incidents, or, Scenes in Life (1797)
Aberford, or, What You Will (1798)*
Mad Man of the Mountain (1799)*
Leopold Warndorf (1800)*
Jaqueline of Olzeburg, or, Final Retribution (1800)
Martyn of Fenrose, or, The Wizard and the Sword (1801)*
The Worst of Stains (1804)*
Happy at Last, or, Sigh No More, Ladies: A Comedy (1805)
Maurice, the Rustic and other Poems (1805)
All Sorts of Lovers, or, Indiscretion, Truth and Perfidy (1811)
Happiness in Retirement: A Poem (1812)
Ferdinand, the Slave of Passion (1818)

* Available or forthcoming from Valancourt Books

LEOPOLD WARNDORF.

A NOVEL.

BY

HENRY SUMMERSETT,

AUTHOR OF

THE MAD MAN OF THE MOUNTAIN, &c. &c. &c.

Imogen.	Why did you throw me from you?
	Think that you are upon a rock, and now
	Throw me again!
Posthumus.	Hang there, like fruit, my soul,
	Till the tree perish!

CYMBELINE.

EDITED AND WITH AN INTRODUCTION AND NOTES BY
STEVE ORMAN

VALANCOURT BOOKS

Leopold Warndorf by Henry Summersett
First published London: William Lane, 1800
First Valancourt Books edition 2013
First paperback edition 2014

Introduction and notes © 2013 by Steve Orman
This edition © 2013 by Valancourt Books

Published by Valancourt Books, Richmond, Virginia
Publisher & Editor: James D. Jenkins
http://www.valancourtbooks.com

All Valancourt Books publications are printed on acid free paper
that meets all ANSI standards for archival quality paper.

ISBN 978-1-934555-79-8 (*trade cloth*)
ISBN 978-1-941147-06-1 (*trade paperback*)
Also available as an electronic book.

Set in Adobe Caslon 11/14.3

CONTENTS

EDITOR'S DEDICATION

This book is dedicated to my family, who never stopped believing; Maria, for her love and patience; and Greg—although I can't write a book with you, I can edit one for you to read.

INTRODUCTION[1]

IT IS regrettable that a writer as diverse and entertaining as Henry Summersett has fallen into obscurity. Perhaps some of this obscurity can be accounted for by the unfortunate lack of extant biographical information surrounding the author. Henry Neville Summersett was baptised on the 23rd June, 1774 at Hadleigh, in the county of Suffolk. Summersett's mother, Hannah, was born in Ipswich, Suffolk in 1749. It is possible that Summersett's father, also named Henry, was baptised at St. George's, Hanover Square, Middlesex, in 1744.

Hannah Summersett died on the 17th December, 1802, aged 53, and the information is recorded in Benjamin Page Grimsey's *Monograph on the Parish of St. Nicholas, Ipswich*, published in 1891. Grimsey notes that in the parish record of her burial, she is called "Somerset".[2] Inconsistencies in the surviving parish records with regard to the family surname make the task of sourcing factual information about the Summersetts difficult, but it is worth noting that Henry Summersett's name on the title-pages of his publications always retains the same spelling of the family surname.

There are no surviving records that indicate that Summersett received a university education, and as James D. Jenkins has previously observed in his edition of *Martyn of Fenrose*, Summersett appears to have been a self-taught man. It is common for Summersett to lament in several of his works his own lack of education as a means of defending his work from hostile critics.

The author of *Leopold Warndorf* may be the Henry Summersett recorded in a marriage registered in 1804 at St. Stephen's

---

[1] As this Introduction reveals details concerning the plot of *Leopold Warndorf*, readers may wish to read it after they have finished reading the novel.

[2] p. 134.

in Ipswich. Archival research also reveals that a Henry Neville Summersett married at Spalding in Lincolnshire in 1813, however, his date of birth is listed as 1778. This latter date may simply be an error in the register, as this would mean that the author was just 16 years of age at the time of publication of his first novel, an unlikely but not impossible event. I have been unable to locate Summersett's year of death and place of burial, although in the late 1810s he appears to be residing in Nottinghamshire.

What we can say with certainty is that Summersett was a prolific and speedy writer, writing in all three canonical literary genres, and that his work, ignored for over two hundred years, has much to say about the psychology of emotions and the stresses of late eighteenth-century and early nineteenth-century life. Summersett's rich and wide-ranging talents were first displayed in the historical romance *The Offspring of Russell* (1794). Published anonymously, the novel demonstrates that at just twenty years of age Summersett could craft an engaging and coherent narrative, complete with a diverse assortment of characters. *The Fate of Sedley* (1795), Summersett's second novel, which survives in just two known copies, one in the University of Pennsylvania library and the other at Ursinus College, was not well received by critics, who took a strong dislike to the act of suicide at the novel's finale. Summersett's third novel, *Probable Incidents; or, Scenes in Life* (1797), was published in two volumes and was the first of Summersett's works to feature his name on the title page.

The short, comic picaresque novel entitled *Aberford* followed, and was published in 1798. The novel, with its subtitle of *What You Will*, immediately identifies Summersett's indebtedness to William Shakespeare, a figure who would influence the entirety of Summersett's literary writings.[1] The novel, by far the most light-hearted of Summersett's fiction, follows the exploits of Mr. Aberford as he returns from France to his home in Yarmouth, and then on a foot-voyage to London. The novel, complete with

---

[1] Summersett's title recalls Shakespeare's *Twelfth Night; or, What You Will* (1601).

hilarious comic scenes, including an early exploit where Aberford accosts a fish-wife and is slapped in the face by one of her
"slimy flounders"[1] and a mock literary criticism of Shakespeare's
character of Richard III,[2] also encourages one to interpret events
as a semi-biographical account of the life of the young author,
with Aberford vocalising his frustrations at finding that writing
poetry can be difficult when you are having an off day. Despite
the rich vein of comedy that runs through *Aberford*, the novel
highlights Summersett's interest in the contemporary issues of
his day, with an extended commentary on the barbarity of slav-
ery and a plea for equality amongst people, regardless of their
race.

Mad Man of the Mountain (1799) showcases many of Summersett's favourite topics that frequently appear in his works
including the wronged lover who descends into madness. In the
character of Francesco Roncorone, Summersett created one of
the most exquisite and complex protagonists in late eighteenth-
century fiction, a figure who sits perfectly amongst the Romantic
sensibilities of Percy Bysshe Shelley and George Gordon Byron
and proves that Summersett was a modern writer, responding
to and challenging contemporary understandings of the individual in his day and age. Published in the same year as *Leopold
Warndorf*, the short novel *Jaqueline of Olzeburg; or, Final Retribution, A Romance* (1800), does not bear Summersett's name on
the title page. This sensationalist piece culminates in the terrifying description of Jaqueline's judgment before God and her
subsequent descent into the depths of hell and contains some of
Summersett's most powerful prose.

Many of the themes and issues stemming from *Leopold Warndorf*, discussed below, are central to Summersett's next novel,
Martyn of Fenrose; or, The Wizard and the Sword (1801). Like its
predecessor, *Martyn of Fenrose* features issues that are pressing to
Summersett: children with absent parents, the spectre of illegiti-

[1] *Aberford* p. 15.
[2] *Aberford* pp. 43–45.

macy, and the powerful bonds made by young people in adversity. Like Leopold in *Leopold Warndorf*, the titular and mysterious Martyn is initially absent from the original story, only to enter with spectacular consequences.

The Worst of Stains (1804) survives in just one copy housed in the massive Corvey library in Germany and is one of Summersett's most shocking novels, which features in the early part of the narrative a young woman reduced to insanity and suicide, but not before she has attacked her own infant with a pair of scissors. Evidently aware that such a moment may cause offence, Summersett writes in his preface that he aims to create realistic and believable characters, and that each of the passions that rules the body imposes its own form of language upon the individual. The lover "uses the sweetest words" whereas madness is "more horrible than the wolf that howls amid the darkness of night". In the same preface, Summersett also defends his writing style from the critics who savaged his works as blasphemous when reviewing *Martyn of Fenrose*. Written just over a year after the death of his mother, *The Worst of Stains* further heightens the importance of Summersett as a novelist, challenging the boundaries of what fiction *should* contain in attempts to create realistic characters.

Maurice, the Rustic (1805), Summersett's first printed collection of poems, survives in just two known copies. One is housed in the New York Public Library and the other at Indiana University. The Preface to the printed volume displays Summersett as a tortured individual, full of self-doubt and ashamed to consider himself a poet. Such claims of unworthiness are frequently made in many prefaces by poets, dramatists, and novelists alike, but Summersett is unusual in the genuine vulnerability that submitting his work for publication seems to have occasioned. Summersett reveals that he has often asked himself the question: "Ought an obscure *uneducated* man to commence Author?" and his reported lack of learning ensures that he is continually plagued with notions that he is unfit to embark upon a literary career. These are no mock stock self-deprecatory statements;

Summersett writes of the "painful mortification" that he felt frequently in his lifetime, leading him to exclaim: "Had I been less
ignorant, I must have been more happy!" Such statements do
much to explain Summersett's frequent authorial intervention
into his own novels to justify his own reasons for writing of a
particular event or in a particular fashion, such as the times when
Summersett interrupts his own narrative in *Leopold Warndorf*,
discussed below, to beg the reader for forgiveness for his own
narrative weaknesses. Such fears of literary dimness are often
revealing of Summersett's own tortuous personality, with the
spectre of learned men and women apparently haunting Summersett, waiting to chastise and mock his uneducated exploits.[1]

Happy at Last; or, Sigh No More, Ladies (1805), which also
reveals its debt to Shakespeare's play *Much Ado about Nothing*
in its title, was seemingly Summersett's first play for the theatre.
The title page confirms that the play was performed at the Theatre Royal in Kendal on March 13th, and describes the author of
the comedy as "of the Kendal, Ulverstone, Harrogate, Beverly,
Richmond, Ripon, and Whitby Theatres". Whether Summersett wrote plays, or was involved in management of these
theatres, is a question for the future. The next publication that
we can positively attribute to Summersett is *All Sorts of Lovers;
or, Indiscretion, Truth, and Perfidy* (1811), possibly Summersett's
final novel, which survives in just one copy housed in the Corvey
library.

---

[1] This is despite the fact that John Locke had suggested in his essay *Some
Thoughts Concerning Education* (1693) that learning Latin and Greek was not
the be-all and end-all for a young man who wished to consider himself a
scholar: "When I consider what a-do is made about a little Latin and Greek,
how many years are spent in it, and what a noise and business it makes to no
purpose, I can hardly forbear thinking that the parents of children still live in
fear of the school-master's rod" (p. 114). Locke further states that, "I imagine
you would think him a very foolish fellow, that should not value a virtuous or
a wise man infinitely before a great scholar" (p. 115). In *The Educational Writings of John Locke*. Edited by John William Adamson. Cambridge: Cambridge
University Press, 1922.

More poetry followed, and *Happiness in Retirement* (1812) survives in just two copies worldwide. One copy can be located in the library at the University of California, Los Angeles, and another survives in the Lincolnshire Records office. Both copies contain the hand and signature of the author; a dedication in one copy and a poem entitled "Friendship" in the other. Seemingly Summersett's second and final play, *Ferdinand, the Slave of Passion* (1818), survives in just one copy which is housed in the Houghton Library at Harvard University, the bequest of Evert Jansen Wendell from the class of 1882. The play, as Summersett reveals in the preface, was not offered to the theatres in London because he "had not confidence enough" to do so. The preface is signed as having been written at the Southwell Theatre, Nottinghamshire, and it is entirely likely that the play was performed there under Summersett's direction. The play was put into print, presumably in a limited number of copies, for subscribers.

Such a brief biography based upon literary output does leave large gaps in Summersett's life that are unaccounted for, particularly between the years of 1806-1810, and 1813-1818. In 1818, Summersett would have been approximately 44 years of age and it is likely that his literary career did continue after this date. It is possible that there are novels and plays published anonymously from these periods that belong to Summersett, or alternatively, perhaps any work written during these years simply didn't survive. The other plausible alternative, that would account for why Summersett seemingly disappears from the literary scene, is the one offered by Jenkins in his edition of *Martyn of Fenrose*, who finds that a Henry Summersett was discharged from the Suffolk militia at 68 years of age, after serving for a period of 25 years and 1 month. The dates do add up. It is therefore possible that Summersett did join the militia in 1818 at approximately 44 years of age. For now, it therefore remains unknown what happened to Summersett after 1843.

Leopold Warndorf was printed in two volumes for William Lane at the Minerva Press in 1800. The novel received an advertisement in the *Morning Chronicle* on Thursday 31st July 1800, informing the public and potential purchasers of its availability. The novel, partly a work of epistolary fiction, is a passionate investigation into the suffering that broken relationships can impart onto an individual, and an exploration of the duties of fatherhood concerning illegitimate offspring. Summersett's novel, complete with shocking moments where individuals almost succumb to madness and the spectre of incest looms over the relationship between two lovers, also contains many moments that are indebted to, and indeed challenge, the great sentimental novel writers of the late eighteenth century.

Leopold Warndorf precedes *Martyn of Fenrose* and introduces many themes and situations that would become a crucial foundation of the latter novel. *Leopold Warndorf* is the tale of a wronged woman, Isabella, and her daughter, Augusta, who have been abandoned by Isabella's long-term partner, Baron Altenburg, who is also the father of Augusta. Altenburg deserts the pair in favour of Christiana, whom he marries, thereby securing his financial fortune. Isabella, however, scorns all offers of financial support offered by Altenburg, and the incensed woman and her daughter cut off all contact with the much troubled Baron and begin a flight into poverty. It is no wonder that Altenburg is so distraught by Isabella's actions. Such a decision could easily amount to suicide in a society where there was little support for the impoverished.[1]

The reader learns that Isabella was not the first woman that the Baron seduced. In his youth, Altenburg seduced a poor villager, Josephine, who, pregnant and abandoned by the Baron, does not live long after the birth of a son, Leopold. When the Baron attempts to locate his long-lost son via the assistance of his friend Count Stendal, Leopold, deeply affected and affronted, refuses to hear even the name of his father and promptly writes to the Baron, forcibly instructing him never to attempt contact

---

[1] For a compelling discussion of the plight of the poor in London in the eighteenth century, see Tim Hitchcock's *Down and Out in Eighteenth-Century London*. London: Hambledon Continuum, 2004.

again. Incredibly, Leopold makes an acquaintance with Isabella and Augusta; the trio are not aware that they are related, however. Somewhat problematically, Leopold begins falling in love with Augusta, which she reciprocates, and Summersett is left to tread a dangerous path with the grim spectre of incest lurking in the margins. Summersett was probably aware of the most famous instance of literary incest in the eighteenth century, Daniel Defoe's *Moll Flanders* (1721), where the heroine unknowingly falls in love with, marries, and has children by her own brother. Unlike in Defoe's novel, whilst the reader is fully aware from the beginning of the exact relationship between Augusta and Leopold, and therefore aghast at the prospect offered here whilst knowing that it is unlikely that Summersett will have the siblings proceed with the marriage, Summersett deliberately prolongs the inevitable emergence of the truth until a powerfully emotive meeting between Baron Altenburg and Leopold ensures that the forthcoming marriage is most definitely off. Summersett may also have been indebted to a novel by Henry Mackenzie, *The Man of the World* (1773), for his interest in the problems that illegitimacy and neglectful fathers could bring upon their offspring. In Mackenzie's novel, Harriet Annesley experiences a terrifying ordeal at the hands of her father, who attempts to rape her before she manages to convert him from his wicked course of action, thereby aborting the sexual violence. The pair's familial bond is unknown at the moment of the planned attack, however, and like Augusta and Leopold, incest is only narrowly avoided.

Leopold flees, utterly crushed, and only returns to Isabella and Augusta after he has learnt to forget all traces of desire for his sister. The reader cannot help but fear that Leopold has gone to perform an act carried out by another extremely popular young fictional letter-writer from the late eighteenth century, Werther, who commits suicide after resigning himself to the fact that he can never marry the woman he loves. Johann Wolfgang von Goethe's incredibly successful novel, *The Sorrows of Young Werther* (1774) appears to have been admired by Summersett. It is not only Leopold who suffers from extreme mental anguish. Altenburg fares badly by the close of the novel; as if the recognition of the pain that he has inflicted upon his family was not enough, Summersett continues his suffering by having Christiana die after giving birth. To heighten the tragedy, the unnamed infant also perishes. There is some comfort and hope restored in the final moments of the novel, however, with Altenburg finally reunited with, and accepted by, his son and daughter as well as Isabella. The reader cannot help but wonder, though, what will become of the titular character, with no prospect of immediate happiness bestowed on him at the close of the novel?

Before addressing Summersett's literary heritage from the mid-to-late eighteenth century, there is another literary giant whose presence can be felt in all of Summersett's novels: William Shakespeare. Late eighteenth-century and early nineteenth-century fascinations with the Bard are evident in much of the literature of this period. Summersett's admiration of Shakespeare, however, permeates *Leopold Warndorf,* and almost all of its fictional characters mirror Shakespearean heroes and heroines at moments in the novel. The title pages of both volumes of Summersett's novel feature a quotation from Shakespeare's play *Cymbeline* (1610). Summersett has altered the quotation from the lines that can be found in the 1623 Folio edition of the text. Shakespeare's lines read:

> Innogen.
> Why did you throw your wedded lady from you?
> Think that you are upon a rock, and now
> Throw me again.

> Posthumus.
> Hang there like fruit, my soul,
> Till the tree die (V.iv.261-264).

In this moment, Innogen is reunited with her husband Posthumus after believing that he is dead, and the happiness at their reunion is captured in their embrace where Posthumus refers to his body as a tree for the fruit-like Innogen to cling onto. Summersett appears to have found such a moment particularly relevant to the characters of Isabella and Altenburg. Isabella, by her own admission, cannot understand why her faithful lover Altenburg has abandoned both herself and Augusta. It is as if Isabella's disbelief is mirrored by Summersett, as at the close of the novel Altenburg does return to his wronged lover and we learn of their imminent marriage. Altenburg becomes the tree to support Isabella in their declining years and the message implied is that he never should have abandoned his *real* family in the first place.

Cymbeline can be perceived to be a major influence on Summersett's novel. The play, a loosely based historical romance, would have immediately appealed to Summersett who had just completed his own historical romance *Jaqueline of Olzeburg*. *Cymbeline* features two sons to the titular King, Guiderius and Arviragus, stolen away from the court twenty years ago as children and presumed dead. Cymbeline's only daughter, Innogen, also flees the court after her father refuses to acknowledge her lover and husband Posthumus Leonatus. A final scene revelation reunites the family and the long-lost children as all ends peacefully. Summersett appears to have been particularly interested in the idea of children wronged, or ignored, by their parents. *Leopold Warndorf* is also heavily indebted to *The Winter's Tale* (1611) which features a child, Perdita, labelled as illegitimate by her father Leontes, who also wrongs his wife. The play also has much to say about children providing comfort to parents and enabling a parental figure to achieve forgiveness after having to live with the burden of a sin committed a number of years ago. Summersett's novel also finds parallels with *Pericles* (1608) which begins with a scene featuring the revelation of incest between Antiochus and his unnamed daughter. The play follows the fortunes of the titular protagonist, who also experiences a painful separation from his wife Thaisa and daughter Marina before a happy familial reunion ensues in the final scene. Asterley falling

in love with Augusta also recalls Proteus pursuing Silvia, despite
her love for Valentine, in *The Two Gentlemen of Verona* (1590).

Writing about the 1790s, the period that saw the initial literary forays of Summersett, Claudia L. Johnson states that the
"fiction of this period is bizarre and untidy".[1] Perhaps some of
the bizarreness can become more familiar in relation to Summersett by tracing the origins of his novel. In the Preface to the
novel, Summersett acknowledges the theatricality of his fiction
by informing his readers that *Leopold Warndorf* was originally
penned as a play. Once again, the negativity and self-criticism
surrounding his own literary talent determined the fate of such
a venture, with Summersett imagining that a laughing theatre
manager would flatly reject such a play. As a result, it appears that
the script was destroyed and Summersett attempted to salvage
his ideas into a novel. Ironically, it was just after Summersett
had finished the first volume of *Leopold Warndorf* that he went
to the Covent Garden theatre to see August von Kotzebue's play
Das Kind der Liebe (1780), adapted into English by Elizabeth
Inchbald as *Lovers' Vows* in 1798. Summersett was right to fancy
that there "was a great similitude between the drama" and his
own novel, and whilst not outright plagiarism, it is easy to see
the influence of the play on volume II of *Leopold Warndorf*. Inchbald's adaptation features a scene between an illegitimate son,
Frederick, and his shocked father, Baron Wildenhaim, which
is closely echoed in Summersett's revelatory moment between
Leopold and his father, Baron Altenburg.

As mentioned above, the authorial voice of Summersett
intrudes into the narrative of *Leopold Warndorf* at various points.
The first moment of authorial intervention occurs near the end
of volume I. Whilst epistolary fiction can provide an excellent
insight into the personal feelings of those characters who wield
a pen, Summersett's narrative strands by the end of volume I
are seemingly too diverse to warrant the practicality of continu-

[1] Claudia L. Johnson, *Equivocal Beings: Politics, Gender, and Sentimentality in the 1790s*. Chicago: University of Chicago Press, 1995, p. 1.

ing in this style. Indeed, at this particular moment in the novel, the reader undoubtedly begins to wonder what exactly has happened to Isabella and Augusta as they appear to become more and more marginalised as Leopold enters the novel and becomes the centre of attention, not only for Baron Altenburg and Count Stendal, but also for Summersett, who is intent on building up a thoroughly virtuous and impeccable young man who puts his father to shame. The very essence of the novel demands a change in storytelling, as the central plot behind *Leopold Warndorf* would be difficult to execute if Summersett were to continue writing in the epistolary form. No doubt buoyed by the fact that others had done precisely this before him—Richardson's novel *Pamela; or, Virtue Rewarded* (1740) had also undergone a transformation in storytelling from letters to a journal that the heroine keeps—Summersett "begs his readers to take the remainder of it in the manner of narrative", and the pace of the novel immediately quickens. Whilst Summersett defends his reasons for altering his narrative style in a manner that is apologetic towards his reader, he simultaneously reminds them that he is in control of the story, and Leopold's last letter to Charles will forever remain unanswered. Summersett's final intrusion into his novel occurs near the end of volume II, where he appears keen to avoid charges of ending the story too abruptly and begs his readers to feel pacified with the conclusion to the tale. In Summersett's opinion, it is better to end his novel fairly swiftly rather than labouring the storyline to fill another volume just for the sake of doing so. Once again, these instances confirm the agitated nature of writing for Summersett, but they also reveal a writer who is determined to provide readers with what they want—an enjoyable and entertaining reading experience.

The change in narrative, however, should not be taken as a weakness on Summersett's part to handle the complexity required in writing epistolary fiction. Summersett is a powerful letter writer. Whether it is the utter wrath of Isabella, the innocent suffering of Augusta, the anguish of Altenburg, or the sagely sentimental and tormented scribbling of Leopold, Summersett reveals a keen interest in the literature of sentimentality and is indebted to the fiction of Samuel Richardson, Oliver Goldsmith, and Henry Mackenzie. Even though he may be slightly unkind to Tobias Smollett in other works, there is no doubt that Summersett had also read the former's *The Expedition of Humphry Clinker* (1771), itself an exquisite example of epistolary fiction. Of equal importance, Summersett appears to be keenly aware of Smollett's tendency to introduce a vocabulary of theatricality into his novels and as Paul Goring has observed, this is a characteristic of many sentimental novels.[1] In relation to Goldsmith's work, *The Vicar of Wakefield* (1766) amongst others, Summersett re-creates that pastoral richness in *Leopold Warndorf*, with Leopold and Augusta both linking their emotive bodies to nature in times of pleasure and distress. Like *Leopold Warndorf*, Goldsmith's novel also features a long-lost son and a family reduced to poverty. Richardson's three novels, *Pamela*, the masterpiece par excellence of epistolary fiction *Clarissa, or, The History of a Young Lady* (1748), and *The History of Sir Charles Grandison* (1753), are all influential in Summersett's investigation into the complex relationships between the sexes and the role that sensibility and personal pleasure play in determining those relationships. Like Sir Charles Grandison and Harley in Henry Mackenzie's *The Man of Feeling* (1771), Summersett has designs in creating the perfect man, but differs from Mackenzie and Richardson in that Leopold, whilst clearly a sentimental character, often experiences great difficulty in explaining and expressing his emotions.[2]

Where Summersett differs from Mackenzie can be seen in

[1] Paul Goring, *The Rhetoric of Sensibility in Eighteenth-Century Culture*. Cambridge: Cambridge University Press, 2009. (See Chapter 5, pp. 142-181).

[2] According to E. J. Clery, Richardson's novel *Pamela* had attempted to develop "a model woman as the agent of moral improvement" (p. 95). In *The Feminization Debate in Eighteenth-Century England: Literature, Commerce and Luxury*. Basingstoke: Palgrave Macmillan, 2004.

moments where his characters are required to express their feelings, usually in a moment that requires sentiment. Whereas Mackenzie's Harley would frequently shed a tear upon hearing or experiencing a moving tale regardless of the company that he was in, Leopold is far more cautious in letting his emotional responses be visible to the wide world. Such is the case not long after Leopold meets Augusta and Isabella, and hearing their plight related to him by the servant of the house, he has to send her away out of his sight and pretend to cough to suppress the outpouring of emotion that would naturally follow hearing such an affecting story. Here, the experience of sensibility is an entirely private affair for the individual to experience. It is not a moment necessarily requiring an audience. What can such a suppression of feeling mean? It is important, however, that even in this private moment of grief it is not clear whether Leopold sheds a tear, and for Summersett, such a moment to indulge in such an outward sign of sensibility is dangerously "unfitting [of] a man". This is a common reaction against sentimentality in the late eighteenth and early nineteenth centuries, but for Summersett, who does intend to present an accurate portrait of a young man of perfect sentiment, the indecision concerning the correct display of sensibility is problematic. Such a moment of indecision governing the sentimental body occurs shortly after the above-mentioned incident. When Leopold decides to bring food to relieve Isabella and Augusta of their hunger, he encourages the reader to believe that this act of charity makes him a worthy man of feeling. But Leopold is also a man of thinking, and after analysing the situation to excess, he decides that he had better not bring the food to the hungry women after all for fear of how they should interpret his actions. Mackenzie's Harley would simply have offered the food immediately.

Susan Manning writes that the "reputation of the eighteenth-century literature of Sensibility has never quite recovered from its embarrassing association with displays of unmeasured, extravagant emotion. It was 'excessive'."[1] Even though it has been suggested above that Leopold is unsure how to respond correctly with regard to expressing feeling and sentiment, Summersett appears to deliberately regulate the excesses of the mid-to-late eighteenth century and provide a new interpretation of sentimentality that is valued and vital in the late 1790s. As Manning also suggests, the "study of sociability was therefore the basis of Sensibility".[2] This is essentially why Leopold has to refine his own views of sentimentality to learn how to accept the role of his father into his life by the end of the novel. Leopold can only be sociable to his father once he has learnt how to correctly channel his emotional responsibilities towards both his father and his sister. Interestingly, solace is found out of the city and in nature by the close of the novel.

As G. J. Barker-Benfield has observed, "tension between the high evaluation of refinement in men and the wish to square it with manliness permeated the eighteenth-century novel",[3] and it is evident that Leopold is responsible for amending and refining the flaws of his father, Baron Altenburg. There is never any suggestion, however, that the refined capabilities of Leopold lead him towards a charge of effeminacy.[4] Leopold is certainly Summersett's revision of men such as Harley from *The Man of Feeling* and Sir Charles Grandison. But this is not to say that Leopold is perfect. Unable to fit into a society that thrives on exploitation and commerce, Leopold seems destined to roam the

---

[1] Susan Manning, "Sensibility", pp. 80-99, *The Cambridge Companion to English Literature, 1740-1830*. Edited by Thomas Keymer and Jon Mee. Cambridge: Cambridge University Press, 2004, p. 80.

[2] Manning. p. 83.

[3] G. J. Barker-Benfield, *The Culture of Sensibility: Sex and Society in Eighteenth-Century Britain*. Chicago: University of Chicago Press, 1992, p. 141.

[4] Critic R. F. Brissenden has stated that Mackenzie's Harley is an "epicene, impotent, passive, almost completely ineffectual character—a set of tender susceptibilities and conventional moral attitudes rather than a living individual" *Virtue in Distress: Studies in the Novel of Sentiment from Richardson to Sade*. London: Macmillan, 1974, p. 251.

world in isolation until he happens by chance to meet his sister. Even at the close of the novel we are left unsure what exactly Leopold is going to do with his life. Augusta and Asterley have their happy ending; Baron Altenburg is reunited with Isabella and his children, but for Leopold, there is no immediate prospect of self-happiness in the closure of the novel besides the final acceptance of his father into his own little world.

Whilst Leopold is aesthetically virtuous therefore, Isabella's sensibility also requires strict policing, not only from Leopold, who acts like a concerned guardian of Isabella in the latter stages of the novel, but also Summersett, who in places seems uncertain whether Isabella is a chaste sufferer demanding pity or an unstable jealous schemer who resorts to dressing up in male attire, seemingly to exact revenge on Altenburg. Clarification does appear in the second volume, and her status as an injured and largely innocent victim is instigated by her sickness which Leopold's assistance helps her to overcome. Isabella's illness, which appears to be a form of extreme mental fatigue and anxiety that induces melancholia, is the direct result of her blurred and burning emotions of hatred and love for Altenburg. Unsure of which passions she should let flow and incapable of casting aside her love for Altenburg, Isabella is overcome by a range of sensibilities that almost destroy her.[1] Even though the reader is encouraged to feel sympathy for Isabella, Summersett also cautiously asks us to remember that the relationship with Altenburg is one that Isabella wholeheartedly enters into, fully aware that without the binding ties of marriage, there is every possibility that the union could be broken at any moment. Summersett also appears to be advising his readers about the dangers of feminine indulgence in pleasing the passions. As Gary Day has commented, the very act of reading sentimental novels could be dangerous for women because the act of reading encouraged women "to indulge their

[1] For a further discussion of melancholy and psychological illness, see Allan Ingram, et al., *Melancholy Experience in Literature of the Long Eighteenth Century: Before Depression, 1660-1800.* Hampshire: Palgrave Macmillan, 2011.

feelings and made them easy to seduce, thereby threatening the home and family".[1] Summersett provides a commentary on one easily seduced woman, Josephine, whose fate is terrible, compared to Isabella, who suffers at the hands of a much condemned relationship that isolates her from her family, yet survives.

As April London has recently stated, over "the course of the eighteenth century, the consolidation of the nuclear family and decline of the extended 'household' one has wide-reaching consequences".[2] And if Summersett may demonstrate this shift in *Leopold Warndorf,* it is at the expense of security. Summersett's family in the novel, however, is far from obtaining that nuclear security that Dr. Primrose and his family initially experience and enjoy at the beginning of *The Vicar of Wakefield.* Summersett's fragmented family are a series of outcasts and should-be societal rejects, but, importantly, both illegitimate children fare surprisingly well throughout the novel; Augusta thanks to the unbroken residence with her mother and later the financial and emotional support of Leopold, whereas the titular protagonist is raised as a paragon of youthful sensibility by the village Rector, a pseudo-father for Leopold. This is all the more surprising because, as Paul Goring has commented, pregnancy "outside of wedlock carried great shame for women, and bastard children were often viewed with contempt, and treated with hostility".[3] The fact that the illegitimate Augusta and Leopold are highly valued by the communities and families that they are a part of in the world of the novel confirms Summersett's notions of the redeeming powers of children in guiding and instructing wayward parents. In *Leopold Warndorf* offspring are the moral and sentimental guides for parents to follow and learn from, and Summersett fre-

---

[1] Essay by Gary Day, "Introduction," pp. 1-16. *The Eighteenth-Century Literature Handbook.* Edited by Gary Day and Bridget Keegan. London: Continuum, 2009, p. 9.
[2] *The Cambridge Introduction to the Eighteenth-Century Novel.* Cambridge: Cambridge University Press, 2012, p. 112.
[3] *Eighteenth-Century Literature and Culture.* London: Continuum, 2008, p. 30.

quently implies that his young characters have much to say about
their own existence, and the world that they live in. Perhaps this
is a very reaction against the distrust of sentimentality that Janet
Todd has suggested existed at the close of the eighteenth century.
Todd writes that by the end of the eighteenth century, sentimentality in fiction was "associated firmly with the under-educated,
the ill-bred and the non-metropolitan".[1] Already anxious that
critics would consider him under-educated, Summersett's decision to wield the double-edged sword of sentimentality could
have posed a serious threat to the novelist's own claims concerning the value of his writing. The threat posed by sentimentality
at the close of the eighteenth century was a very real and pressing concern that occasioned great debate about the state of the
nation. As Todd states, to "many in Britain the cult of sensibility seemed to have feminized the nation" and created a breed
of emasculated men.[2] To combat this, Summersett's new interpretation of the sentimental body at the end of the eighteenth
century redefines masculinity, as the rakish father Altenburg is
portrayed as morally inferior and lacking the refined sentiments
that his son Leopold possesses with no suggestion that Leopold
is unmanly or effeminate for possessing such virtues.

Despite Summersett's insistence in the preface to *Maurice, the
Rustic* that he had not been "reared by Science, and fashioned
by Taste", his writing demonstrates a conscious and compelling
engagement with the philosophical and scientific debates of his
age. It is likely that Summersett would have heard of, if not read,
Adam Smith's successful book *The Theory of Moral Sentiments*
(1759). Many of Smith's statements about sensibility and humanity are evident in the entire range of Summersett's writings and
are particularly pressing to the chief concerns of *Leopold Warndorf*. Summersett's exploration of Smith's ideas is most evident
in the characters of Leopold and Altenburg. For Smith, we "can
never survey our own sentiments and motives, we can never form

[1] *Sensibility: An Introduction.* London: Methuen, 1986, p. 133.
[2] p. 133.

any judgment concerning them, unless we remove ourselves, as it were, from our own natural station, and endeavour to view them as at a certain distance from us".[1] Altenburg can only seemingly comprehend the barbarity of his actions in the medium of letter-writing, whether it is to the abused Josephine, or to his daughter Augusta, where he manages to achieve some form of penance for the wrongs of his youth by expressing his sins and asking for forgiveness. The process of writing a letter, allowing the individual to express his thoughts on a blank page, generates the necessary distance for Altenburg to retrospectively regard his character and recognize his faults. Smith's writings also influence the character of Leopold. As noted above, Leopold is an individual who is set up as a moral paragon of sensibility, but such a depiction is problematic when it comes to expressing one's emotions. However, for Smith, this is entirely reasonable: "A man of sensibility may sometimes feel great uneasiness lest he should have yielded too much even to what may be called an honourable passion".[2] Leopold's body is constantly referred to as a site for confirming and redefining sentimentality and once again demonstrates that Summersett, therefore, is intent on exploring the psychology of the individual in *Leopold Warndorf*.

Writers in the Romantic period continued to turn to the sentimental genre as a means of expressing their thoughts about the world that they lived in. As Ann Wierda Rowland reveals, the culture of the last few years of the eighteenth century and the first couple of decades of the nineteenth were "preoccupied with the workings of passion, the anatomy of feeling, and the communication of emotion".[3] As a writer producing literary works across the period that Rowland identifies, Summersett, perhaps

[1] *The Theory of Moral Sentiments* (1759). Edited by Ryan Patrick Hanley. London: Penguin, 2009, p. 133.
[2] *Id.*, p. 147.
[3] Ann Wierda Rowland, "Sentimental Fiction," in *The Cambridge Companion to Fiction in the Romantic Period*. Edited by Richard Maxwell and Katie Trumpener. Cambridge: Cambridge University Press, 2008, pp. 191-206, p. 192.

unsurprisingly, explores with keen interest the issues that were a part of his society and culture. Parental duty, affection, love, illegitimacy, filial duty and the bonds of friendship are all subjected to an exploration and analysis of the capability of human beings to make connections through emotional and physical attachments. Summersett's investigation into the workings of the body and the mind provides a refreshing and compelling take on the importance of sensibility at the start of the nineteenth century. Despite the fact that Summersett may have fallen into obscurity, the issues and topics that he discusses and raises have not and are still current in this day and age. Such an observation goes a long way to quantify the statement that Summersett is an important, and modern, writer.

STEVE ORMAN
Canterbury Christ Church University
March 9, 2013

Acknowledgments

I would like to thank the English Department at Canterbury Christ Church University for their unfailing support and enthusiasm over the years, particularly Dr. Peter Merchant, who was inspirational in fostering my love of eighteenth-century fiction. I'm also grateful to Dr. Andrew Palmer, who kindly found a gap in the Departmental budget for me to fill with a printing request. Finally, my thanks to Jay at Valancourt Books who answered all of my queries swiftly and with kindness and interest.

Note on the Text

This edition follows the first and only published edition of *Leopold Warndorf*, printed in 1800. I have used the edition housed in the British Library as my copy text. Only one other copy of the first edition is known to survive and belongs to the University of Alberta. In keeping with the editorial policy of Valancourt Books, this edition reprints verbatim the text of the 1800 edition without any alteration in spelling or punctuation. The following obvious printer's errors have been corrected:

Vol. I. p. 20, l. 17   died]   dyed
Vol. I. p. 175, l. 6   sericusly]   seriously
Vol. I. p. 195, l. 3   mann r]   manner
Vol. II. p. 60, l. 15   call it."]   call it.
Vol. II. p. 87, l. 2   better services.]   better services."
Vol. II. p. 182, l. 1   gentlemen]   gentleman
Vol. II. p. 274, l. 11   discoveryof   ]   discovery of
Vol. II. p. 281, ll. 2-3   writer Having]   writer. Having

LEOPOLD WARNDORF.

A NOVEL.

IN TWO VOLUMES.

BY

HENRY SUMMERSETT,

AUTHOR OF

THE MAD MAN OF THE MOUNTAIN, &c. &c. &c.

Imogen.   " Why did you throw me from you?
　　　　 " Think that you are upon a rock, and now
　　　　 " Throw me again!"
Posthumus.   " Hang there, like fruit, my soul,
　　. " Till the tree perish!"

CYMBELINE.

VOL. I.

LONDON:

PRINTED AT THE

Minerva-Press,

FOR WILLIAM LANE, LEADENHALL-STREET.

1800.

PREFACE.

THE author of the following sheets is unwilling to obtrude on the public any superfluous matter; but he conceives that his reputation, if any has, or ever shall be awarded him, demands a few words by way of preface.

Leopold Warndorf was, about two years ago, cast in a dramatic mould; it contained characters which have since been put aside, and attempts at humour which will not be found in these volumes.—"Oh! that I could see the inimitable Kemble assuming the passions of the Marquis—that I could hear the exquisite tones of Mrs. Siddons swelling with the rage and resentment of Victoria; and the almost magic voice of Mrs. Jordan repeating the hopes and the sorrows of the simple Antoinette!"—These words I have not unfrequently uttered.* The reader may smile at my vanity;—I have smiled at it myself. My ambition faded: the fancied laugh of the Manager was a death-blow; and I put aside my papers, because I would not be reminded of my own folly and presumption.

At length I brought them to the light again, and at intervals began to form them into a Novel. I changed the scene of action from France to Germany, gave new names and titles to my characters, and had actually written the first volume, when I went to see the representation of a new Play, which deservedly became a favourite with the town. I was agitated by the excellence of the performance: and when I left the Theatre, I fancied there was a great similitude between the drama and what I had then written and designed.* Self-assured, however, of my honesty, I proceeded in my work, which I completed in the manner as it is now presented to the public; and I shall never think myself more indebted to the German poet, than he is to me. Indeed the likeness has since appeared to me *very faint*; and I am persuaded that my book contains not a sentence that may be traced in the author to whom I have alluded.

It may be said by some, that, even in this short appeal, there is much ado about nothing; and the sense of my own feebleness prevents me from aiming at such a stupendous giant as Kotzebue. But I know the prejudices arising from comparison; and I do not think it improbable, but that a certain set of monthly critics (I speak not of the *Monthly Reviewers*),* may, in some after season, assure their readers that my book bears a resemblance, though such an one as *by no means is favourable to the imitator*, to Peregrine Pickle, or to the facetious Humphry Clinker.*

> *Hamlet.* Methinks it is like a weasel.
> *Polonius.* It is back'd like a weasel.
> *Hamlet.* Or, like a whale?
> *Polonius.* Very like a whale.*

Some of the inconsistencies of the Danish Courtier may be found in the ingenious critics of the eighteenth century; among whom I shall not be surprised to discover those who will consider me as a pigmy, too diminutive to be bound on the wheel of torture.

LEOPOLD WARNDORF.

Isabella to Baron Altenburg.

ALLOW me to offer you my congratulations on a late happy occasion—congratulations which flow from the heart, not merely from the tongue. Coming from me, and on such circumstances, they should be unbounded, many, ardent—animated by fancy, enforced by sincerity: they should give to you and to me an equal pleasure. And do you not enjoy pleasure, fascinating pleasure? Do you not sink on the bosom of love, and hourly clasp beauty in your arms?—Yes, these joys are your's, Baron. And am I without *my* felicities? No, no; I am happy in the completion of my hopes. I have attained my wishes, been favoured in my expectations, indulged in every——But hold! your happiness is the subject; let me not, therefore, unseasonably talk of my own.

You have married, and I have pondered on the circumstance: you have married—hear the prayer that I utter for you:—

May God place a curse on you for ever! on every thing that concerns, on every thing that belongs to you—on your wife, on your children! May he bring poverty to your house, misery to your heart, and affliction to your body! May your wife be barren! If she has issue, let it be marked by ugliness and disease! But, for a final curse, may life be misery to you, death excruciating, and hell an eternal torment!

Villain! monster! devil! how did you dare to use me thus? Do you remember, Sir, who I was, and who I am? I sacrificed the opinion of the world and every thing to you; and when the finger of derision and contempt has been pointed to me, I have scorned it on your account, and gloried in that connection with you which the world loudly called my shame.

5

What if I had deserted you, and fled to the arms of another, would you not have upbraided, scorned, cursed me? Why then should I not upbraid, scorn, and curse you for your treachery and hypocrisy? But my lips shall be sealed on this subject for ever. Remember, however, that my enmity will not sleep: at some future day I will be revenged, amply revenged. My malice will ever be waking; rest not, therefore, in security: I will plot mischief, and execute it. The law shall not reach me; your power shall dwindle into impotence; and if any horrid disaster should befal you, regard it as the revenge of

Isabella Marilli.

———————

The Baron to Isabella.

YOUR frantic letter has reached me; the language of it shocks me. I am, however, inclined to view it as a burst of frenzy, and cannot think but that, when reason returns, you will regard it with horror and repentance. Were you not fearful of having your hand stiffened by the anger of Heaven when it was employed in giving characters to your dreadful execrations? Did the hyena possess the powers of the human voice, it could not, even in its most savage moments, express any thing more shocking and atrocious.

Isabella, I know the strength of your mind, the fervour of your passions, and the irritability of your disposition: but there have been times when your sentiments have charmed me—when love has been predominant in your bosom, and when your temper has followed mine through all its mazes, and shewn itself with superiority.

Hear me, Isabella—I entreat you to hear me with patience. I think I can extenuate the crime of which I am accused, for my own conscience has already acquitted me of it.

You will remember that seventeen years have passed since we

first met in Italy. Finding you regardless of certain forms and establishments observed in society, I began an acquaintance with you of such a nature, I conceived, as the dissatisfaction of either of us might readily dissolve. I admit that I was the first object of your choice, and also that I have never had any reason to suppose that I was only a sharer of your affections;—you yielded to me, and surely I made equal sacrifices.

Did not my father on his death-bed declare that my connection with you had been the most severe of his afflictions? Did not my uncle, his surviving brother, dispose of his immense property to enrich shrines, and to fatten Monks, in order that he might reduce to poverty the man who refused to abandon you? After that, limited as I was, did I not for several years attach myself to you, support you with elegance, resent each injury that was offered to you, and make you an object of greater consideration than myself?

My conduct and propensities have been of a very faulty nature; they led me into such extravagances, that I lately found ruin staring at and menacing me. My fortune was reduced to the lowest state, and I was almost wild when thinking on the means of re-establishing it. I thought of marriage, but at the same time thought of you, Isabella, and was pained. I had many internal struggles, and the combat between love and necessity was obstinate;—the latter, however, convincing me that it were better to place you in single independence, than plunge you into the distress that threatened me, I resolved to persevere in my new-formed intention; and, during my absence from you, which you so forcibly urged me to account for, and which the want of fortitude prevented me from doing, I selected a woman, young, beautiful, and rich. I married her; and I confess to you that I love her. The passion which I entertained for you must, if I wish for happiness, be suppressed—it is my duty to conquer it: but if you will in its place allow me to substitute friendship, it shall attend you till my heart grows cold in my bosom.

Your threats, Isabella, are futile; made in a moment of passion, they are, I hope, already forgotten. Retire from Vienna, and you shall receive an annual sum sufficient for your support: make a proposal yourself; let me know your wishes on the subject, and I will readily, cheerfully accede to them. Remember, however, that you must retire from Vienna; Isabella and Christiana must not be near to me at one time, lest my new-formed principles should be destroyed, and my old habits again imperceptibly steal on me.

Your cool judgment, not your passions, must direct you; and I think, Isabella, however severe are your invectives, I think it is not possible for you to hate me—to curse me *twice*! Necessity has of late been my directress; and, as my heart did not wilfully stray from you, pity and forgive me.

One subject I have not yet touched upon—our daughter, the child of our love:—God bless her! I am *indeed* her father—I feel it, I feel it this moment in my soul. She is now sixteen—sweet, blooming, beautiful! Isabella, yield her up to me; I will place her with an accomplished lady, who, I am convinced, will give the finest polish to this rich diamond.

I will see her often—you shall see her at certain periods; and when she arrives at the age of twenty, Christiana's dowery shall provide a fortune for Isabella's daughter. Think of this seriously. Kiss my dear girl for me, and prepare her to accompany the person whom I shall send for her in the course of a few days.

And now, Isabella, I am writing a painful word—Farewell! I see you at this moment; your rage is hushed, you are sad, dejected; you pity, you love

Altenburg.

Isabella to the Baron.

IT was my intention, Baron, to have remained silent after having written my last letter to you; but it is necessary I should address you again. The winds laugh at the poplar that bows at their passing; you, probably, exult with the idea of having bent me down with your consequence: but you are deceived in respect to my state; my soul is still great in its monarchy, and as much as ever despises your perfidy and hypocrisy.

Your last epistle has caused me to smile, but not to weep; no, Sir, I have done with sorrow;—if I must be tormented, it shall be by active pain, not by that dull anguish which makes the sufferer contemptible.

You have not yet convinced me but that you are a proud, insulting monster—a selfish being, who, for his own preservation, or for the pleasures of a dainty mind, scruples not to sacrifice his honour, and the peace of those to whom he is forsworn. A spider, hideous and venomous as yourself, would spin a stronger web than that of your arguments; flimsy in its texture, and sorry in its construction, a breath, a vapour will destroy it.

Baron, I once loved as much as I now despise you. I have blessed you a thousand and a thousand times; why have you given me cause to curse you eternally? From a passage in your letter, it might be inferred that you stepped from poverty by your late pleasing gradations, merely to save *me* from it. Worthy man! I want a new heart to thank you for it.

To be near you was once to be happy. In the days of our acquaintance, had you, in consequence of crime, been sent to any distant country to be made a common drudge, or to the gallies, or to the mines, I would have been your associate prisoner. In the winter, I would have retained only one of my coverings, and warmed your limbs with the others; and in the summer, my hand should have removed each drop of sweat as soon as it started upon your brow. These are not the boastings of romance; but whatever they are, they shall sink, and be forgotten.

You have been very elaborate in stating your compulsions and your motives for withdrawing yourself from my society, and given yourself much unnecessary trouble in repeating stale incidents. Sir, did you conceive yourself as appeasing an incensed prostitute, or as pleading to the ear of ignorance and stupidity?

Insulting man! do you not remember that I am allied to a family, the honour of which was not blemished till I foolishly attached myself to you and your fortunes? My father cursed me, my mother abhorred me, my sister turned from me, my friends contemned me!—Wretch, wretch! all this they did, and thus was I lost to them, because I loved, and so madly gave myself up to you. Preach no more, then, on necessity—my dare was the greater; but your's is the triumph over misplaced love and infatuation.

Baron, I will leave Vienna when I please; I will have no stipulations. If my continuance here can either pain or perplex you, I will be rooted.—You will provide for my necessities!—*You!* I would hunt with dogs in the street for food, beg it from door to door, supplicate every passing stranger for charity, rather than receive the sorriest pittance from you—famish, perish first. I reject all your services; and again avow myself your implacable enemy.

Our daughter!—Think you I will give her up to you—that I will entrust her with the man who betrayed and deserted her mother, in order that she may receive a provision from the dowery of Christiana? Pitiful man! to kill her would be better than to betray her.

On hearing the news of your marriage, I sent for her;—she stood before me as a mark of my shame: she at that moment seemed to bear a stronger likeness to you than ever. I struck her with violence, and made her bleed!—Oh my beloved child! pardon the action of a frenzied mother! I kissed off all the blood, and dyed my lips. I love her fifty thousand times more than ever. You should have my heart from my bosom rather than my adored child. What if I had murdered her? God would have made *you* answerable for the crime, and acquitted me. I struck my daughter!—Oh I shall remember it on my death-bed!

Altenburg, you are deceived; I have no more love for you than for any of the brute creation. My passions may, in some degree, subside; but the spirit of revenge I will not attempt to conquer.

Isabella.

Baron Altenburg to Count Stendal.

SOME few years ago, dear Count, I sent you my congratulations on your having attained a wife; and in your answer you
laughingly wished that I would afford you the opportunity of
shewing to me an equal civility on a similar occasion;—the time
to felicitate me is arrived, for I am married.

About a week has elapsed since I became the husband of a
charming woman, with whom I hope to live in true happiness
and enjoyment, forgetful of the errors of youth, and of the follies
of riper years, and in directing my views towards such objects
as an improved and corrected conscience shall point out to me.
So have I resolved and sworn myself to do, and I daily discover
a growing stability in my mind, which assists me in my best
projects; and from which I infer that I shall be enabled to tread
the paths of honour and of rectitude without deviating into those
of dissipation and extravagance, in which I have too long been an
unwary and idle traveller.

Many of my follies, which my late father so much lamented,
and which, in his latter days, added poignancy to his afflictions,
originated even from his own inattention; for when I was a mere
boy, he not only allowed me a free command of money, but
prompted me to a profuse expenditure, unwisely thinking that
the liberality of the hand would create liberality of heart.

Sent into the world at a very early age, the good precepts
which had been laid down for my edification, were soon put to
flight; and my young companions laughed at my morality, till
I myself began to ridicule it. Italy is not the soil for virtue; and
thither I was sent, under the direction of a tutor, who frequented
the bath of Venus more often than the temple of Minerva;* and
who would rather step into the steamy refectory of Epicurus,*
than into the schools of philosophy, though to my father he

had shewn himself a stoic, and animadverted on the practice of morality as earnestly as on the culpability of the minor and elder vices. A punishment of the greatest severity ought to be inflicted on such dangerous hypocrites; so, however, at that time I did not think. I regarded him as an obliging, accommodating person, and was glad that he would not only allow, but also partake of the gaieties of life.

I was scarcely nineteen when I became acquainted with Isabella, who from that period, till very lately, continued to reside with me, and by whom, you know, I have a charming daughter.

My companion was a most extraordinary young woman; she was held as a singular character; and her peculiar sentiments almost entirely excluded her from female society: such society, however, she did not court. She had the mind of a man, combined of judgment, wit, and fancy: in associating with the opposite sex she was happy; and being in some degree discountenanced by her family, she resigned herself up to me, and our gratification was mutual.

At certain different periods I have proposed to marry her, when she has assured me that her happiness was complete, and that neither law nor custom could possibly improve it. Isabella was deficient of property; and for the first eight years I lived with such freedom, that I found the inconvenience of it: and my father and family were so disgusted with my habits of life, from which, however, I was not to be diverted, that they made my fortune considerably narrower.

When they left the world, I found my expectations greatly baffled; and I confess that I regarded them as rigid moralists, who, naturally too coldly constituted to participate in pleasure themselves, churlishly thought my trifling indulgences serious vices, and all my pleasing gaieties unpardonable levities. Even my external mourning was limited: the world soon received me again, and its pleasures I pursued with increased avidity. To be coldly prudent I thought unnecessary and absurd; to be gay, and to seek for pleasant varieties, I only seemed to live. My mind, therefore, seldom dwelt upon my father; and my cynic uncle, who had removed all his gold from my grasp, I blotted out of my memory.

From thoughtless expenditure, I ran to extravagance; dissipation was sweeping away my property; and the pleasure that I courted, and in which Isabella joined, would not, I conceived, be succeeded by any degree of pain, or of repentance. But I was deceived; an attachment to gaming, and a series of ill fortune, made me a complete bankrupt; and I was reduced almost to poverty, though Isabella had no suspicion of my circumstances being even impaired.

Dear Count, I am afraid that I have already tired you with the repetition of my follies; with some of them you were before acquainted, but the worst of them I have hitherto concealed from you. I will pass hastily over the subject by merely saying that the reduction of my fortune and consequence I had not sufficient philosophy to withstand—it tortured, almost distracted me; and I reflected seriously, as at such times most prodigals do, on my extreme folly and culpability.

Forming an excuse of business, I quitted Isabella for two months, and retired into the country, having previously, but with considerable difficulty, bound my most serious creditors to a temporary forbearance and secrecy.

An accusing conscience haunted me: my eyes were no longer misty; and the conduct of my father and my uncle now appeared to me to be the result of caution, rather than of vindictive malice. I went to the house of a friend, at some distance from Vienna, and to that friend I made known all my indiscretions, which created pain, and even drew tears from me. He pitied me when he found my repentance sincere, and endeavoured to console me with good hopes. His fortune was not very large, but he generously tendered me a part of it; and having begged me to pardon him for his freedom, he censured many of my past faults, and laid down to me a regular plan of life, to which I seriously attended.

He advised me to re-establish my fortune by marriage, and

introduced me to a lady of birth and education, seriously advising me to make myself as agreeable to her as possible. I thought of Isabella with pain, and at first could not listen to his advice; but my ideas wandering again into their late perplexing track, I agreed to endeavour to insinuate myself into the favour of Christiana, and to aim at securing her affections.

This task, however, I was scarcely equal to;—Isabella opposed it, honour opposed it: still I carried on my designs with all possible ingenuity. I confess I used many little artifices; which, in the course of two months, I discovered had secured me her heart. I now really loved her, and resolved to offer myself to her;—I did so, and was accepted. But before I could do this, I had a thousand internal struggles; necessity, however, urged me on, and my friend applauded and encouraged me.

Christiana's fortune was very large, and at her free disposal. Unwilling that so young and excellent a woman should be deceived in her object, I stated to her my reduced wealth, laid my heart and its transgressions open to her, and ingenuously shewed myself as I had been, and then was. She thanked me for my openness with a sweetness that reached, and almost melted my soul; smilingly offered to countenance the daughter of Isabella after she had been brought into notice by an amiable female friend; and entreated me to appropriate a fund for the use of her mother, my late companion.

The sentiments of Christiana raised my admiration; these truths which, as a man of honour, I thought proper to make known to her, and which many women would have shut their ears against, she placidly listened to; and in the plan of her own gratification, she did not neglect the happiness of those with whom I had been so long, so intimately, and I may add, so dearly connected.

I married; received the congratulations of my friend, and carried my lovely bride to Vienna just four months after I had left it; and, at her earnest request, immediately paid those creditors, the fear of whom had driven me from that city.

I was preparing to apprize Isabella of my marriage, and to make such pecuniary arrangements for her as my friendship prompted me—(*friendship!* perhaps it was something more), when I received from her a letter, written in a style of frenzy, and not only intimating a knowledge of my union, but also a rooted hatred to me, expressing many curses, and declaring eternal enmity.

Though her letter led me almost to suppose that she had been deprived of reason, I immediately answered it. Feeling most sensibly for her situation, I endeavoured to sooth and tranquillize her; and, after making some proposals for her future accommodation, entreated her to yield her child up to me. This has only served to strengthen her resentment. She replies that she detests me, that she despises assistance, and that she will not part from her daughter. Her letters agitated and affected me; for my own tranquillity I put them into the flames. I fear, Count, that I have——I ought not to proceed.

I trust that the present storm will soon be hushed by serenity, and that I and Christiana shall be uninterruptedly happy:—she is a noble creature, and I cannot love her too well; she wins upon me in a moment, and in an hour she absolutely fascinates. I must be compounded of all the different vices if ever I abuse her love and generosity.

Oh dear Stendal! I think I am now secure in virtue and happiness. The sea-boy falling from the tallest mast, and caught midway by a fellow-mariner, cannot more rejoice at his preservation than I do. And yet poor Isabella!—my sweet daughter! Count, surely I may, in some degree, still love the former; for what is the difference between love and friendship? and as to the latter, not even Christiana is dearer to the heart of

Altenburg.

Count Stendal to Baron Altenburg.

AN account of your wedding, dear Altenburg, had reached me

before I received your letter; which, however, does not prevent me from wishing you every possible felicity, and much permanent happiness. Rumour has been of late very busy with your name; and in the loquacity of her gossipings, I must add, she has not been tender of your reputation. Her accusations against you are numerous; and she has given out that with your mistress you have been cruel and perfidious, and with your wife designing and hypocritical.

These are the journeying stories of the day—the tales of those who are better pleased in attending to the concerns of other people than to their own. You must not be angry with me for introducing them here, nor regard me with resentment till I join the gabbling party of your censurers.

And yet I am tempted to risk your displeasure in speaking of the subject to which you have led me: you have not, it is true, enquired the nature of my sentiments; the tenor of your own language, however, encourages me to treat you with little ceremony, and to speak freely of those matters concerning which you have been so unreserved. You have indeed, Altenburg, laid yourself very open to me; the causes that you assign for your early deviations, have considerable weight; and the character of your tutor I hold to be odious, and also know to be just.

I have at different periods taken some pains in examining the qualities of which you are composed, and many times lamented that habit should have destroyed what Nature had so well and generously executed. I must not forget that I am addressing a man equal to me in years and understanding—who was my schoolfellow, my earliest associate, and the merry companion of my liveliest days. I nevertheless wish to deal frankly with you, and to speak in the same manner that you have in past times freely sanctioned.

Your first acquaintance with Isabella was unfortunate, your closer connection still more unhappy. To begin at the age of nineteen too!—mere boy and girl; and yet, forsooth, in your own opinions you were philosophers! Isabella was a deluded woman;

but though she continued so long in concubinage, I cannot rimple my brows at her according to the rules of our rigid moralists—I cannot help pitying her.

Altenburg, you should not have deserted her: your errors were mutual, your pleasures mutual; and your distresses ought to have been the same. You stepped together into guilt; you did not take her stained from its school. You admit her fidelity for sixteen years—that she was wise, tender, affectionate, and that she brought you a lovely daughter. Such a woman I cannot call a prostitute, and such a woman you ought not to have wronged.

I wonder not at her present distraction. Remember, Altenburg, that you admit she has never offended you since you offered to make her your wife, and which proposal she did not catch at, merely because she was secure in your love and honour. You have done wrong:—marry to remove your embarrassments! Why did you not apply to me? Did I not once accept of a loan from you, remain a long time your debtor, and even pay you by instalments? Why then, in the days of my prosperity, could you not condescend to ask me for a similar assistance? I can scarcely pardon this pride.

Dear Altenburg, whatever harshness this letter bespeaks, I am most truly your friend; I wish sincerely for your happiness, and for the happiness of Christiana, of whom you have drawn so lovely a picture. Your situation is peculiar, and you must cautiously frame your actions according to it, or your felicity will pass over as a vision. You must not trust yourself with Isabella even for a moment; there would be most imminent danger in it. Do her justice as far as you can; and retire for a while with your wife into the country.

Though you have forgotten your old vows, remember, I conjure you, your new ones; those which are made in the open air, ought to be as religiously observed as those uttered at the altar. I hope you are firm, my friend, in your resolutions; and yet I am almost afraid to trust such a heart as your's. I again entreat you to leave Vienna: I shall be prevented by a visit that I am going to make, to offer you an invitation; but I wish you to write to me frequently, and to direct to me at W——. Happiness to the friend of

Stendal.

To Isabella.

THE enclosed bills are presented to Signora Marilli with all possible respect; and the person who has taken the present liberty, entreats her to do him the honour of accepting them. He hopes he shall not be accused of indelicacy in mentioning the name of Altenburg, and in assuring her that the Baron has no knowledge of, or interest in the transaction.

Stranger as the writer of this is to Signora Marilli, he feels a more than common interest in her fate, and in that of her lovely daughter—an interest which no selfish or improper view has created, and from which nothing more than their accommodation and happiness is expected.

If the Signora should be returning to Italy before her supplies from that country arrive, and will still further oblige an unknown friend by allowing him to do away that inconvenience, he will be most truly happy, and any sum may be readily commanded by her. She is entreated to give the stranger an answer, directing it to Mr. H——, at the post-office at B——; and again assured that her acquiescence to his request will be in the greatest degree pleasing, and also that the obligation will be ever considered to rest on him alone.

To Count Stendal.

ABOUT two years ago, you, my Lord, spent a few days with

Baron Altenburg, a man who was once known, and dearly loved by me. I was then an inmate of the same house; and whenever in your company, the goodness of your heart, the richness of your mind, and the delicacy of your manners could not fail to impress, and to shew me your genuine merit.

The peculiarity of my situation quickened my remarks on society; I endeavoured to discriminate as justly as possible, and I think it was not often that I looked with the eyes of prejudice. I deal not in flattery, Count, but must say that your manners and deportment excited the admiration of Altenburg's mistress, which was my worldly appellation.

You may, perhaps, remember that you once presented me with a written copy of some beautiful verses; it was made by your own hand, and conjecturing it was also your own muse that gave birth to the ideas, I have till this hour preserved the lines, and very often read them with increasing admiration.

Some few days ago I received an anonymous letter, enclosing notes of value, and speaking, I think, the language of Count Stendal. My surprise at first was more than common; and it was not till after many readings that I thought the characters of the hand familiar to my eye. Perusing it still more seriously, and thinking of your verses, I immediately compared them, discovered them to be the same, and knew that he who styled himself a stranger, was the generous Count Stendal.

My Lord, my Lord! your kindness has found a passage to my heart, which is impatient to pour its whole store of gratitude before you. I cannot select words, I cannot study a dress for language—but indeed I thank you, most sincerely thank you.

You must, however, pardon me for returning that part of your packet which I hold the least valuable: the bills you will receive again with this, but your letter I retain; and having stamped it on my memory, shall place it foremost in the depository of friendship. I may hereafter be very poor; and if poverty *can* make me humble, I may then probably apply to so excellent a friend and benefactor.

My daughter—Oh these foolish tears!—my daughter will cheer me in every distress; her smiles will irradiate the cells of want; and her sweetness, her innocence——Dear my Lord, beware of the professed friendship of the Baron. He who can act as Altenburg has done, can step beyond the devil in villany, can slur religion, violate sanctity, spread corruption, and blow a pestilence around him.

Deny not, my Lord, your generous imposition, for I am sure my suspicions do not deceive me; and though I decline your friendly services, I bless you for the motives that prompted you to offer them. I am not returning to Italy—I have no country, no friends! I am an outcast, a forlorn and miserable alien! The perfidy and cruel desertion of Altenburg may corrupt my heart, and cause it to act desperately, but shall never make it insensible to such a friend as your Lordship.

Isabella Marilli.

———————

Baron Altenburg to Count Stendal.

STENDAL, what a letter have you written to me! I read it with horror, remorse, and anguish; and fearing to trust my eyes with it too often, I put it into the fire, and endeavoured to forget all that it contained: but every sentence, every word was impressed firmly on my mind; I alternately thought you cruel and just, unmerciful and candid.

Surely, my friend, you deal too hardly with me, and make me more culpable than I really am. You know not the nature and extent of my late pecuniary obligations; they were too heavy and too many for friendship to bear, nor could I have applied to you to be the witness of such immense follies. Had not the demands of my creditors been immediately attended to, I must have resigned my liberty, and entered a prison; and in such a state, what could I possibly have done for the support of Isabella and her daughter? Nothing;—distress must inevitably have fallen on them, and they might have been even the victims of want.

If my arguments are fallacious, for God's sake do not endeavour to crush them! Some sense of the propriety of my conduct it is absolutely necessary to retain, or I shall be wretched indeed. I must enter no accusations against myself; should I do so, my present state of content, which I admit is not perfect, would be fatally disturbed, and the lines of misery would be drawn over the plan that happiness has begun to sketch. If I am deceived in myself, let the illusion continue; the veil withdrawn, my eyes might ever thereafter be open only to wretchedness and sorrow.

You cannot conceive, Stendal, in what shocking language Isabella has expressed her sentiments on my marriage; it is so ungovernably wild, so rude and savage, that I am fearful her intellects are affected: and yet now and then a softness glides in undesignedly, which dissolves my soul, and gives her again to my imagination, not as a friend, but as the woman who fascinated and held me in a long and willing bondage. Still she vows eternal resentment, talks of bringing something fatal on me, and obstinately refuses all manner of assistance, preferring poverty and pain, beggary and contempt, to any services which I have offered her!

Oh how miserable should I be were she to experience the horrors of want! and I know not what means she has of keeping them from her; for she has resigned every valuable to me, even her trinkets and *clothes!* and those diamonds which, in the moments of love, I purchased to give brilliancy to charms that I adored, she has sent back to me—back to, as she styles me, "the venal Baron of Altenburg."

Count, in talking of this woman, I almost start from reason; and if I do not soon put her from my memory, I shall be unworthy of the love of Christiana, whose gentleness of conduct, and mildness of sentiment, entitle her to admiration. Is it not uncommon that a wife should be interested, and even plead for the discarded mistress of her husband? Christiana has done it with great fervour; but the subject distracting me, and an apparent indifference to the object being on my part necessary, I have entreated her to speak no more on the subject, and she promises to obey me.

The resentment of Isabella I find to be implacable; and your advising me to fly from her is judicious, and has been attended to. I must indulge no criminal affections; but it follows not that I must perforce hate where I ought not to love. I cannot do it, though she curses me so dreadfully; and as to her daughter—*my* daughter—Oh Stendal, Stendal! have I reared this lovely flower merely to blast it, and tread it to the earth?

I shall leave Vienna in the course of a few days: the Baroness has an estate near Brinn; I have proposed to retire thither for a short time, and to this she readily acceded. Indeed, my dear Count, she is an exemplary woman, and I wish I could bring her to your acquaintance. I must, and will do justice to her virtues; and when I cease to love her, may I instantly cease to breathe!

In our proposed retirement, I shall have leisure to make my arrangements, to regulate my actions, and, I hope, to mould my heart anew. If you love me, upbraid me no more; advise me how to act in what is to come—censure me not for what is past. There is an accuser sufficiently severe in my own breast: add not, therefore, to my torture; but rather, by your better and cooler judgment, soften the distresses of your friend

Altenburg.

———————

Augusta Marilli to the Baron.

FATHER! Father! My dear, cruel Father! have you really deserted, and left us for ever? No, I am sure you have not: I know you will come to us again, and soon; and then, Oh how happy we shall all be! *You* cast us from your heart!—you never return again!—aye, those who say so can have but little knowledge of you. Good God! how can people tell such wicked lies? I shall really despise them for it.

And yet, Oh Heaven! my mother says it is true—she says we shall never see you more—that you are married, and that your love for us has perished! Is this, can this be true? She also says that you hate us: do you indeed, *indeed* hate us? Very well, father—Baron, my mother now calls you: very well, Baron! we can both die; and then, you know, when the grave hides us, we shall not feel your cruelty.

Do as you please, Baron; do as——Oh pray, pray come back to us! My mother has been deceived—I have been deceived; and your absence has been necessary. But so very long—well, that may be accounted for; and I know there are not two people in the world that you love so well as your Isabella and *her* and *your* Augusta, for you have said so a thousand times.

My mother is coming; I must hide my paper, for she would hate me if she knew that I was writing to you; and she is the only person who is dearer to me than you are—I think she is a little more dear——no, no, she is not.

$$* \quad * \quad * \quad * \quad * \quad *$$
$$* \quad * \quad * \quad * \quad * \quad *$$

Oh you have made my mother crazy! She is certainly distracted, and my terror will destroy me. I am afraid to look at her; her actions are growing more strange, and her words I am obliged to shut my ears against.

"Augusta," she says, "curse your father!"

"Madam—mother, did I understand you?"

"Curse your father!"

"Oh no! I dare not."

"God—God will do it!" she exclaimed; and then she sat a long time silent, staring at me with distorted features. Something which she had done to me before increased my fear, and I was rising to fly from her; but she took me in her arms, and having kissed me almost a hundred times, told me I was the only link that bound her to life. Then she again relapsed into profound silence, and for a while fixed her eyes on your picture, which she held in her trembling hand. She looked dejected—more mournful still—still more miserable: she sighed, she wept, pressed the picture to her breast, and afterwards to her pale, quivering lips. Her passions again changed; her features swelled with indignation; she gazed with horror on the painting, and throwing it into the fire, ran shrieking out of the room, and locked herself within her own chamber. I have not seen her since; she refuses to admit me, but tells me that she shall soon be composed again.

Father, remove the anguish of my mother, or I fear I shall soon see her raving in chains. Remove the anguish of your Augusta also by proving that the aspersions of the world are false and malevolent—at least convince her;—I want no assurances; for I can almost as soon believe that God himself were our foe, as that you, my dear parent, are.

How dull we were after you left us in the country! I neglected all my walks. The weather was gloomy, and the birds were mute; like inconsiderate man, the little ingrates forgot to carol their praises to Nature because a temporary gloom succeeded their joyous summer days. Oh ingratitude! we find thee every where; I wonder thou dost not vex Heaven out of its patience.

Let me see—when shall I see my dear father again? I will give you three days, and I am sure that is a long time. To-day is Monday—that must be one; then there is Tuesday and Wednesday—and then on Thursday—Oh my heart is beating with pleasure!—on Thursday I shall be in the arms of my father, and my mother's sadness will disappear!

I will make some little arrangements for the day:—you shall see my improvements in drawing; and a piece, that I have just sketched from my own imagination, I am anxious to place before you; it is a rude, winter scene, a wretched cottage, and two females of miserable appearance, each bearing in her arms a scanty bundle of wood, and standing near the door of the hovel. There is another object; I have introduced a noble looking man, richly dressed, and comfortably clothed with fur; he is gazing with compassion on the strangers, and offering to the elder woman his purse. But what do you think I have further done? I am sure you will say it is ingenious;—to the man I have given your countenance, copied with exactness from the miniature you left with us; my mother appears as one of the cottagers, and I as the other: and the resemblance of each of us is so strong, that I think you will be delighted with my performance.

I however fear there is a small fault in the eyes of my mother— they are not equal to those of the original; but you can compare them when you come to us, and direct me in giving them a darker shade. God bless my dear father till he meets his

Augusta.

Baron Altenburg to Count Stendal.

SOON after I had written my last letter, I left Vienna, and with my lovely companion journied towards our country retirement, in which we have now been nearly a fortnight established. It is indeed a lovely place; Nature has been profuse in adorning it, and made it a residence where the philosopher might reflect unmolested, and the poet quietly indulge himself in the beautiful excursions of imagination.

But I have not yet discovered whether Solitude be the nurse of tranquillity, or the subtle promoter of unhappiness; whether she lulls the turbulent passions to repose, or cunningly prepares them first for mutiny, and then for open rebellion. I am still divided between hope and anxiety. In some moments a thousand blessings seem within my grasp; but in others the tear-swoln chalice of grief, and the dark-shaded vista of disappointment only meet my eye.

The war of conscience has not yet subsided: your letter, my friend, gave new vigour to it; and, till the hostilities of the mind are over, it were folly to expect even a moment of ease. Man possesses but few fixed principles; he is an eternally deviating object: at different periods he has certain notions and ideas, which, bearing in some degree a similarity, he foolishly calls rules: the fluctuations of his sentiments are, if he acts with privacy, only known to himself; for his mind can always be an undetected monopolist, and those who pretend to determine on his established character, are absurdly presumptuous. In early life he may draw plans of future conduct, and for a while adhere to them; but the consciousness of the propriety of acting rightly cannot always keep him in the performance of it; he cannot resolve himself to be what he wishes, and his perseverance is hourly, nay, almost momentarily either strengthening or relaxing.

The days of practical philosophy are, I fear, over; and of those which are said to be past, considerable doubts and suspicions may be entertained. A mere man of the world may sometimes be deemed a sage in his closet; but bring him to the light, and the deception will be wondered at. I was once acquainted with a professed moralist, a lover of literature, who told me he was preparing to publish a treatise on the practice, universally and individually, of humanity; but I afterwards discovered that he had the soul of a negro-driver. Another person, with whom I was for a while in habits of intimacy, would melt at the dramas of Schiller and Kotzebue;* but in actual distress, I could have dug a softer heart from a quarry, or tore a better one from the breast of malice.

Man, therefore, knows little of himself, and his fellows know less of him. Such reflections as these, and the conviction of their being just, sometimes spread a gloom over my countenance, give a pang to my heart, and make me fear the birth of hidden events.

I find it is necessary, as well for the happiness of my wife as of myself, that I should not suffer any appearance of dejection to hang upon me. I yesterday discovered her in tears, though she endeavoured to conceal them: concerned, and even alarmed, I ran up to, and entreated her to inform me of the cause of her sorrow, and also conjured her to banish it immediately if it depended on no very serious circumstance.

"How can you, Altenburg," she replied, "expect to see pleasure in *my* countenance, when *your's* is so gloomy and clouded? For some days past I have observed it with extreme pain: your frequent reveries, your absence, and your musings—all, all bespeak anxiety; and there appears a restlessness in you that I have imputed to dissatisfaction: but of what? Surely, surely *I* am not the cause of your discontent?"

"Oh no, by Heaven!" I exclaimed, pressing her to my heart; "Oh no, by Heaven, Christiana!"

In soothing her I made use of a falsehood:—begging her not to smile at the idea of periodical affections, I assured her they actually visited me, and that I had always found the approach of the autumnal season very oppressive to my spirits. But I promised to bear against them; and in order to appear a more reasonable being, I keep constantly in her presence at home, and when inclined to walk abroad, I now always request her to join with me, and to break the solitude. Still, however, I feel the weakness of my own deception; and though I sincerely love Christiana, yet in my heart poor Isabella, poor Augusta—I am leading myself into dangerous paths.

Previous to my leaving Vienna, I executed some writings which entitle Isabella to an independence, and put them into the hands of my steward, desiring him to wait on her, and present them. On the back of the principal paper I have written with a pencil, "To Isabella, and to Altenburg's beloved Augusta."

I have not yet heard the event of the embassy of Grotz, but most fervently hope it has been successful. If Isabella should be still obstinate, in spite of the love and tenderness of Christiana, I shall anticipate a long winter of sorrow.—Oh indiscretion! though we feel no compunctions at the time of yielding to thee, what a black train of plagues, all the progeny of thy secret womb, and by ourselves begotten, do we afterwards open our disgusted eyes upon!

Altenburg.

Joseph Grotz to the Baron.

MY LORD,

YOUR Lordship may probably have wondered at my silence in respect to the affairs that you commanded me to execute; but circumstances have so happened, that till this time it was not possible for me to give you any intelligence. What I have now to communicate is by no means of a pleasant nature. I however assure your Lordship, I have not wanted exertion in the business, though I have unfortunately failed in the completion of it.

The lady, whom you desired me to wait upon with the writings, has removed from her late place of residence, and with so much privacy, that it was with difficulty I lately traced her to an obscure lodging in the suburbs of the city. Having discovered her abode, and being desirous of relieving the anxiety of your Lordship as early as possible, I immediately went to the house, and begged permission to speak with her; which request, after some little delay, she consented to, and I was brought before her.

Oh my Lord! what a dreadful alteration in Madam, and in Miss Augusta, your Lordship's daughter! At sixty-five we are enfeebled, both in body and in mind; it is not strange, therefore, that my breath grew short, and that I burst into tears to see the eyes of the lady, once so brilliant, now sinking into their sockets; and the sweet cheeks of her child without a tint of those roses which once overspread them—all faded! pale and drooping, like a storm-beaten lily!

She sucked at the breast of my wife, my Lord; she was fostered in her infancy by the milk of poor Susan: she has since, till within a few months, cursed months! flourished, and gambolled, and sported before my eyes! Pardon, therefore, the pratings and sorrows of your old servant Grotz.

My Lord, Augusta's mother has seen the writings, heard a full explanation of their import, and read the short note addressed to her. Her answer was this:—

"The Baron knows my sentiments—they are fixed, established; he therefore must not, shall not trouble me any more. Henceforth I will owe nothing to him: were I friendless and famishing, passing by his door, or bending with burning thirst over his canal, I would yield to death rather than take a morsel of bread from the one, or a drop of water from the other."

"So would I, so would I!" cried the daughter, clasping her mother's neck.

"You hear," said my poor Lady; "tell your master this, and God bless you, old man!"

The same words were repeated by your Lordship's daughter, who pressed my hand, and then went out of the apartment, leaning on the arm of her mother. I did not immediately leave the room—I could not—my nerves relaxed; but when they strengthened a little, I collected the papers, and departed from the house, which is but a sorry place for one who has long been accustomed to the elegancies of your Lordship's mansion. But to the heart of grief what is the difference between a palace and a dungeon? The letters which were sent to your Lordship some few days ago, did not pass through my hands, or they would have reached you earlier; but I hope they were of no great importance. Command in what manner the rejected writings are to be disposed of by your Lordship's old and faithful servant,

Joseph Grotz.

Baron Altenburg to Count Stendal.

STENDAL, there is no happiness for me! I have, I fear, precipitated myself into misery, from which there can be no extrication. The slave of passion, and the fool of impulse has now nothing left to cover his extravagances but a sorry repentance. Good God, what a part have I acted!—I look with wonder on my past deeds, and am shocked even by my present presumption.

Count, read the enclosed letter; it is written by Augusta, by my beloved child, by the daughter of the abandoned Isabella! Oh you know not how I have loved this girl! you know not how her innocence, her simple accusations, and her sweet sensibilities have torn my heart!

I have scarcely possessed my senses since I received this letter; it has brought my depravities fresh into my mind, and cast an ugly soil upon my nature. You are a father, Stendal—Oh how I envy you!—Had I, like you, been virtuous, like you I had been happy. I likewise am a father: I have children—yes, *children*;—but I gave them being merely to make them objects of derision, of shame, and of poverty! I have been base beyond your imagination; and the curses of my progeny are likely to pass over my grave. I am a seducer and betrayer: in the exploits of the one I thought myself admired; in the baseness of the other I find I am despicable.

Hear what my poor little girl says; how affecting, how pathetic!—Read, read, and think what my tortures must be. Be careful of the letter, and return it to me; I will carry it always near my heart: it shall be an eternal punishment to me for my sins; and I will read it every night, in order that, as a penance, it may keep me anxious and waking. What a shocking picture has she drawn of her unhappy mother! Oh I see in it the delineations of insanity! That beauty which I once admired, to be distorted! that mind which was so sweet and strong, to be overthrown!

Mark how my child pleads for my return; how unwilling she is to believe that I *can* desert her. She saw Monday, Tuesday, and Wednesday pass over; and on Thursday—torture must have wrung the innocent's heart. Perhaps she then, indeed, joined with Isabella in cursing her father!

Do not you feel the force of the preparations that she was making to celebrate my return—of the drawing that she intended to place before me? The horrors of winter, the distresses of poverty, the relief of humanity—Isabella and herself the miserable women; I the administerer of comfort—*I!*—She has, I dare say, removed me already from the scene, and substituted a robber, a murderer, or a beast of prey!

I have not yet heard from Grotz, in respect to the writings which I executed in favour of Isabella. His silence alarms me; I cannot conjecture what is the occasion of it: but the fidelity and integrity of the old man have been long known to me. After I had dissipated my fortune, I was obliged to discharge the honest fellow; but on coming into the possession of that of Christiana, it was with pleasure that I reinstated him.

Ah, my dear Count! you cannot conceive the difficulty of the part I am now acting: like a compounded character in a drama, I cover my baseness with hypocrisy, and hide habitual vices beneath an indiscriminate heap of artificial virtues. I have hitherto deceived my amiable wife; and pray Heaven the deception may continue till I shall become more worthy!

*   *   *   *   *   *

Letters from Vienna are arrived—there is one from Grotz: I have read it, and my afflictions are increased; for it informs me that Isabella hides herself in an obscure lodging, and that both she and her daughter are resolved to bend to the rigours of want, rather than receive from me the most trifling assistance. Obstinate women, perish then!—Oh no, no! Isabella, Augusta, why will you not still let me be a friend and a father to you?

Christiana calls me to walk with her. Count, were you to see this woman, you would admire her. Think me not licentious for wishing a plurality of wives; but in the division of my love between Isabella and Christiana, the sun would not bid good-day to a happier mortal. Aye, I know I talk madly; and confess there is at this time a great fault in my brain.

My wife calls again:—I come, deluded woman! Adieu, dear Count. My intellects want a new arrangement, and there is an oppressive sickness in the heart of

Altenburg.

Baron Altenburg to Augusta.

AUGUSTA, my beloved child! you must not deny me the comfort of writing to you; you must not prevent me from telling you that I am still your affectionate parent. I have not had a moment's tranquillity since the arrival of your letter, which, on the first perusal, filled me with indescribable anguish: to reply to you now increases that anguish; and I think I see my dear daughter regarding me with contempt and horror.

Be patient, Augusta, and hear me.

I am married: I can no more return to your mother—duty to my wife forbids it; we are therefore parted for ever! The connection that once subsisted between us is dissolved, and we must not expose ourselves to the danger of any future meeting. Still be tranquil, child:—your mother is wild, and will not listen to me; but to you I think I can shew some extenuation for my conduct.

Had I not acted in the manner that I have done, the sad remainder of my life, Augusta, must have passed in a common prison; and my last breathings must have been within the damp walls of a dungeon. Could you, could you, dear daughter, have seen the days of age creep on your poor father in a place like that? Carry your eye to it, and to the soul-weary captive;—see his wants, his misery, his despair! Relieve him—revive the sickly flame of life—lead him again to the free enjoyment of the pure air; you cannot, you have no means. His fate and your own are combined; his sufferings, his poverty, his dreadful wants, all attach themselves to you. Alas, alas! Altenburg, Isabella, and Augusta are expiring; they grow more weak—weaker still—they perish! they perish!

Such must have been our general fate; and what I have lately done could alone save us from it. I have not painted an unnatural scene, but such an one, dear Augusta, as misfortune would have presented to us. To avert the impending evil, to rescue myself from imprisonment, and to give comfort to those whose happiness was of no less consideration to me than my own, I was compelled to change my system, the result of which is now known to you and to your mother; and though she refuses to listen to my reasonings, I trust that your more tranquil mind will feel for my condition, acknowledge the necessity of my actions, and pity me for being so cruelly driven to them.

Endeavour to sooth the passions of your mother;—plead for me; tell her my sufferings have been, and still are dreadfully acute; that my memory will never discard her, and that my heart can never wholly throw her from it. Pursue the subject farther; talk to her till she agrees to accept the writings which old Grotz lately offered to her; and, if possible, get her to consent that you should quit her for a short time, in order that you may come under the protection of your father and the Baroness, who is anxious to take you to her heart. This desire must make her appear amiable in your eyes; and her connections are such as will probably ensure you the most considerable advantages.

Your mother has refused to comply with this proposal; but as your elevation and happiness may perhaps depend on it, I would have you employ your most forcible arguments to put aside the hasty determination of Isabella, from whom I would not separate you entirely: for she might, at certain periods, see and converse with you, though to me she must be ever hereafter invisible. To meet were again to love; and to love were assuredly to be wretched.

Let the necessity of these conditions do away the hardness of them. Soften the obdurate heart of your mother; accept the writings yourself if she should again refuse so to do, and they shall be accordingly altered: and, dear daughter, pray, pray take the diamonds which Isabella lately returned to me! In spite of your peremptory commands, I have desired Grotz to obtain a private interview, and to present you the trinkets in the absence of your mother. Discover not my intention to her; admit the old man, receive from him the jewels, and look on them as coming from him to whose heart you ever have been, still are, and while he breathes, will be most dear, most precious.

Attend to all that I have said; obey me as far as you can, and let your affections be proportionate to mine. The Baroness will love you; she has seen your picture, and is filled with a lively admiration. Come to us, though you return again soon. Admit old Grotz, and refuse not the jewels. God bless you, child! God bless your mother!

Altenburg.

The Baroness of Altenburg to Miss Messein.

I HAVE been long silent, but forgive me, my dear Charlotte; there have been times, you well remember, when you have fallen into the indolence of correspondence, and when I have silenced all your excuses with a ready and voluntary pardon, which ought now to smooth your brow, if it be ruffled, and cleanse your heart of every particle of anger.

I told you in my last letter that I and my Altenburg were preparing to leave Vienna, in order to take a view of our estate at F——; we accordingly quitted the former, and have since been residing some little time at the latter place, the natural beauties of which are heightened by a most luxurious and fruitful summer.

Bountiful Father of the heavens and earth! thou who sheddest thy fostering dews, who causest the blossom to open, the fruit to ripen into perfection, and the corn to wave on the plains, on the hills, and in the valleys, which thy mysterious hand formed from the shapeless mass of chaos—Power of my adoration! were I to forget to bless thee in the morning, I were unworthy to live throughout the day; or were I to neglect my orisons at night, I should be undeserving of the protection of thy soothing spirits, who give to us in our temporary oblivion, the dreams of pleasure, and the visions of delight. Having made me what I am, with such liberal endowments, never may the seeds of penury root in my heart! never may I, with criminal thoughtlessness, with-hold my superfluities from those who have missed thine envied bounties!

Charlotte, I really think I may, without vanity, say that I pos-sess no inconsiderable strength of mind; for I learn that my name has been abroad of late, that the prudes have condemned me for marrying a libertine, and that much evil is augured from my temerity. And yet I have listened to these tales of idleness, these accusations of folly, and forebodings of ignorance, without either pain or anger. To smile at impertinence is the most effec-tual method of crushing it; gravity merely provokes it, and anger only serves to give elasticity to its springs.

Either the world, or your friend, is miserably deceived in respect to the character of Altenburg; I think he has been rudely calumniated, and many of the vices which the self-sinning mor-alists of the times have been pleased to annex to him, my heart has willingly softened into improprieties, which may yet be effectually purged away. I knew him not in the days of error, nor did I see much of him before I became his wife; but I did not unite myself to him without love: he planted that passion first in my heart, and his sincerity and frankness rooted it most firmly. He gained me not by hypocrisy and canting, nor wished to pass himself as immaculate: he shewed his very soul to me; I deemed it a noble prize, and never may I repent the claiming of it!

Altenburg is several years older than myself, though the dif-ference is not very conspicuous, and the beauty of his person cannot easily be excelled; he has also a very superior mind, and since our connection I am sure it has been strictly governed by reason. There are moments in which his tenderness almost over-powers me; and his language is of such a peculiar nature, that I could almost persuade myself Sensibility was his mother.

While I retain the love of Altenburg—and may that and life fly from me together!—let the loquacious few, who arrogantly call themselves the world, arraign me as they please, and exercise their spleen even till it becomes vapid to themselves.

In my former letter, Charlotte, I made you acquainted with the connection that for many years subsisted between the Baron and an Italian woman of the name of Marilli, by whom he has a daughter of the age of fifteen or sixteen; and, judging by a miniature which he has shewn me, she must be a truly lovely girl. The mother has accepted a provision from the Baron, and is retiring to her native country. Being willing to take the daughter to my own protection, I hinted my desire to Altenburg, who instantly applied to the Signora for that purpose; but could not induce her to part from the girl, of whom he is exceedingly fond.

This refusal has, I know, given him extreme pain, though he endeavours to conceal it; but as they will soon leave the country, it must be my task to bring him again to tranquillity, and my hopes of success are strong ones.

I wish the application of Altenburg had been attended to: his Augusta would have made me a sweet companion; and I fear the sentiments of her mother may be dangerous to inexperienced innocence. I believe the model of your heart, my dear Charlotte, is so much like mine, that I do not fear it will condemn the actions of your friend towards the former associates of Altenburg, the elder of whom I pity, and the younger, though unknown to me, I really love.

The fastidious sentiments of many of my acquaintances actually make me smile, and some few of them have completely disgusted me. You remember the old Baroness of L——; having no longer charms for admiration, youth for gaiety, or health for amusement, she has assumed the garb of a devotee, and become a professed censurer of the prevailing habits and customs; and though, in days that are passed, reputation vowed no longer to be her handmaid, her intimacy with the Margrave of B—— having assumed an unquestionable appearance, yet now she would place her foot on the neck of Virtue, and cast the shadow of prejudice on the face of Innocence.

She has been talking to me concerning my late connection, with matchless confidence; I resented it with an unaccustomed spirit; and now, perhaps, the gossip is going her rounds in Vienna, with my name and a bag of venom hanging on her tongue.

Our German ladies have certainly many infirmities and bad propensities. I wish my dear Charlotte would, to make their national pride and characteristic impertinence of still less importance than they are, come to her friend

Christiana.

Augusta to Baron Altenburg.

HOPE had lulled me into a pleasant dream; the moments fled; I awoke not: the illusion was still fair, beautiful, and the creator of it watched over me with delight. You have now roused me; the vision no longer glows, and the forms which were moving gaily in it, have yielded to the intrusion of demons. Peace has wrapped her white robes around her, and fled; and Misery, in her tattered sables, and sighing in the sickness of her soul, approached near to me, saying, "Girl, thou art young, and not long ago thy prospects were sunny, though they are now dismal. Let me take thee in my arms; live with thee forever; travel through life with thee, and be near to thee on thy death-bed. Come, here are garments for thee; such weeds as these distinguish my followers from the offspring of happiness: come, quit thy pleasant home; bring thy mother with thee, and let us all seek the dark ways and flinty passages!"

Oh unbelieving fool that I have been! The present sickness of my heart might have been less, had I shaken off credulity, and not so firmly relied on the virtue of man's nature. Scourges and unceasing reproofs await the disobedience of children; but the inexperienced triflers must neither murmur, nor turn a dewy eye upon the oppressions and cruelties of their parents. Oh father! so well did I love you once, and so much were you in my mind, that there have been times when, praying to my God, my thoughts (Heaven pardon me for it!) have wandered from my devotions, and fixed wholly upon you.

To make you great, I lessened every other object. Where was there so noble a mind—where so good, so generous a heart? When you have been heaping kindness on me, what ecstacy it was to break from you, and to exclaim, "He is my father—he gave me life! I owe my being to this beloved, this excellent man!"—It was in these moments pleasure to weep; many a time joy has swelled my tears. Past, past, Augusta, are thy sensations of delight!

My Lord, I did not acquaint my mother of the letter you sent to me: I admitted Grotz privately; I suffered him to place before me the jewels which once ornamented me and the parent with whom I used to be happy. But I delivered them again to the old man, retaining only a string of pearls, as a remembrance of a cruel father, whose desertion could not make me hate him. Take them back again, my Lord—they would only mock my wretchedness; and if placed upon my bosom, like those which lie midway in the mine, would sparkle over a gloomy and comfortless abyss. Take them, my Lord—they are in the possession of Grotz.

I told you that I kept a string of pearls as a remembrance; but finding it a pain to look on them, I have disposed of the baubles. One day, when my mother was not present, I put them for a little while round my neck; but a chain of iron had afflicted me less. I tore them from me, opened the window, and threw them one by one into the street.

A little beggar girl was standing below; she picked them up as I dropped them, and when she had got possession of them all, she sat down on the threshold, smilingly untied a string of beads, and having carefully intermixed her toys and the pearls, went her ways on her supplicatory errand.

Oh that I had been the insensible little wretch! Perhaps her father gave her the poor ornament that she wore; and perhaps, after a day of severity and hard living, when she enters her sorry abode, *that father* may take her in his arms, and say to her, "God bless thee, poor child!" Oh that I were her, rather than what I am! And yet our worldly situations will soon be similar.

My Lord, I never, never will leave my mother;—happy together, or miserable together. I applaud the independence of her spirit, and will frame mine according to it. While I have a nerve in my arm, I will exercise it for her support:—it is true I have not been used to work for my bread; but custom, that will soon teach the Baron of Altenburg to forget the creatures who have perhaps too long checked his pleasures, and impeded his happiness, may also teach me to think without regret on the sorry alteration that has already happened, and on the poverty that is likely soon to wrap itself around me and my dear mother. We go from hence to-morrow. Farewel, farewel! and cruel as you have been, God guard you, father!

Augusta.

――――――――――

The Baroness of Altenburg to Miss Messein.

CHARLOTTE, my dear Altenburg is ill—very, nay I fear dangerously ill! The first appearance of his indisposition alarmed, and an increasing fever has terrified me; it was preceded by a depression of spirits that he was not able to conceal, though he evidently strove to do so, and by an absence of the mind that plainly shewed its internal disturbance. Oh what can be the occasion of it?

Seeing my agitation, he entreated me not to alarm myself unnecessarily; but I could not be in any degree tranquil till he consented to the attendance of a physician, which he was previously much inclined to dispense with. The Doctor does not speak very unfavourably of his patient to me, but to others I have reason to suppose he is less cautious: I know he entertains some serious apprehensions, and regards the progress of the fever with great concern. Oh Heaven! if I should lose my Altenburg! Charlotte, there are a thousand agonies in that thought!

He even strives to laugh away my fears; but in that expedient I can discover the opposition of Nature, against whom he is weakly struggling. Whenever I take his hot hand, he tells me he shall soon be well, and that to his affliction a child would scarcely yield. My continuing in his chamber, I perceive does not please him; his motives, however, for wishing my absence spring from love and fear, which serve to fix me near his bed, rather than drive me from it.

He had not slept for a considerable time till last night, when, about nine o'clock, he fell into a slumber, and I laid myself by his side. He continued to sleep for some time, alternately quiet and disturbed; for his breathings were frequently hard, his hands hot, and his forehead dewy.

The hour of midnight went over, and the second of morning was come, when he started up, and looking around him, and then at me, enquired the time; on my replying to him, he gently chid me, and desired me to retire to bed. I was obeying him, when he called back, and pressing his burning lips on my hand, "God bless you, Christiana!" he cried; "and may his angels watch over you, as you, their sister, have watched over me!"

"Heaven protect you, my Altenburg!" I exclaimed, as I went out of the room in tears, which I wished him not to notice. I was in his chamber again early in the day, but found nought of comfort there, no happy alteration being discernible. On many occasions I have hitherto thought that I possessed much fortitude and confidence; but to see my kind, my dearly loved Altenburg on the bed of affliction—God! perhaps on his deathbed—Oh how shocking is that idea! I have now no strength, no courage!

Charlotte, grant me the request that I am going to make:—come to me as early as possible; with all the force of friendship I entreat you. On this spot I have no friends; and if any fatality be awaiting my dear Altenburg, not one consoling voice would reach me while I gazed on him in his coffin, or dragged my weak limbs after him to the grave.

The Doctor is now coming from his patient, and I go to him trembling, and tortured by fears. Come, come, dear girl, as early as possible; and under this roof put up your prayers to Heaven for the life of the husband of

Christiana.

The same to the same.

YOUR letter, my friend, has reached me, and given pain to my heart. How concerned I am that, while I was pressing you to come to me during the affliction of my husband, you should be closing the eyes of a mild and venerable parent, and weeping over the corse of her who gave you to the world, fostered you at her breast, and watched you with tenderness through youth to your late state of happiness!

Soon, soon may that happiness return! Let the tears of affection and regret take their course, and then recal your former serenity to your bosom. The thoughts which attach themselves to death may be gloomy; but those which range to immortality, are bright as the clouds of summer.

Good God, what transition! To breathe oppressively, to strive to raise the heavy eyelid, to touch the warm hand that gives no heat, and cannot be pressed, to fall from the supporting arm cold, stiff, totally insensate;—then the spirit—wonderful essence! to burst from its secret prison-door, to ascend, to travel through the ways of light on the wings of rapidity; and, unobstructed, to call at the gate of heaven, saying, "Open, Almighty Father! admit thy expected servant: open, Almighty Father, and let me dwell with thee for ever!"

Oh Charlotte! I am thrilled with an inward rapture; my feelings at this moment are very strange. If imagination has its victims, and I sometimes believe it, I fear I shall fall a sacrifice. Dry up your tears, my friend; remember Nature enforced not her demand till a long date, and even then did it with an unusual degree of mild resolution:—dispel, therefore, the clouds of sorrow; turn your eyes from the body of your mother, and direct them towards her remaining family of love.

My Altenburg—Charlotte, he will live, he will live! My fears made me wild, but they were groundless; the fever that preyed upon the poor sufferer is gone over; his mind is become tranquil, and nothing remains but a languor which will I hope soon disappear. Gratitude has ever been in my nature: but Oh the gratitude that I am anxious to offer to the Supreme Being on this occasion, flows incessantly, still without any pomp of words or studied form.

I seem to be newly created; I go about the house, smiling; I meet the Chaplain.—"Friend," I exclaim, "my husband is recovered. Remember to whom your praises are due—to God! worship him for it." I make my servants assemble together, tell them of the happy change, and bid them rejoice;—then I fly to the chamber of my Altenburg; my lips fix on his still pale cheek; I throw my arms around his neck, and place my very heart before him, in order that he may see the characters of love upon it.

Enthusiast!—Well, be it so, while my enthusiasm is not injurious. Farewel, my dear friend! Peace be to the bosom of your yourself, and to the kindred mourners who surround you!

Christiana.

Count Stendal to Baron Altenburg.

WHY this long silence, Altenburg? What is the cause of it? Have I, in my plainness of speech, advanced any thing to give you displeasure? If so, trust me I am sorry for it. There are some qualities in me which will, in their obstinacy, discover themselves. I have never been accustomed to strangle my thoughts; and have so long indulged myself in the free utterance of every thing allied to truth, that in this age of fashion and ceremony, when polite lying is thought an accomplishment, and harsh facts are held to be odious, I believe there are those who, seeing me approach them, would be ready to exclaim, "This barbarian must be avoided till he has gone through the rules of civilization."

Remember, Altenburg, I am a plain, rusticated mortal; one who is little pleased with ceremony, or proud of riches; one whom state and pageantry disgust; no cringer at Courts, no smiler at levees; nothing more than an unaspiring being, who, for his happiness, must discourse with Nature, and suffer her to regulate his days in those retirements, where winter makes him contemplative, and summer joyful; where love comes willingly to bless him; and where he, who is fond of prattling on little concerns, finds too much poverty of circumstance to feed on.

The world has said (it may still say) Stendal is not old; he has rank, fortune, is married to a lovely woman, and his means are nearly princely; yet, for all this, he is cynical and mean; he retires from the sphere in which he should move, merely to accumulate wealth; affects simplicity to cover his parsimony; keeps his wife in obscurity through similar motives; and has too poor a soul to support that dignity which attaches itself to his name.

Oh ye sorry observers! my happiness is well secured against your malice, too remote for your sarcasms to reach; it is in the beauty and fertility of my demesne, in the prosperity of its cultivators, in the smiles and fidelity of my dependants, in the caresses of my sweet wife and blessed progeny!—such is the constitution of my happiness; and in my retreats, heard are the effusions of genius, and the deeper tones of wisdom, arising from enchanting poetry and divine philosophy.

Altenburg, break your stubborn silence, and write to me. I need not repeat that you are in my heart, and that I wish the felicities of life upon you. I am going a little tour of friendship, and shall on Thursday be at N——, where I would have you direct to me. Adieu! the best wishes of a friend attend on you and the Baroness.

Stendal.

The Baron in Reply.

THE cause of my silence, friend, is not that which you conjectured: though your truths have carried conviction, and your accusations reached my conscience, which went the greater way to meet them, yet none of them should have sealed my lips, lest it should have been suspected that my taciturnity arose either from insensibility, or the spirit of obstinacy.

I was preparing to write to you at the very moment your letter arrived; and have now to inform you that I have of late been deprived of the pleasure of corresponding with you by a severe affliction. Yes, affliction, my friend; indisposition is too forceless a word to express my late situation; it may, indeed be applicable to the state of my body, but is not important enough for the malady of my mind. The former is again assuming its functions, and the latter I am striving to amend: there must be resolution on my part—I find it necessary; and if my exertions be not great, my relapse may be fatal.

The cause of all this internal pain and intellectual warfare is, as you may conjecture, in Isabella; my misery arises from her and from her daughter; and they have so opposed my projects, that my reason almost sunk with them. You know my natural rashness and impetuosity: there have been moments when I almost cursed these women, but the imprecations were immediately succeeded by blessings; and I have shuddered at my own impiety, and called back again the discarded objects to my heart.

Isabella and Augusta are the voluntary victims of poverty; the fortune of the one, it is resolved by them, shall be the fortune of the other; every valuable has been rejected; and by a letter which I have lately received from old Grotz, I find that even the greater part of their clothes have been packed up by them, and sent to my house; and also that they have again removed their lodging, and with so much privacy, that nothing can be learned of them.

They will starve! they will perish! Isabella and my girl will die in want and wretchedness, even while luxuries spread the board of the man who has deserted them, and who once was, and perhaps, in spite of their protestations, still is, remembered and beloved. Presumptuous, unnatural thought!—Dearly as I have ever prized my daughter, her actual worth was not known to me till I lost her; for I knew not till of late that, possessing the similitude, she had the mind of an angel.

She has written to me a farewel letter; it is a composition that would melt the most iron-hearted mortal, and a savage parent might weep over it. Oh Stendal! that very letter laid me on a bed of sickness; I read it till I was almost distracted; my heart sickened, and nature was nearly subdued. A fever succeeded; but, thank Heaven, it did not reach my mind; I have therefore retained my senses, and consequently been very guarded in my expressions.

What a good angel is Christiana! Divided as my heart is, she must ever be a dear object to it; and if my love wants that fervour which it possessed when directed towards Isabella, still my attachment to my wife is tender, and firmly fixed. She has been my nurse, her sweet bosom my pillow, her eyes the anxious watchers of my restlessness; from morning till night she has attended me, and again from night till morning. When I lay faint and exhausted, I saw the terror of her face, and heard the murmurs of her breast; but now I have, in some degree, regained my strength, and since danger has left me, mirth presides over her countenance; she laughs, she sings, and shews such proofs of love, as, even in my present debilitated state, awaken my admiration. Dear enthusiast! never will I forget my duty to thee:—duty! the word is insignificant, and does not reach my meaning.

I have kept her in ignorance respecting Isabella; she believes that my mistress and daughter are gone back to Italy, and that they have accepted from me a competent provision. Amiable being! how few of the prejudices of the sex obscure her nature! She can pardon those frailties over which at first she sighs; and her compassion and humanity are directed towards those places from which some women would fastidiously turn, or look upon with affected disgust.

I dare not, at this time, trust myself in saying any more respecting these unfortunate creatures: happy, happy should I be, could I put the same restraint upon my mind as on my pen; but every effort that I have hitherto made to direct the former, has been totally ineffectual. The brain is an obstinate republic, and it is difficult to account for the anarchy that breeds in it.

Dear Stendal, I feel a languor creeping over me. I promised my wife not to be absent more than half an hour, and therefore must fold my letter, and dispatch it. But first let me wish you pleasure in your tour of friendship. As you did not mention the name of those whom you were going to visit, I presume they are unknown to me. There is a circumstance of which I wish to speak, relating to the village in which this letter will find you; it is——But I am faint, and cannot now proceed. Within a few days, perhaps to-morrow, I may address you on a subject which I am, at this time, too weak and irresolute to mention.

Altenburg.

_____

The Baron to the Count.

YOU are a man of virtue; in the paths of rectitude you have been steady, never deviating therefrom: your pursuit has been happiness, and you have attained it. I—but no parallels, lest they should appear tinged with sycophancy. I am a poor extenuator of my errors, and can plead infinitely better for those of other people than for my own. I am convinced of the fallacy of the doctrine, that a man's optics make not the imperfections of himself visible:* he may, I admit, for a while close his eyes upon them; but the time cannot be long before he must open them to a full disclosure of his deformities, whether he confesses it, or not.

The sequel to these reflections may probably make me appear to you like a sorry author, who having something base to obtrude upon the reader, would fain attract him by some artifice in a laboured preface.

The letter that I wrote to you two days ago, must have led you to expect another. The subject, however, which I am desirous of entering upon, embarrasses me; and, fearful of your further censures, I have been much inclined to do away what I said, by silence. But to retract would not be honourable; and to proceed will be, I fear, to lead myself into merited disgrace. Were I of the Catholic persuasion, I should weary even the most patient confessor, whose absolutions of my multiplied transgressions would necessarily come with tardiness and reluctance.

About twenty years ago, and when I was not quite eighteen years old, I and a juvenile acquaintance, whose habits and idle propensities were kindred with my own, retired from Vienna, and for the course of three months resided in the village where you now are. We had a large supply of money, which enabled us to keep a more than ordinary appearance; and we lived in the extravagance which had become habitual to us. To prevent the impertinent enquiries of our friends, we assumed fictitious names; and as the spot was particularly favourable to hunting, and the season being that of sports, it formed our principal amusement.

My dissipated associate had accommodated himself with a temporary mistress, whom he brought from Vienna: and as I had neglected to do so, and possessed no more virtue than my young acquaintance, immediately on our arrival at the village, I began to look for an object of similar gratification.

Vice, I soon discovered, was little known in the hamlet, and wantonness not to be found in it; still I saw women, young, blooming, and modest; and that to seduce any of them, was to be a villain, neither perplexed nor entered into my mind. Being an epicure in my sensualities, my heart bounded when I discovered a girl of about seventeen years of age, and of singular beauty, residing in a cottage at a little distance from the house which I had engaged: I marked her as my prize; my imagination rioted, and I was impatient to obtain possession of the lovely rustic.

In the present days, as it was in those to which I am now alluding, to seduce the affections of a wife, or to pillage her of her honour, is looked upon and pardoned frequently with a smile; and to decoy a mistress from a friend, is applauded as an act of heroism and ingenuity. I was acquainted with the tenor of my companion's sentiments, and knew the strength of his passions; therefore, to effect my security, and forward my own vile plans, I kept him ignorant of my designs, and did not point out the charming cottager to his notice.

One day, taking advantage of his absence, I sauntered past the lowly habitation of the stranger, and saw her knitting at the door: her beauty heightened as I approached near to her, for as soon as her eyes came upon me, blushes rose in her cheeks, and she looked down on the ground, rather than on her work. This evident confusion only served to embolden me; and to subdue a timid woman was, I thought, more easy than to prevail with a confident one.

Her countenance was truly sweet; she had not the appearance of a ruddy rustic; there was a grace about her so natural and fascinating, that I looked on her with increasing delight. Opening the wicket of the garden, I walked up to her, and with some degree of respect, asked her whether she had seen a lady and gentleman go past the cottage within the last half hour; she answering in the negative, I advanced some further questions, and attempted to begin a conversation, when I found that, with her beauty, she had no mean intellect, and that the sweetest simplicity accompanied every word she uttered.

We were soon, however, interrupted by her mother, who came into the garden; and as the old lady seemed to scrutinize me, I thought it proper to retire from the cottage till opportunity better favoured my project.

Stendal, the recollection of the means which I used in order to bring innocence and unwary youth into ruin, at this moment chills my languid blood, and gives sickness to my heart. Moralist, what must you think of your unworthy but repentant friend?

I contrived to see and to talk with her again on the following day: several other meetings succeeded. I forced her to accept some little presents, professed an attachment for her, and by a masterpiece of dissimulation, and after an acquaintance of two months, she gave her virtue up to me. Barbarian like, I seduced her with lies; swore that I was the son of a merchant, that I sincerely loved, and would marry her, and that I would never, never forsake her. She yielded to me; our intercourse was continued with privacy, and she had no suspicion of the deception that I had practised.

But she had scarcely entered into the errors of love, before she heard the upbraidings of conscience, and felt the pangs of guilt. I had much difficulty in soothing her; and whenever I found her inclined to melancholy, I cheered her by talking of the union that would soon subsist between us, which generally dispersed the clouds of anxiety.

I found that the village priest was the friend of my lovely victim; that she had been his favourite from her infancy; that he had given her an education, and in some degree improved her mind, and carried his attachment so far, as to persuade her parents, one of whom was since dead, to name her after his wife, who had been recently wrested from him. Neither of these circumstances, however, impeded me in the progress of villany: my religious tenets were very weak; and if ever I felt any respect for the sacerdotal character, an intrusion of some of the glare of false philosophy, which had led away my understanding, would almost instantly overthrow and destroy it.

I had not hinted at my amour to my friend, who now began to talk of returning to Vienna, as the means of prodigality were failing him. He urged me to accompany him; I assented to his request, and an early day was fixed for our departure.

I now felt the pangs of self-reproach; the cottage of poor Josephine I could not look indifferently on; and when in a moonlight evening, and in the absence of her mother, she stole to a little thicket, the usual place of our assignations, and crept to my bosom, Oh then I began to suspect I was a villain! Still it was but a suspicion, and it abided not long with me.

Count, I will abridge my tale.

I left the ruined girl without taking any leave of her. Returning to Vienna, I strove, like a monster, to forget her; but it was impossible to expel her immediately from my memory, because Vienna offered not so lovely a woman to my notice. The varied dissipations of six successive months could not wholly drive her from my mind; that time had elapsed when I wrote a letter to her, in which I enclosed a bill of some value: and, still using the fictitious name of Rostock, assured her that I should ever love her; but on the subject of marriage I was very much guarded, if not wholly silent.

After waiting with great impatience for the course of a month, I received an answer to my letter, not written by Josephine, but by the Priest, of whom I have before spoken; and being in a serious mood when it reached me, the edges of a thousand swords could scarcely have mangled me more than the good man's words and intelligence. He first expatiated on the crime of seduction, and on the prevalence of vice; then painted the poor cottager in all the colours of innocence—colours which I had sullied, innocence which I had defiled! He spoke of her confession, her consequent shame and agony; and shewed her to my imagination broken-hearted, and sobbing on the bosom of her unhappy mother, in an advanced state of pregnancy, and of ruined health and mind.

Had he presented her to me at that moment, I could have exclaimed, "This woman has been injured by me; but as my wife, and with the sincerity of love, she shall have reparation."—Oh Stendal! I cannot now proceed; the next post shall bring you what I am at this time unable to send. You may never have felt

the pangs of conscience; I have—I do; at this moment they rack
the breast, and almost distract the brain of

Altenburg.

─────────

The Baron to the Count.

IF I did not weary you, dear Stendal, with the beginning of
my tale, I entreat that you will listen to the remainder of it. The
picture of the good old Priest disturbed my imagination, and I
thought myself cursed in being the cause of all the misery that
he had so pathetically described. Conscience is never so susceptible of any wound as of the first, because there is no previous
suspicion of its being merited; every other attack on it is less
severe; frailty grows more palpable, and the repetition of faults
seems more deserving of punishment: precautions, therefore, are
taken against those inflictions, to which at length it becomes
habituated, and which sink the acute sense into comparative
indifference and apathy.

Preparations were then making for my going to Italy. My
father was busy in arranging my concerns, in reproving me for
my former levities, and in entreating me to be more guarded and
prudent in my future conduct. He was unwilling that I should be
much with my thoughtless associates, and seemed desirous that I
should spend with him all the intervening time till the day fixed
for my departure from Vienna. This restraint I found highly disagreeable, particularly as I had formed a project of seeing the
poor unhappy cottager again, and of making her some reparation
previously to my leaving Germany.

Six weeks after receiving the probing letter of the Priest, and
also after having persuaded my father to grant me a few days'
absence, I hastened down to the village where I had led the fond
and unsuspecting Josephine from innocence to shame. It was
my intention to direct that a sufficient sum of money should

be annually paid for the support of herself, her child, if it lived, and her mother;—when I should come into the possession of the expected fortunes of my father and my uncle, I wished to do more for them; but till those events happened, I meant to conceal my real name and quality, and again to use that under which I had become her seducer.

I knew that I could not attend to all the promises I had made her, that of marriage being included: such an union was impossible; and greatly as I loved her, I believed her to be much too good, in spite of her frailty, to become my mistress; still I hoped to accommodate matters with some degree of satisfaction, though the idea of seeing her confused, and of encountering the eyes of her godfather, abashed me.

It was evening when I entered the village; the sun had gone down, and twilight was travelling over the forest, which lay on the one side, and falling on the hamlet that rose on the other. Nothing broke the silence but the salutations of the retiring peasants, the repeated "Good night" of the little children, who were playing in the road, and the sound of the bell swelling from the village church.

My horse was tired, and I was glad to find myself so near a resting-place. Calling to a boy, who was running along the path, I requested him to lead my horse to the inn, as I wished to dismount, and to walk either to the cottage of Josephine, or to the Rectory. The lad, however, told me that he could not oblige me, because he was hastening to see the funeral that was proceeding towards the church.

"Simpleton!" said I, "here is money for you. Whose funeral is it?"

"Poor Josephine's!" cried the young son of Nature; "poor Josephine's!" and he ran away from me with swiftness.

"Josephine's!" I exclaimed; "not *my* Josephine, surely! There may be many women of that name in the village; and yet—and yet grief may have broken the heart of my victim! My cruelty may have blasted her in the spring of life!"

My heart was growing sick with conjecture; I dismounted from my horse, tied it to a tree, and followed the steps of the young informer.

In a few minutes I was in the church-yard: a solemn procession was moving near to me; it still approached—it came close to me. I stared upon the slow-pacing and unobserving attendants. Before went the pastor, bending towards the earth, and sighing as he passed.—"He must sigh for Josephine!" said my frightened soul. Then came the corpse: the wind blew the pall against my cheek; my shiverings increased—*If* it be Josephine!—The first mourner followed; it was an old woman, who staggered as she walked; her hands were clasped, her eyes fixed on the coffin.— "Oh my God! Oh my child! Oh daughter, daughter!"

I heard her, knew her voice; it was Josephine's mother! I was supported by a tombstone, which was not colder than my body. I sunk into a short insensibility; and when I again unclosed my eyes, discovered no one near me. I rubbed my forehead, fearing a distemperature of my mind; but seeing light from the windows of the church, found that there was no delusion.

I went towards the house of God (unfit place for me!), and entered it. I did not suppose that I should be recognized, as I wore a great coat, the collar of which I had pulled above my head; beside, it was the hour of general sorrow, not of curiosity; and the eyes of the Priest and the mourners were fixed on the coffin, seldom straying towards any other object.

My vital powers became still more cold and languid; and in the dark recesses of the edifice, the optics of imagination collected all the ugly forms of fear.—"I have accelerated the death of an innocent young creature," I inwardly murmured; "I have given birth to a child, and been the instrument of tearing the nipple of its mother's breast from its little mouth! I have planted sorrow in the bosoms of the sympathetic! I have stabbed the heart of old maternal fondness, and agonized the mind of one of God's most holy servants!"

I could not bear these quick reflections, could no longer look on the sorrowing group; but, hurrying out of the church, soon after remounted my horse, and rode precipitately from the village, regarding myself as a friend more cruel and sanguinary than the Devil when he was flying from the corruption that he had implanted in the sweets of Eden.

Returning hastily to Vienna, fatigue and heat brought on a fever, and my mind was almost in a state of distraction. My father was alarmed, and entreated me to explain the cause of my malady and mental disorder; but I was not to be brought to confession, and remained with the secret in my tormented breast. My fever declined as rapidly as it had risen, and I was determined on leaving Vienna immediately; and though my father wished me to delay my journey for a short time, I would not be thwarted in my purpose.

Before I left Vienna, however, I wrote, under the name which I had formerly assumed, to the minister who had buried poor Josephine.—"I have been guilty of a most serious crime," I said; "it presses on my heart, still more heavily on my conscience. I abhor myself—you must abhor me; and Heaven will, I fear, scowl on me for it. Man feels no compunction for little vices; he rarely becomes a penitent till his deeds have been monstrous. I entreat your forgiveness, good and holy man! Take care of the child of my poor Josephine; I will provide for her mother, and for her infant; and in the name of mercy, of charity, I entreat your pardon!"

I wrote in the fulness of my heart, with an agitated hand, and with watery eyes. The answer of the virtuous pastor I need not repeat: he promised to be the agent in the business, and to apply my remittances; but assured me that, if the widow were not afflicted, and his pecuniary means were not much confined, neither the old woman nor the child should subsist on the bounty of Josephine's betrayer.

My journey to Venice could not disburthen my mind of its melancholy; all the sensibilities which Nature had implanted in me, were in activity; and reason, for the first time, appeared to be breaking through the clustering levities of youth and intemper-ance. I shewed my mind to my tutor, and told him the secret that had long oppressed me.

"You think too seriously of this affair," he replied; "while we lament the effects of our actions, if we turn our eyes towards Nature, in her shall we discover the compulsive source of them. Those principles, or instincts, which are known by the appel-lations of virtue and vice, are consequences resulting from the different springs of our passions: and I hold it to be equally rea-sonable that a watch should stop after repleted motion had been given to its wheels, as that a man should check the impulses by which, at the very time of his formation, the secret artifi-cer intended he should be ever thereafter actuated and biased. Seduction is a chimera: I affirm it to be impossible that even an idiot should be seduced. Cohabitation is the mere blending together of two wills; and if there is a mutual acquiescence, how can a single charge be afterwards made or supported?*—Woman repines not at the act, but she knows the prejudices and hypocri-sies of society; to keep herself above the waves of contempt, she therefore puts on the customary garb of penitence, which, by the bye, is nearly threadbare; and turns her accusations against him who only participated in, and acceded to a joint proposition and corresponding instinct." ——

Youth is credulous: I listened to the voice of a man whom many had called a philosopher; and though I did not imme-diately feel the force of his observations and sentiments, yet a repetition of them, and a continuation of his theories afterwards strangled the monster Conscience; and, expelling the gloomy ideas of my mind, I again began to seek for the pleasures of the world.

Still there were moments in which I pitied poor Josephine, and mournfully reflected on her premature death; my tutor, however, told me that it was weak and absurd to wrap the heart up in sorrow, and voluntarily to cloud the intellectual brightness for a common state of mortality, to which I might myself be reduced before the re-appearance of the sun. I fell into the hands of a pernicious, dissembling villain, and my progress in vice you are well acquainted with: my follies my connections are known to you; my heart would sicken at a repetition of them.

An annual sum has, till within four years past, been paid to the mother of Josephine; the last tender, however, was rejected, though I have never enquired into the cause of it. It was not till lately that I discovered any beauty in virtue; and my sandals are yet covered with dust collected in the road of vice. I should suppose that the Rector and the mother of Josephine have ere now retired to a happier world. My son I never saw; his fate I never had the humanity to enquire into, and scarcely have I thought of him.

Dear Stendal, learn the situation of the poor lad, and apprize me of it. What if he has been reared in ignorance? The event was adventitious, and he is not less entitled to kindness and support. I would do something for the son of the sweet Josephine; find him out; tell him his father wishes for, and will promote his prosperity; and also that a sufficient sum of money shall be advanced for that purpose, and be at his entire direction.

I beg you not to mention my name; you may, however, state my quality, and acknowledge that the character I passed upon his mother and the humane Rector was fictitious. Yet, on reflection, I see not the necessity of this confession; but do as you like, and think proper. The boy is doubtless ignorant, has been inured to labour; and, as agriculture has probably been his employ, I will purchase for him a farm, and at some future period cast my eye upon the cultivator and produce of it.

Ah Stendal! I can never do justice on earth. My eyes are open to the worthiness of Christiana; but they are not shut upon Isabella and her daughter.

Altenburg.

Count Stendal to the Baron.

THE Rector is still living, and every soul in the village rejoices at the prolonged existence of such an excellent being. The ashes of Josephine and her mother repose together; four years have passed by since the latter entered the grave, over which she had long bent with an aching heart, and with an eye of sorrow; the rustics speak compassionately, affectionately of them both. Your assumed name is still remembered, still execrated! You know my love of truth; I flatter not—I tell no lies!

I have seen your son. The village is very small, and thinly inhabited. I sought for your boy among the cottagers; and seeing a healthy lad following a plough, I asked him whether he was the son of Josephine.

"No," he answered; "I wish I were."

"Do you know him?"

"Oh yes, very well."

"Has he left the village? Is he still living? Can you, young man, direct me to him?"

"Enquire of those who are coming across yon meadow," said the labourer, abruptly leaving me.

I looked towards the place to which he had pointed, and saw an aged man leaning on the arm of a tall and elegantly formed youth. Concluding that the rustic had piqued himself on his cunning, and wished to lead me into an embarrassing situation, I did not intend to trouble the strangers with an enquiry concerning a person whose insignificance I thought had doubtless kept him from their notice.

But as I approached nearer, in the elder of them I beheld a venerable Clergyman, and in the younger I fancied that I saw Baron Altenburg stepping back to the age of twenty, and assuming a form and countenance more graceful, more impressive than they had actually been at that period of his life.

This was your son—the son of Josephine—the scion that you

planted, but which you neglected to foster. I knew him instantly; astonishment possessed me for a moment; but I was immediately after affected as much as if the youth was my own discarded son.

I was determined to speak to him, though I scarcely knew in what manner. Their slow approach, and my own tardiness, enabled me to collect my ideas: still, when I came close to them, your boy cast upon my face a pair of eyes so exquisitely bright, beautiful, and expressive, that I even feared to name to him the seducer of his mother;—I could not then do it. I suffered him to pass, strove to follow, but was unable; and therefore the opportunity of executing my commission entirely failed.

To-morrow, however, I will see and converse with him; and after my interview, will write to you again. The youth is handsome; and though I did not hear him speak, I dare affirm that he is wise. The locality of the brain does not prevent it from extending its influence over the countenance, which is often infinitely more eloquent than the tongue, the volubility of the latter being frequently poor, compared with the lightnings of the former.

Oh that my little ones may one day be such as your boy now is! And would to God, Altenburg, you could be as happy a father as I am! I shall write to you to-morrow, and I doubt not but that my letter will be earnestly looked for.

Stendal.

Baron Altenburg to Count Stendal.

HAVE you seen my boy again? Have you spoken to him? Does his mind accord with the beauty of his person? and is he——

Oh Stendal! how unjust have been my actions—how reprehensible my conduct! Your letter has greatly agitated me—pleased, pained, delighted, and distressed me.—"What ails my Altenburg?" says my wife, while leaning on my shoulder.

"Nothing," I reply; "nothing, sweet Christiana!"

"Nothing?—Ah now you are deceitful! Why did you start on reading that letter? why fall back in your chair? why laugh? why, almost in the same moment, suffer those tears to flow into your eyes?—and all this is nothing! Ah Altenburg! I will not strive to rob you of your secrets, but I entreat you to be more careful in the government of yourself."

Dear Stendal! I cannot make my wife acquainted with this last discovery. My present consequence is all derived from her; love, delicacy, and gratitude therefore ought to be ever directed towards her. She has pardoned many of my errors; and her affection has made her blind to many of my serious faults.

Yet my boy shall be no longer neglected. My fortune is very great: should my wife bring me any children, noble provision shall be made for them; but my newly-discovered son shall be independent, and Isabella and my Augusta—Ah perverse women! why do you torture me by your seclusion?

I could almost quarrel with you, Count, for suffering your sensibility to master you when you ought to have resisted it; and yet your weakness certainly arose from the most amiable propensity. May the God, whom the good minister so righteously serves, shower millions of blessings on his aged head, for the care he has bestowed on the son of Josephine and Altenburg!

Write to me instantly, dear Stendal; you may believe that I am impatient, but cannot tell how much so. Take my boy to your heart—press him to it strongly; assure him that——Christiana is coming towards my room; I cannot repulse her; she is too good, too gentle, and too excellent; and she must not see this paper. Farewel!

Altenburg.

Count Stendal to the Baron.

THE generality of men are nearly alike in their construction; Nature does not often evince any extraordinary partialities, though every vain creature of her hands fancies that those partialities are actually to be found in himself. Sometimes, however, we discover some things which resemble peculiar kindnesses in the universal goddess; we see, or fancy we see, them even in infancy, trace them more strongly in ripening youth, and find a full confirmation of them in the meliorated state of man.

This trite remark has been drawn from me by the qualities of your natural son, which appear to me of the highest order. His education, I conceive, not to have been a mean one; he has a superior mind and an excellent heart, though you may presently be ready to affirm the contrary; sensibility seems to preside over his soul, and I perceive that he is sometimes guided by enthusiasm.

I have before spoken of his form and features; from his statue a sculptor might catch a graceful Apollo, and his face would supply exquisite materials for an Adonis.*

Blaming myself for my irresolution on the appearance of the minister and his young friend, immediately after breakfast on the following morning, I went towards the Rector's house, with the intention of introducing myself in the best possible manner to the venerable old man. But in a meadow through which I had to pass, and sitting on a hillock, I saw your son earnestly, and with apparent pleasure, perusing a book; and he being the more immediate object of my intended visit, I made towards him, instead of seeking his disinterested guardian.

The use of language was at that time scarcely remembered by me, and the manner of combining words absolutely appeared a difficulty. The idea of bruising honour, and wounding sensibility, as well as that of pleading the cause of dissimulation and cruelty (I have written the words, Altenburg), nearly again frustrated my design.

His eyes are almost magical; there is, not to speak poetically, fire in the centre of each ball, generally beautifully sparkling, but sometimes kindling into the brightest flame. I advanced still nearer to him, when he looked up to me, and on my bowing, rose from the ground, and returned my salutation with ease and gracefulness. I entreated him to pardon a stranger for abruptly disturbing his mental repast, and that he would not accuse me with impertinence if I begged to know his name.

With some little appearance of surprise, but without any intimidation or embarrassment, he immediately answered, "Leopold Warndorf."

"So I had conjectured," I said; "and you are the person for whom I was seeking."

"For whom you were seeking?"

"Yes. Will you allow me a few minutes' conversation with you?"

"Readily, Sir," he answered; "will you go with me into the house yonder?"

"With your permission," I said, "I will speak to you here; for the present summer has not given us a finer day, and I am loth to lose an hour of it. My motive for now appearing before you is an important, but a painful one. I have perused your face, young gentleman, and formed a most valuable opinion of your heart;—but to that heart, what I am about to say will, I fear, give a severe, though not a mortal wound."

"You alarm me!" he cried;—"I guess at it: you bring me ill news, perhaps fatal news of my friend Charles! His iron-hearted parent has probably carried his rage and malice to their extremities, torn him from Elizabeth—imprisoned, murdered him! Heaven! speak your errand quickly, Sir; for you have made me all anxiety."

Had you heard the varied tones in which these words were spoken, the chords of your heart would have thrilled as mine did, though Charles, his parent, and Elizabeth were strangers to you. If this youth can feel so exquisitely in the cause of a friend, Oh how would he have repaid the love and tenderness of a *father!*

As this thought was passing in my mind, he caught hold of my arm, and looked impatiently in my face.

"You are agitated," I said; "be composed, for I do not come from the person of whom you speak—he is totally unknown to me. I am deputed to address you by——"

"By whom?" he enquired eagerly.

"One who has much injured you, and is anxious to make reparation; one who is stung by the recollection of his past errors, who loved your mother—who said to me, "Go to the son of Josephine, and bring him with you to the arms of his father.""

Leopold shrank from me; he appeared to be falling to the earth, and I clasped his body to save him from doing so. Almost immediately, however, he recovered his strength; but he looked with a considerable degree of wildness on me.

"And you are the friend of my father?" he cried: "he lives, and you are his friend?"

"He lives, and I am his true, his confidential friend, and have been such many years."

"Then your countenance has greatly deceived me. We may look on corruption, and pass untainted; but if we become familiar with it, we must necessarily be infected by the putrid juices. The man to whom you allude, has been twenty years a villain; and if you have known him so long, you ought, Sir, to have forgotten him sooner."

"You are severe!" I cried: "your father, indeed, has been unjust—"

"Unjust!—artful, cruel, and designing!"

"But he repents sincerely. He has never seen you; his arms, however, will take you in, his breast cherish you, and his fortune enable you to execute any plan which you may form for your establishment in life. Go with me: I must convey to him some token of his former love for Josephine."

"Love!—Sir, you should have said lust. Carry some token to him! Why then, go to the church-yard yonder; you will see my mother's grave near the west angle of the edifice; at the head of it is a stone, on which is cut her name, her age—eighteen years! Dig up the earth; you may find a piece of rotten plank, a remnant of the shroud in which she was buried, a bone!—carry these to him—Oh they will be fit remembrances!"

"You talk wildly," I cried; "you have too much sensibility—indeed you have. You may obtain happiness if you are willing to stretch out your arm for it. You will hereafter love your father; you will be ever cherished by his affections."

"And if I were to go to him—and if he were to smile on me, which I cannot wish for, would not every gross tongue be ready to exclaim, 'How kind he is to the bastard!'—I knew not till now that I had a father. Leave me, Sir; Oh you have interrupted my tranquillity!"

My heart melted; he burst into tears; but in a minute, with indignation, he wiped them away.

"I can listen to you no longer, Sir," he cried; "and I must not be rendered contemptible by my weakness. But perhaps I have—I hope not—I thought not of it before—perhaps I have been talking with the actual seducer of Josephine?"

"No, by Heaven!" I exclaimed; "but if you were my son, I should with pride acknowledge you."—He bowed.—"Your father," I continued, "will do the same; and the prejudices of society you will soon disregard. The levities of my friend are gone over, and virtue and honour are now stationed in his heart. He is a man of birth, of rank——"

"Of birth, of rank!"

"Yes, he has a long line of ancestors, a high station in the world, and his name is——"

"Good day to you!" he said, abruptly leaving me.

He would not be recalled, but ran into the house, leaving me surprised and embarrassed, perhaps a little offended. I went back with disappointment, ruminated all the day and half the night on the singularity of your son's conduct; and this morning received from him a note which I now transcribe.

———————

"Secluded as I have been, retired as I have lived, and little as I know of the world, still I am not altogether ignorant of the forms of society. I am awkward in apology, for the language of fashion is not much known by me; but I entreat Count Stendal, for such I have discovered is the gentleman who took the pains of conversing with me yesterday, to pardon me for some harsh personal reflections which I recollect I then suffered to pass from me. The abruptness of the interview, the astonishment that seized me, and the pangs of my heart, made me almost frantic. My sentiments, in regard to your character, are softened, are changed; but the destroyer of my mother must ever be abhorred by me. If you respect the peace of the human mind, if the happiness of a fellow-creature be dear to you, attempt not to see me again: and I conjure you, by every thing that is holy, never, by words or writing, endeavour to make the name of my father known to me, for I know not what my passions might induce me to act. Convey to him, my Lord, the inclosed letter; and forgive the past rudeness of

"Leopold Warndorf."

―――――

Thus you see, Altenburg, ends my embassy. I shall offer no additional reflections of my own, no advice; you must hereafter determine for yourself, and as you may think proper. Leopold is an uncommon character; and I have written, without remark or comment, the very words which were spoken by him.

The old Rector is, I hear, confined to his chamber, and his grateful boy tenderly soothing the infirmities of age. I am obliged to go from hence to-morrow; and were my continuance here to be prolonged, I do not think I should venture to speak to your son again. But I shall never forget him! If I condemn a part of him, my admiration will be insufficient for the other part.— Adieu! I feel most sensibly for you, my dear Altenburg.

Stendal.

―――――

*To the Person who twenty Years ago
assumed the Name of Rostock.*

I HAVE requested Count Stendal to convey this letter to you—to you, who, aided by the laws of Nature, brought me into existence: those laws demand that, in speaking to you, I should call you by the name of father—a name which has often thrilled me when I heard it come from the poorest peasant, from the ignorant who knew not the meaning of a hundred different words; but in pronouncing it myself, it stabs my heart, compresses the passage of my throat, and conveys a frightful sound to my ears.

Can I for a moment think you were serious in deputing the Count to bring me before you; or that, after your heart has been for so long a period incased with ice, the stranger sun-beams of humanity should thaw any of its frozen springs? I will not believe it.

Suppose I admit the inclination, and reject the impulse? Thus then, I account for it.

In an hour of mirth, when the feelings of no individual were regarded by you—when the prurient sensations of your own heart made you indifferent to the aches and contortions of others—when your goblet sparkled to the eye, and the fumes of your potent libations were mounting, and creating a wild revelry in the brain—when, perhaps, a group of noisy Bacchanals* laughed around you, you thus addressed the Count:—

"When you pass through the village you have just mentioned, and which I had almost forgotten, enquire for a boy of the name of Warndorf. Nearly twenty years ago, I gained the heart of a poor country girl, who, I believe, within a twelvemonth died, leaving behind her this male bastard. Nay, do not laugh so loud, gentlemen, for there is nothing uncommon in it; though I confess all these things are a little whimsical. If the cub be living, Count, I will humanize him; and if the seal of stupidity be not too fatally pressed upon his brains, he shall have the management of my hounds, and perhaps sometimes take the end of my table."

Nature! Nature! Nature!—goddess bounteous and beautiful! Were I to live a thousand years, my first debts of gratitude could never be paid. Thou sawest me helpless and abandoned, left by a dead mother, and forsaken by an unnatural father! but thy animating and inspiring breath came upon me from the woodlands and forest haunts; thou gavest a vigour to my body, and a spirit to my soul; one of which affliction has never aimed at—the other, exquisite gift! has been often subdued by the wrongs of my lost parent, but never shall be affected by the hypocrisy and cruelty of my living one.

My Lord, I am not for your purpose. You murdered Josephine, and I will avoid you with the greatest caution. Your name, your actual quality, and your fortune are alike unknown to me, and may they be so for ever! You deceived my mother with a lie—a complicated, despicable lie! and Leopold will be ever wary of your artifices.

You told her you would marry her; you told her you were a merchant. Thinking you might still probably be such, sometimes in the evening, when the grave of Josephine was beneath my eye, a storm has risen, clouds have collected, winds roared, and lightnings darted athwart the dreadful face of heaven: I have gone home, slighted my food and my bed, and alone in my chamber heard the increasing roar of the elements. It has filled me with a sensation of pleasure: what struck others with a panic, gave a warmth to my soul; and while each shuddering individual has thought only of his solitary self, I have been almost unconscious of my own existence, and filled with the idea of my father.

"His ships, the greatest part of his treasures may," I have said, "be tossing amid the hollows of the frighted sea; the huge waves sweep away the cables and the anchors; the blasts tear the shrouds, and snap the cordage; the crew sink into despair, and the black horrors of surrounding rocks frown upon their terror-stricken eyes. *He* is among them! *he* is the saddest of the sad!—Retributive Providence! let his vessels divide, and his riches sink to the unsearchable bottom of the ocean! Drench him in the billows; carry him, shuddering, half way down to death and darkness, and raise him, hopeless of life, on the highest waves! Fill him with fears, and plunge him in a thousand horrors; but spare his wretched life, that he may hereafter have calm hours for repentance and contrition!"

Was this language unnatural? Think from whom it proceeded; think also of your former actions: reflect on the strength of many of the passions which Nature gives to us, and of the peculiar circumstances on which I had to ruminate. I am not inhuman; mine is not a savage heart. All God's creatures are dear to me, except my father and those whom vice distinguishes.

My history is a short one.—After my mother was buried, I became the care of her poor, old, heart-broken parent, who passed her hours in sighing for her dear Josephine, and in sobbing and weeping over her infant's cradle. I afterwards had the breast of a healthful nurse to cling to and thrive upon; and I did thrive. The first things which I remember are the smiles and the kindness of the Clergyman of the parish, who was the godfather of my injured mother; and my tongue cannot express what he has since been to me. God will give him his ultimate reward.

He educated and made me what I am; he has taught me how to be happy, and his examples ever coincide with his precepts. When he dies, and the melancholy day is, I fear, very near, I shall possess his little property: it will be enough for a good and virtuous man; and when I cast away that character, may the insufficiency drive me even to the den of wretchedness and famine!

I was at an early age informed of the circumstances of my birth, and they no longer make me blush. The mother of Josephine was for a long period supported by the seducer, the murderer of her daughter; affliction lay upon her for fifteen years, and during the last five of her existence she never left her bed. Miserable creature! who brought thee to this state of wretchedness? Had she not accepted your money, she must have perished in want.

But after her death, and when the next secret payment was tendered, Oh I was blasphemous!—God pardon me for it! I thought I could have trampled on my father's heart, as I did on his proffered gold. He could provide provinder for his horse, could chastise his groom for not giving it good attendance, could admire, and almost love it; but he thought it enough to offer his son bread; his happiness, his education, his morals were nothing! Had my body festered on a gibbet, my father would, unpitying, have looked on it, execrated my vices, and swore he had done his duty!—Oh my soul sickens!

I have said enough. I hope I shall soon forget all that now agitates me—forget that you ever made a claim on me; all then will be well again. My life was, before this interruption, beautifully serene; and this little storm must not ruffle all my summer days. My ideas and reflections will, I trust, hereafter be calm and unimpassioned; and perhaps, at some period not very remote, I may cease to curse the seducer of my mother, though I shall never bless him. Think not that you have in me a son; for that name I shall ever renounce, and start from.

Leopold Warndorf.

The Baroness of Altenburg to Miss Messein.

OH, I hope I have not been deceived, Charlotte! I hope what I lately regarded as beautiful realities were actually such, and not the exquisite visions which the mind will sometimes throw before the fascinated eye.

Did I not describe to you my happiness, paint to you my felicities, tell you I was the most joyful, the most animated creature of the earth—that Altenburg was nothing less than the ardour of his Christiana would wish him to be?—Yes, I remember that

I spoke to you of all these things, and cannot suppress my sighs when I remember it.

From this you will infer that I am unhappy: well, perhaps I am; and perhaps I ought to be so for my fears, my suspicions, and my unjust surmises. But what magician can strangle the fretful offspring of the brain? Thought will not be impeded in its progress; and the human mind, whether agitated or tranquil, I must ever consider as a democracy.

I find, Charlotte, that I have been wrongly educated:—my preceptors were too soft to me; I have been led into a maze of sensibilities which attack me at every turning; they infuse each moment a poison into my soul which often thrills me with a delicious but dangerous sensation, and frequently shakes me almost to annihilation.

I will alter all these things; I must—it is not too late; and I will hereafter strive to direct myself by new systems and by more determined rules. I am, I believe, too nicely suspicious; I must indeed be so when I fancy that Altenburg loves me not: and yet I have fancied this, though I blush, as I ought to do, at my confession of it. The whole store of my affections I joyfully surrendered to him; and if he returns me only half of his own, can I be otherwise than unhappy?

Let no one smile, or tax me with enthusiasm, or dare to call me a rhapsodist when I declare that my love for him is infinite! I feel it as a friend, as a wife, as a mistress; it is the chief passion of my soul, and I pour it upon him sometimes with smiling, and often with tearful eyes;—tearful! yes—joy is superlative when it comes from a humid source.

"And does he fly from your embraces? does he disregard your smiles? is he sated with joys which he thinks too liberally offered—offered without being demanded, rather than granted on solicitation?"—Ha! are not these your questions, Charlotte? Though you are so many leagues distant, methinks I hear your voice.—God shield me from these thoughts! My suspicions will undermine my reason:—*my* suspicions! no, they are your's,

Charlotte; but they are unjust, indeed they are. Take them to yourself, dear girl, and recant as I do: let me never hereafter think that I had them for a moment in my brain.

*   *   *   *   *

I am much inclined to tear the paper on which I have been writing. No, it shall pass; it will serve you, Charlotte, as a specimen of my talents for romance. You will laugh over it as I have done; though few people can be sportive with their own errors and absurdities, I protest I have been so over mine.

I certainly have freed myself from a strange humour; its singularity surprises me, and I wonder that I should ever fall in such an one, so degrading to myself—its consequences so injurious to my beloved Altenburg. I ask your pardon for having forced the monsters of spleen and discontent into your company, and promise to shew myself to you hereafter as a more rational and considerate being. I protest I am not only angry with, but also ashamed of myself: I have told you already that I have laughed over my own folly, and must confess that I have likewise wept over it.

Many times have I been on the point of casting myself at Altenburg's feet to implore his pardon; but it may be better to conceal the weakness of my heart and understanding. I have, however, sobbed out my girlish sorrows on his beloved breast, and been hypocrite enough when, with a soul-dissolving voice, he has said, "For God's sake, my dear wife, tell me from whence arises this distress!" to impute my unjustifiable sorrow to a remote and inconsequential cause.

Charlotte, my grief has been self-imposed, and my pains were not more severe than I merited. All my concern has been excited by an impertinent curiosity, and by some absurd remarks on the countenance of my husband. Because he received a letter which startled him, and because my too scrutinizing eyes discovered a few contractions in his face, I must take into my bosom a large share of multiplying doubts; and conduct myself more inconsiderately than I ever did at the age of thirteen!—Strange, misguided, infatuated Christiana!

Surely I was not till lately a versatile character. That I am such now, even to a degree of absurdity, this letter will probably evince. Pardon, however, dear girl, the errors of your friend, of which no one can be so truly sensible as herself.

Christiana.

The same to the same.

THE quiet of myself and of Altenburg was interrupted yesterday by the appearance of the old Baroness of L——, who is going on a visit about ten leagues from Brinn. She had necessarily to pass our chateau; and I was walking with my dear Altenburg over the grounds, holding some of the tenderest conversation since our marriage, when we were met by the Dowager. You know I do not esteem her, that I think her garrulous and highly censorious; and if you recollect the manner in which she talked to me at Vienna, and my resentment on that occasion, you will perhaps be surprised that she should ever seek another interview with me.

But there are women whom no circumstance whatever can abash. Her Ladyship was perfectly at ease; she addressed both the Baron and me without any embarrassment, and declared herself extremely happy in meeting us, though the rencounter was owing to chance alone.

The wheel of her carriage had broken within a league of the chateau; and on learning that we were then residing there, she thought she could solicit of us the hospitality of a night, and till the vehicle could be put into a proper condition for travelling. Altenburg gave her a polite welcome, and I followed his example, though the eyes of my husband declared that he thought me unusually ceremonious. I have never acquainted him with the nature of the last interview between me and the Baroness; did he know what sentiments she then expressed relative to him, he would doubtless catch some of my reserve, and also act upon it.

Our visiter's tongue was, till we separated at night, in constant activity; her anecdotes tire with their multiplicity; her remarks are severe, often unjust, sometimes indelicate: and having lashed the vices of society, she concludes with thanking Heaven that she has no such propensities. She is proud of what she now pretends to be, and has no recollection of what she was.

I must own she possesses a considerable degree of discrimination in some particulars; and this morning she ruffled me very much. After breakfast my Lord went out, and the Baroness accompanied me to my dressing-room;—seating herself near the toilet,* she looked earnestly in my face, and smilingly held out her hand to me.

"I perceive," she cried, "that you are yet harbouring an idea of things which are past; you have not forgiven me for what, in the warmth of friendship, I said to you at Vienna; your formality to me declares it. You must give me your pardon for the unintentional offence; you must not bear enmity any longer about your heart; assure me that you will not, my dear Baroness."

In the preceding minute there certainly was a cause for her suspicions; but it fled on the instant, and her words, and her peculiar manner of speaking touched me sensibly; and taking the hand she proffered, I assured her that her surmises were entirely groundless.

"I rejoice then," she cried, "in my deception, and in the afternoon shall pursue my journey with a greater degree of pleasure and satisfaction. Yet how much would that pleasure be increased, if I were to depart with the assurance of your being happy."

I started; my face glowed, and I looked strongly at her.—"If you were to depart with the assurance of my being happy!" I exclaimed; "good Heaven! am I not so? Do you doubt it?"

"Ah no!" she replied, "I have no doubts: mine is an unpleasant confirmation. I protest your situation creates an interest; your infelicity excites regret, it does indeed. Dear lady, what can thus disturb your peace?"

"You astonish me," I cried, "by your conjectures! I assure you I am most truly happy."

"Ah!" cried the Baroness, shaking her head, "those who possess true sensibility are loth to make any person uneasy by recounting their sorrows. *You* happy! would to God you were! You have, since I came hither, been acting with a delicate hypoc-risy: you smile, you laugh, you talk, and attempt to appear as if all were tranquillity and joy in your heart. But I have observed you with a friendly earnestness. The tide of your blood is strangely irregular; for it rushes into your cheeks, and then rapidly forsakes them, leaving them almost deadly pale. You often fix your eyes on a particular object; they moisten even while you are smiling: and when you join in a calm common conversation, your voice falters, and you are in an absolute state of trepidation."

I knew that she described me as I actually was, but had thought myself secure in my follies, and was vexed by her remarks, though I endeavoured to crush them with a laugh.

"Nay, this is still worse, my dear young friend," she contin-ued; "these tones are far from being natural; and your present mirth is an *effort*, not an *impulse*. I ask for no confidence, but would entreat you to be more attentive to your health and hap-piness. Believe me you are strangely altered of late; your new complexion really astonished me when I met you yesterday. You have a beautiful seat here; the building is noble, the grounds are delightful; but pray is not the situation rather unwholesome?"

"I have never heard it so called," I replied, in sickness and confusion; "my own opinion was always contrary."

"Your own opinion, I fear," she said, looking more earnestly in my face, "your own opinion, I fear, has been wrong. And then, my good friend, the Baron—Heaven, what a melancholy change!"

"Good God!" I exclaimed, incautiously, "are then my suspi-cions true? Tell me, Madam, does my Lord *really* look unwell?"

"Very much so, very much so indeed!"

"And—does he appear to you unhappy?"

"It strikes me that he is *most* unhappy: a secret misery seems to prey upon him; and yet I dare say you are in his confidence?"

"Oh no, I am not!" I cried; "he places no trust in me: if he be mentally afflicted—"

"He certainly *is*."

"Then," I replied, deeply sighing, "the cause is unknown to me."

"Strange!" cried the Dowager, "very strange! that recently married to a woman who (I compliment not) was so extensively admired and solicited, he should sink into visible distress and melancholy, without assigning any cause for the change—it is most extraordinary! I knew the Baron almost twenty years ago, and happened to be at Venice when he first became acquainted with——Bless me! when he first appeared, and was known in that delightful place. He met with admiration every where; a constant smile sat upon his face; and when in motion, he displayed the airy graces of a Mercury."*

"I have heard," I replied, "that he was of a lively disposition."

"Lively disposition!" said the Baroness; "he was truly the son of vivacity, the polished mirror of elegance; and till a little while, a very little while, he has not abated a scruple of his fascinating ease and gaiety. But the change in him is more alarming than that which I have discovered in you, my dear young friend;— paleness, flushings, visible anxieties, and unseasonable musings! I hope his Lordship will not long continue in a state which appears to me actually alarming."

I could not bear to hear any more; besides, I began to suspect some unfriendly designs in the woman who so ingeniously tortured me; I therefore left her, and have since been writing to my dear Charlotte. I am, I believe, much too credulous. The Baroness, I am persuaded, wishes to vex me; but indeed Altenburg is unhappy, and I consequently am the same. I had regained much composure; but the remarks and insinuations of this pretended friend have disordered me again.

*   *   *   *   *

What am I to think of the conduct of my husband? Dear friend, what am I to think of the pain and mystery of my Altenburg?

Politeness would not allow me to be long absent from the Baroness; therefore I put aside my pen, which had almost run before my thoughts, and met her in her dressing-room: we afterwards went into the apartment in which we had breakfasted, and within a little time were joined by the Baron, who had just returned from his walk. He addressed us in no very lively manner; and my eyes encountering those of the Baroness, I perfectly, though with pain, read their language, and could scarcely restrain my tears from shewing themselves. Our visiter, asking a number of questions, each of which related to a different concern, and receiving from my Lord sometimes a languid answer, and at other times only a monosyllable, viewed him attentively, and exclaimed, "Bless me, Baron! you certainly are not well?"

"I acknowledge," he replied, "that I am not very well."

"My God!" I cried, "what is your malady, my dear Altenburg? You alarm me by this confession. Take advice immediately; let me dispatch a servant for—"

"Softly, softly, my good, my tender Christiana!" he said, catching hold of my hand, and pressing it with tenderness; "this mighty affliction is nothing more than a pain in my side; and as I intend within a few days to give my arm to the lancet,* I do not suppose that I shall long have cause for complaint."

The Baroness looked at me again, and I thought incredulously: but the pressure of my Altenburg yet thrilled my nerves; and his kind, his exquisite smiles raised my love, and totally vanquished my suspicions. His spirits seemed to acquire a sudden vigour; he spoke in a strain almost lively, and smiled at the manner in which I had expressed my fears. My wounded heart seemed to take in a most delicious balm; but the gravity of the Baroness increasing as that of Altenburg relaxed, in an instant

I was again torturing myself with conjectures, and said secretly, "The cool discernment of this woman is faithful and just; she calmly views and examines what tenderness and love close my eyes upon."

I again grew uneasy, and was so much under the influence of Lady L——, that her nods, her shrugs, and gestures, which, though observed only by myself, were plentiful, filled me with doubts, tremors, and apprehensions. At length a servant came in with letters which had just arrived from the post-house at the next town. The Baron saw the man at the door, and starting from his seat, rushed forward, seized the different packets with a strange anxiety; and having looked at the superscriptions, his face crimsoned, and he placed himself hastily, or rather seemed to fall upon his chair.

"Your side, my Lord?" cried the Baroness; "I fear it is extremely painful."

"No—yes," he answered, and was again rising in order to leave the room; but Lady L—— begged him to use no exertion, and to break the seals without apology or ceremony. Seeing him gaze strangely on the letters, and singularly irresolute and undetermined, she beckoned me to retire with her; but before I could get upon my trembling limbs, he had risen, bowed, and withdrawn himself.

The Baroness ran up to me.—"Do you see," she cried, "do you not perceive it? Ah! dear friend, compassionately, most compassionately do I feel for you!"—I ought not to have listened to her;—so however I did; and I am grieved to confess that, when I should have exerted all my strength of intellect as well as of body, I suffered both to forsake me, and wept upon a breast which perhaps contained a guileful enemy.

Within a few minutes, however, the impropriety of my conduct struck me; and raising my head, I freely confessed to her that I deemed my weakness and folly contemptible. I saw her labouring for an arrangement of features to correspond with some smooth-tongued speech. This artifice, palpable in itself,

served to rouse me; and I left the room with an assumed composure, though indeed I had little peace within my breast.

Altenburg has since continued in the library—I in my chamber, writing in tears, and troubling my Charlotte with my
sorrows; and the Baroness—But I must go to her, or she will
draw the most strange and injurious conclusions from the conduct of me and my Lord. I wish I had never seen this woman; I
have been fascinated even by her tormentings.

* * * * *

Thank Heaven, she is gone! She departed immediately after
dinner, and I sincerely hope I shall never see her again: such a
woman would banish me from the world beyond recal, if I were
to be long in her society. Altenburg partook of our repast, and
behaved with so much ease and propriety, that I could scarcely
think he was internally agitated, though our visiter evidently
seemed to consider him as a polite impostor. When she afterwards stepped into her carriage, she said some words to me in a
low tone of voice which I did not fully understand; but I judged
that they were insinuations levelled at my quiet, and am now
glad that my ear did not catch them.

My husband and I had walked with her across the lawn; and
after her carriage was driven away, he drew my arm through his
own, and in sauntering with him over the turf, I was really as
happy as I had been before the Baroness interrupted my quiet.
We rambled till almost the close of day. Discoursing on dear and
delicious subjects, our eyes frequently met each other most tenderly. My heart fluttered with rapture; my head inclined towards
him, and my lips coveted the kisses which he pressed on them.
I told him I was glad of our visiter's departure, and hoped we
should have no more such intruders. He expressed the same
wish, and confessed that he had imbibed a sudden dislike for the
Baroness.

"We will be no longer separated, my Christiana," he cried,
"no not even for an hour. You are so essential to my happiness,

that every little minute which divides me from you, becomes a tedious age: you are the life, the heart, the soul of Altenburg."

What an ecstatic creature I became! The sun went down in glorious splendour, and the delightful colours of the western heaven were widely stretched. Surely no breezes so soft had ever passed over creation; the face of Nature had never looked half so beautiful. It was the most precious hour that had ever intervened in the annals of time! How I secretly praised the great and invisible Spirit! Oh how I thanked my God!

We returned to the Castle: he led me to the library, where I threw myself on a sofa, and his arms clasped me, his breast was my pillow. Neither of us spoke for several minutes; but at length I raised my eyes, and saw above our heads the portrait of my softer parent—"Look there, Altenburg!" I cried; "my mother, she smiles!"

"Yes," he replied, "at the happiness of her beloved daughter."

"At the love, at the tenderness of her dear daughter's husband!"

"Her eyes are on us both," he exclaimed, "Dear saint, we are both thy children!"

I will say no more, Charlotte. I have no suspicions, no doubts, no apprehensions. The Baroness is a vile tempter, and I was too easily betrayed. My Lord will hereafter account for all those little circumstances which struck me as peculiar; and if he should not, I never will renew the self-tormenting arts of which I have so recently divested myself.

Christiana.

***

Baron Altenburg to Count Stendal.

THE summer tempest is awful while it continues, and its tremendous bursts and vivid fires may appal the stoutest traveller. But sink not, shuddering mortal! under the weight of thy terrors; for the labouring clouds will ere long smile over thine head, and instead of the wild lightnings which blaze around thee, the rays of the sun will soon salute thy face again. And if evening be drawing nigh, and thy dwelling is yet far distant, the milder beacon of the night; and the gems of heaven shall smile most lovely on thee, and thou mayst go forward, musing on the sublimity and beauties of Nature, and no longer trembling for her past wrath and uproar.

I thank you, dear Stendal, for your care and solicitude. Ah, God! how you have pained my heart! but it is now at ease; it is again at ease. For the last two days I have governed myself with a power which I feared I had not been able to assert; anarchy had obtained an ascendency over reason, but has at length been made to retreat by the force that I had conceived to be entirely unequal to the contest.

My son!—I will think of him no more, or rather will feel for him no more. And yet what an extraordinary youth! beautiful in person, rich in understanding, and noble, though eccentric, in sentiment. Oh! he might have drawn my heart into his own bosom; but, assassin-like, he stabs it in an hundred places, still deeming the bloody marks too few! I cannot repeat any part of his letter; I scarcely dare reflect on it; it almost roused me into madness; it made me shudder with a thousand agues, and sent scalding tears into my eyes.

"Curse the boy!" I have exclaimed.—"God pardon me, and bless *him!*" I have added in the same moment, and before the imprecation could be registered.

He tells me we must never know each other:—I do not wish it. I have looked confidently on the world for many a year, sometimes encountered the serious form of danger without shrinking; but I should have no courage to meet the eyes of my son: they would petrify me, convert my body, my limbs, my veins into marble, and fix me a senseless statue for men to gape at. Yet he is a noble fellow! Why did he refuse the embraces of a father? Why would he not let me take him in my arms, and while fondly pressing him, examine the uncommon particles of his heart?

Now I wish it not: he is superior to me, and I will not step forward to meet degradation. But I would give all the world, would freely abridge my life if—

Ah Stendal! pardon the weakness and inconsistencies of your agitated friend!—Agitated! I told you just now that I was calm, and so again I presently shall be. Leopold, without my assistance, will, I think, be hereafter prosperous and happy; for it is evident that he possesses rare talents: and when I am in the grave, the excellencies of his heart, and the genius with which he is gifted, will bring him a thousand smiles, though the flesh of his father's face be eaten away.

I have thought much of this boy of late: but my mind at intervals has also dwelt on two other painful objects—on those who, once dearer to me, treat me with equal disdain and cruelty. Still I cannot say this youth's pride and inflexibility are deserving of scorn and resentment; I cannot say the silence and contempt of this woman and her daughter fully entitle them to my neglect and indifference.

Leopold, Isabella, and Augusta!—can three such characters be found in existence? Their circumstances are nearly alike, and their passions similar; were they not so widely separated, I should be inclined to believe that they had entered into a conspiracy, in order to deprive me of reason, if not of life; and sometimes I am half persuaded that they are the agents of Fate, that they have a delegated power over me, and that they are commanded to lead me into madness and destruction.

But they shall not: there is a saving angel near me, who has a ready hand. Sweet Christiana! thou art the good spirit to whom I owe my preservation, and to whom I must confidently look for future protection. I have wronged thee, love, but will make atonement. Thy smiles are precious, and thou art liberal in bestowing them on thy Altenburg. Oh my wife! as thou seemest to me the most perfect of women, surely thou art deserving of being most happy: yet thou hast lately wept—hast hung in grief around my neck, and sobbed upon my breast!

I was the cause of this sorrow, and will henceforth strive to be the cause of thy happiness:—yes, by my redemption from poverty by thee, by thy soft pitying eyes, by my love, my honour—by the Almighty God, I will!!

This is a voluntary, a willing oath; and while I have life, will I abide by it. Shall I, like an insensible villain, dash from me the hand that so generously saved me? or, like an assassin, stab the heart that so tenderly loves me? Every day I feel a thousand self-reproaches for my conduct towards my wife; and her mild forbearance, the softness of her voice, and her silence on my errors, which must be palpable, make her a thousand times more dear to me.

And I will deserve the blessings that she offers me; my mind, shaking off its heavy encumbrances, shall calmly dwell on her alone; and my heart, putting aside its inconsistent sympathies, shall cling affectionately and devoutly to her while it has warmth and motion.

Altenburg.

Leopold to Charles.

MANY of your letters, my dear friend, have actually frightened me by their violence; but in the last that you wrote to me, there is a tranquillity which has banished every apprehension. It shews you to me just as you were before our separation; at least I thought so when I first perused it, and that idea has made me read it over an hundred times since.

In this age of disguise and affectation, when sentiment is dressed by the rules of fashion, and when few will allow that they are without the commodity, and the art of adorning it, a man's mind can be little understood by the style of his epistles; you, however, are fully known to me, for I have read the faithful volume of your heart, and found it genuine, pure, and unmutilated.

Cherish the stranger Peace, and hold her long and fast to your breast; she will repay your endearments with substantial blessings; and her love at length will grow so strong, that she will never again abandon you. She delights in the ready smile: and were man more grateful, more frequently would her sandals pass over his threshold, and longer would she sojourn in his dwelling.

I willingly allow that the vicissitudes which have of late awaited you, were sufficient to discompose the calmest temper, and to trouble and afflict the firmest heart. I am often inclined to disbelieve the tales and legends of the extraordinary strength of the human mind; many of those of antiquity I deem fabulous and absurd:—in such situations man can be the only judge of himself; for bystanders and observers must be incompetent, and not know any thing respecting that on which they attempt to decide.

I am bending over a dying friend; I shew no grief, heave no sighs, shed no tears. What impulse, therefore, governs my heart? What ideas have I in my mind? I am consoled by the knowledge that every other mortal must go the ways of the departing soul, and my thoughts are becalmed by the sweet assurance of immortality? No such thing: whatever my countenance may express, whatever philosophy it bespeaks, my heart is pierced to the centre by anguish, and a stream of blood seems to flow from it in extreme pain. Those who are around me praise, and are ready to proclaim my superior wisdom and fortitude, while I know myself to be the most imbecile and wretched creature in existence.

The best written piece of biography must for reasons like the present, contain many errors, if it be not the performance of the very person of whom it directly speaks: and allowing it is so, we shall more readily admit the incidents than the sentiments; the actual resuscitation of ideas is, I think, impossible; we may indeed conjure up a shadow, but the substance is for ever gone beyond recal.

I am, however, wandering; strange that it must be always thus with me! Should I ever attempt the task of a poet, I must avoid touching on the epic and the dramatic, having so little knowledge of the unities.*

I congratulate you, dear Charles, on your present state of mind; and the description of your situation, and of the manner in which you are passing your days, is truly pleasing. In the warmth of imagination I have transported myself to your quiet dwelling, have walked with you in the surrounding groves, held converse with the first friend of my heart, and heard the sweet voice, and also seen the sweeter smiles of his Elizabeth.

How unenviable is that mind which has no powers for such excursions! The very visions that cheat us are delightful; and knowing them to be too splendid for reality, and too happy to be changed into the certainties of life, we see them disappear without any extraordinary regret, and again indulge ourselves in mental sorcery. Since you left the neighbourhood, I have cultivated no society, formed no connections whatever; but I have severely felt the loss of your friendship: and when I turn my eyes on him who banished you from hence, for uniting yourself to youth, to innocence, and to loveliness, in opposition to a stubborn will, I can scarcely smother the strong resentment that lodges in my breast.

Some few days ago I met your father in the coppice, where you and I have so often, and so happily walked and talked.—

Solitary, discontented, self-afflicted mortal! if thou wouldst but bring thyself once more to strain thy son to thy heart, and press thy lips on the rosy face of Elizabeth, thou wouldst no longer appear wrapped in the glooms of winter, but with all the radiance of autumn gleaming around thee.—

I bowed to him, but did not speak; he saluted me in the same silent manner, and passed on. My eye, however, was much deceived if it did not see a faint smile steal upon his cheek—a smile which may hereafter diffuse over the whole countenance, and which also may, at no long distance of time, beam upon my deserving friend and his beauteous wife. Yes, I anticipate the time when your offended parent will call you back with a thousand times more joy than if you had never been separated, when you will be reinstated in all the honours which it was once his command should wait on you, and when the *fête* of the happy tenantry, and the merry peal of the village bells shall celebrate your return to your native shades.

I indulged these reflections last night near the walls of the castle, and directly under the window of the chamber which you used to occupy. The season was as delightful as my meditations; the moon was smiling unveiled; the tall trees near the western corner of the building, nodded to the breezes; and the flute of poor blind William sent some strains of tender sweetness from the door of his cottage:—Ah it was a delicious hour!

* * * * *

After thus calmly thinking, thus calmly writing, can you, dear Charles, believe that I have lately been nearly deprived of reason? that my heart has been pierced as with a dagger, and that I have already sobbed like a child, and raved like a maniac? I *have*. But my senses are again compact, and I have talked myself into firmness.

At the time of your father's coming to take possession of the castle, and when you were first inclined to allow me your friendship, the prejudices of the world, and the distinctions of society were not unknown to me; and I thought it not improbable that a young man, educated as you had been, might have strongly imbibed those notions which are widely diffused, and generally adopted.

"I will see whether my conjectures are right, or not," I said to my guardian, my protector; "I will confess to the young gentleman my actual situation:—a repulse at a season like the present I should soon forget; but were I to meet it after a mutual declaration of friendship, and after my heart had admitted him as a brother, it might long continue to mortify, to scourge, and to torment me."

When I next saw you, I opened myself; told you that I was a creature of the Rector's bounty, a bastard; the son of a man whom I had never seen, who had abandoned me and my unfortunate mother, and of whom I thought with horror and disgust!

What did you do?—gave me an embrace as strong as if your mother's womb had produced me. What did you say?—"Leopold, by the God whom I believe in, and worship, you shall be as dear to me as if you were my brother!"—Oh Charles, Charles! I then wept, and my eyes even now are growing blind with tears. My generous Charles—exemplary friend!

*   *   *   *   *

These passions must not have such domination; for on the ceasing of every fit, I think my heart is more and more impaired!

*   *   *   *   *

Well!—This father of whom I have spoken is, I find, still living—is a man of rank and fortune, and not what he declared himself to be when he ruined, and gave the death-blow to my mother. After a silence and neglect of nearly twenty years, during which time his pursuits may have been in the highest degree vicious and disgraceful, he has offered me his protection, and sent an ambassador to bring me before him. I was astonished, nearly mad, for a while I believe *actually* so. I thought that I had received an invitation to league with a murderer, and recoiled from it with indignation!

I never knew my mother, but her wrongs have been told me by my dear benefactor; and he has spoken of her in such terms, that my heart for her has become all love and tenderness. I scarcely disbelieve in spirits. Last night she rose from the grave, and smiled on me. I was alone in the church-yard—the hour late. Last night I saw her; my substance was too gross for an embrace; but her arms were opened. It could not be merely fancy!

I must now attend my venerable friend, who, I fear, has but

a little while to live. Though the functions of life are nearly put aside, and though the renovating spirits of immortality are at hand, yet I shall follow his body to the grave with sadness, and sigh for him many an hour in the days of winter. But his ashes will comingle with those of his god-daughter—with those of my mother.

Soon, dear Charles, I will write to you again more fully, and I hope more calmly, though I felt no discomposure till within a few minutes. Farewel! a kind farewel to you and Elizabeth.

Leopold.

THE story has hitherto been told in the epistolary form; but the author begs his readers to take the remainder of it in the manner of narrative. His adopting the latter style will not, he trusts, be deemed injudicious, or less interesting:—his characters are shifting widely; and as some of the principal ones have long been silent, and somewhat obscured, owing to the difficulty of making them form a natural correspondence, he is inclined more strongly to alter the original plan of the performance. Whatever the opinions of other Novelists, or of readers, may be, the writer of these sheets does not remember to have ever read a single work of imagination in letters, which might not have been improved, and made to appear more probable, consequently more interest- ing, had the author been less uniform, and occasionally spoken for himself.

Besides, not to anticipate, when friends part, and are after- wards divided by foreign lands and seas, letters become more rare, and are transmitted more tardily: ships are not often so exact in their arrivals as our inland mails; and the children of Astræus* are seldom so accommodating as a single postboy. The rules neces- sary to be observed in a Novel and in a drama are nearly similar. What chance of success would a modern play-writer have, if he were to transport his personages as Shakespeare has done in most of his enchanting pieces? Perhaps it may be augured, that when a modern poet shall discover the strength of sentiment, the grandeur and beauty of imagery which distinguish the British idol, an audience will forgive the magical migrations, the inconsistencies of time, place, and action; and not only allow him to skip across the Channel into France, but also to step from Milford Haven to Italy in the shifting of a scene.*

*   *   *   *   *

Some few days after Baron Altenburg had written his last letter to Count Stendal, he and the Baroness returned to Vienna. They were thus suddenly recalled by letters from Grotz, which announced the arrival of a lady of the name of Gardiner, who had been admitted into the house as a relation of the family, and who, since her coming thither, had been much indisposed, and very solicitous to see those friends for whom she had a considerable time been seeking.

The Baroness did not recollect the name, which sounded foreign to her ear; the intelligence of the steward, however, highly interested her; and on her return to Vienna, she discovered, in the supposed stranger, the only surviving sister of her late mother. She really felt the pleasure she expressed; for she had long concluded her aunt to be dead, and had heard, several years previous to this meeting, that Mrs. Gardiner, then bearing another name, had been lost in a storm near Barbadoes.

The life of this relation had been, indeed, a strange mixture of successes and mischances; but as this book is not intended as a vehicle for episodes, it will only be said that the person newly introduced to the notice of the reader, had recently stepped into a state of second widowhood, and was soon going to England to receive a large fortune, which her last husband, a native of that country, who had been a merchant in India, bequeathed to a truly excellent wife.

The tender, the studiously humane Christiana served to remove the indisposition of her aunt, which arose partly from fatigue and anxiety; and Altenburg was pleased in the discovery that had been lately made. But the necessity of Mrs. Gardiner's early departure was very displeasing to her niece; and as neither the journey could be protracted, nor the regret put aside, one morning when they had been in Vienna somewhat more than a month, Christiana entreated her Lord to go for a while to England.

Altenburg, not expecting such a request, started on her making it, and was inclined to opposition; but the petition was urged again with a thousand new smiles, and granted by him with a thousand new pleasures, though every one of them was quick in dying.

The Baroness and Mrs. Gardiner were delighted with the acquiescence of Altenburg; but he, going soon after to the library, found that not a single ray of their happiness had been diffused in his almost comfortless breast. He paced the room in great disturbance, and folded his arms, as if by that means he strove to alleviate some inward pain. Having murmured a few words, but what they were he scarcely knew himself, he took from his bosom (was he culpable for the act?) a miniature of Isabella.

He did not immediately bestow on it any particular mark of favour: on the contrary, he held it at some distance from him, and looked on it only with the eyes of pity. *He held it at some distance from him*; but a more than common thought seemed to strike the center of his brain; and he hugged the resemblance of her who was once so dear, so precious to him, as if he wished to incorporate it with his heart.

He wept a flood of cruel tears, and burst into many exclamations, denoting pain and wretchedness.

"And must I leave thee?" he cried, gazing on the picture of Isabella; "must I leave thee and our daughter, our innocent child, perhaps to perish for want! These eyes smiled on me seventeen years: so long did this lovely bosom bear within it a true and ardent love; so long were these delicate arms thrown with a dissolving tenderness around my neck. Yet I left thee—in a moment of womanish fear I left thee! And while thou wert journeying on the road of grief and disappointment, I was posting, on the wings of a new-created love, to the goal of wealth and pleasure. Base, hypocritical Altenburg! Unhappy and neglected Isabella! thou mayst be compared to a tree, which was beautiful in its blossoms, and delicious in its fruit;—I looked, admired, and feasted; till, by repeated thefts, and by the boughs being too rudely shaken, they became stripped, and were incapable of bearing bloom, nay, even of putting forth their leaves. The sated robber fled, but not till he had carved upon the tender rind his infamous and cruel name—the name of Altenburg!"

In such ruminations as the foregoing, and with his mind frequently reverting to the extraordinary son of Josephine, passed his time till the arrival of the day on which he left Vienna; nor could the bustle, occasioned afterwards by the embarkation for England, rout the strong images from his mind. Christiana often smiled on him, and as often did he press her to his breast; but he frequently stole away from her for a few minutes, and going to the stern of the vessel, looking on the bed of waters he was leaving behind, and murmuring those names which were never to be erased from his memory, he would indulge the spirit of melancholy: and it was not unusual for him repeatedly to lay his hand upon his heart, and sorrowfully exclaim, "Ah! here is much amiss!"

END OF VOL. I.

LEOPOLD WARNDORF.

A NOVEL.

IN TWO VOLUMES.

BY

HENRY SUMMERSETT,

AUTHOR OF

THE MAD MAN OF THE MOUNTAIN, &c. &c. &c.

———◦◦◦◦◖◦◖◗◦◗◦◦◦◦———

Imogen.	" Why did you throw me from you ?
	" Think that you are upon a rock, and now
	" Throw me again !"
Posthumus.	" Hang there, like fruit, my soul,
	" Till the tree perish !"

CYMBELINE.

VOL. II.

LONDON:

PRINTED AT THE

𝕸𝖎𝖓𝖊𝖗𝖛𝖆-𝕻𝖗𝖊𝖘𝖘,

FOR WILLIAM LANE, LEADENHALL-STREET.

1800.

LEOPOLD WARNDORF.

THE season was come in which many regrets begin to steal into the breast of man; in which his mind more strongly inclines to whatever is pensive; when an almost unconscious sadness infuses itself in his imagination, and when he often sighs, scarcely knowing the cause, and even while his countenance expresses neither pain, nor regret, nor anxiety.

It was the departure of the third pleasant season. The verdure of the meadows was gone; the yellow corn, which beautifully waved in the fields, had been cut by the sickle, and nearly a month conveyed to the stack-houses; the forests no longer invited with their freshness; the sear branches of the trees had shed their golden honours, and the leaves were choking up those mazes through which it had recently been delightful to wander. Not a covert remained for the Muse; not a rose was there to be found by her, not a flower that could be placed in a garland. The eye seemed slowly to wander over nakedness; and, if it rested on the fadeless holly, it only conjured up the idea of storms and of freezing skies: if a branch of yew waved before it, the mind reverted to death and the grave, and to those cold and comfortless spots of earth, where the hand of gloomy man more generally plants that melancholy tree.

The jasmine had fallen from the cottage wall, and the sun no longer gleamed on the window in the evening; the hedge, that fenced it, displayed only its thorns, and the brooklet that wound around it, began to be incrusted with ice. Only one bird would carol, and he, like a little interested warbler, seemed to expect a reward for his song from the hands of the housewife and her children. There was nothing delightful in the days, and the evenings were thick, damp, and cheerless. The village sports were forgotten, and the flute of poor blind William was

no longer heard in the season of quiet: the deep murmurings of
the wind, the lowing of the stalled oxen, and the rustlings of the
wary partridge among the stubble, or the startling noise made
by the up-springing covey, alone disturbed the gloomy tranquillity. Every thing appeared to anticipate the season of rigour and
distress; gratitude survived not the blessings which had passed;
even the first blasts that were felt seemed to have blown it out of
man's selfish breast.

It was on a dull and melancholy night in November, and at
an hour somewhat late, when Leopold was walking round the
village; his musings made him regardless of the coldness of the
air, and there were neither pleasure nor happiness in his heart
sufficient to warm it. That species of discontent which has just
been alluded to, perhaps had taken possession of his bosom.
Superior minds, at many periods, are subject to common influence, and nature cannot always be restrained by habit. Such a
lover of retirement as Leopold was, could but mourn to see how
greatly the prospect had changed; the stiffened ground told him
it would be long before the flowers of the earth would rise again,
and the naked trees informed him that many long and dreary
days must pass by before the nightingale would fly from the
changing climate afar, to warble and repose among their fresh
leaves and branches. The spring that was next to come would,
doubtless, produce many a charm, and the ensuing summer
might be as bounteous and delightful as that which had gone by.
The few solitary sheep would bring forth their playful lambs; the
rough waters of the river would calmly flow between the flowery
banks and among the osiers, and the sweets of May be liberally
diffused.

"But where shall I be then?" said Leopold, "where shall I be
then?"

It was not an unoppressive sigh that accompanied these
words, which, being spoken, he seemed to fold his arms mechan-
ically, and as he walked on, his eyes were seldom raised from the
ground.

His reverie was at length broken by his arriving at a stile which divided one of the meadows from the church-yard; he laid his cold hands upon the upper rail, and slowly climbed over it: but he went not forward for several minutes, and his head dropped low upon his breast. Still the wind blustered, but he heeded it not; and though the fog was succeeded by a thick drizzling shower, which was penetrating his clothes, yet they seemed not to him uncomfortable. The moon was full, but invisible; and by the melancholy light which broke through the starless heavens, he afterwards stalked over the graves till he came to the west angle of the church.

"This has long been thy sanctuary, mother!" he cried. "This has lately become thy resting-place, father!—Is it ignorant to weep for those who are for ever wrested from us? I cannot think it so. The common and inevitable circumstance for which thousands daily mourn, I will not have the vanity to think myself superior to. They have least philosophy who the most vaunt of it: and I neither am nor would presume to be above the general weaknesses of human nature. Cleave, spirit of my mother, to him who has lately met thee in the world of bliss! Take him to thy bosom for the bounties which he has bestowed upon thy unfortunate son! Were he to be restored to me again, and again to live an age equal to that which he had first attained, my gratitude and tenderness would not perish even at the end of the second state of existence. I have had few to love me since my birth; of friends not many; of relations none; and in the present hour, if I could derive aught of good from human consolation, who is he that would willingly offer it? My memory, dear father, from thy precepts shall not stray; and while I bear myself according to thy directions and examples, I shall fondly think thy mild and approving spirit loves, and is permitted to associate with me. How weak is that man who, believing in the visitations of the dead, quakes at the idea of a re-appearance! His fear must arise from a foul imagination, and be occasioned by the absurdity of legends, rather than by the smallest degree of evidence. I have seen my relation, or my friend convulsed, laid stiff and cold in his shroud, and afterwards consigned to the bosom of the earth; still I admit that he may come again, and believe that at any hour or season he may stand before me. But how? In what form?— As a horrid phantom, as a meagre skeleton, or as a corrupt and bloated corse? Contemptible and absurd!—No; in no other form than that of an angel, for has he not become such?—with the placid looks, the soothing smiles which, in life, he was wont to wear; so must I view him, or see him not at all.—What madman first taught that the pure spirit, having passed the body, would, merely to abuse the world, resume it in a vile, corrupted, or mutilated state?—Ye whom this earth covers, to whom I owe my being and my preservation—ah! if permitted, sometimes deign to appear before the eyes of your Leopold; meet him at the hour of midnight; he will be confident of your love and protection, and not weakly shrink from you."

He stood ruminating on the same spot almost till the first hour of morning, when he returned to his home. An old woman, who had lived with the Rector upwards of thirty years, opened the door for him; she had been terrified by his absence, and seeing him wet and pale, she took hold of him with her palsied hand, and drew him near to the fire.

"Bless me!" she cried, "how could you frighten me so? Dear Leopold, I have had a thousand fears for you; my heart has been quite sick with them. I have been looking out at the door and at the window, but the night is so thick, and the wind so sharp— ah! I was afraid that you had fallen into the river.—How late the hour is! And you are wet and cold as the dead, and your cheeks are pale. Dear child, where have you been?"

"To the grave of my father!"

"Oh master! Oh my poor master!"

"Ah, let me not distress you, good old woman, by my sorrows; I have been to blame in disturbing your rest."

"Sleep, child, is not so sweet to me as it has been."

"But it will be hereafter, Gertrude."

"Yes, when I sleep like the Rector: he sleeps soundly, sweetly; and my long night of peace is nearly come. But, Leopold, we were of an equal age, both born on one day. We have been like two old trees in the forest; and I always prayed that the axe of Death would fell us both at one hour. Still I must remain withering a little longer."

"Good Gertrude!" cried Leopold, "you are a sorry nurse to the melancholy. Good night! and for my impropriety in keeping you from your bed so long, do not rise early in the morning."

"Good night, God bless you, Sir! God bless you, child!"

Leopold immediately went to his chamber, and soon after to bed; but he lay thinking on recent events almost till the appearance of day. By the will of the Rector, who had no kindred, a small annuity was left to the faithful Gertrude; a yearly donation directed towards the indigent parishioners; and the remainder of his fortune was, in terms of tenderness, bequeathed to Leopold.

Two months before his decease he had been speechless; but every necessary arrangement in his last concerns had been made before that period. He had often previously talked of his dissolution to Leopold, telling him what he was to expect, and advising him on his future manner of living; however, when the powers of speech failed him, he made it known to his favourite that he had something further to propose, and something to withdraw. He began to write on the subject, and employed himself two mornings in his study; when he delivered a sealed packet into the hands of Leopold, on which was written—"When I am buried, peruse these papers. Dear boy, I will not any more lead your thoughts towards death."

His voice had failed about a week before the arrival of Count Stendal in the village; and Leopold had never made him acquainted with the interview which had taken place between him and the friend of his parent, fearing that the agitation it would occasion might be too severe for his feeble frame, and also that, if he were to know of it, he would advise a reconciliation with the father, which the wounded son could not bring himself to agree to. He died, therefore, unknowing of the circumstance; and the youth thought that, in suffering him to do so, he had saved the old man's heart many a pang.

The grave had been closed nearly a week before Leopold broke the seal of the packet; on the morning following the visitation in the church-yard, he took up the paper, with the intention of learning its contents: but he gazed on it some minutes motionless, and in silence, and afterwards laid it down several times unperused and unopened.

Gertrude brought in his breakfast, and observing the melancholy of his face, affectionately asked him how he did, and expressed a doubt of his being well. This roused him. He replied, with a thankful smile, that he was not ill: and as soon as she had withdrawn, he put aside his morning repast, and unsealed the letter of his benefactor, the tenor of which he found as underwritten.

———————————

"Though my God has deprived me of the powers of speech, yet not an atom of my love and reverence for him has been crushed. Visited as I am by affliction, I should be an ingrate to murmur; and if an eternal silence be imposed on my tongue, I have faculties and means still remaining to shew my Leopold my mind, and also to hear the sentiments, and peruse the characters of his own. How idle, wicked, and presumptuous therefore would it be for me to say, either in bitterness or in grief, the blessings of the Almighty are not with me! and how unjust is he who could say so, while he can raise his eyes to the glories of Omnipotence, and while he can feel the breath of heaven!

"I have lived a long and a happy age; have survived every companion of my youth; have marked the growth of forests, and even the mouldering of turrets, which were strong in my spring-days. Shall I mourn that I must moulder likewise? Shall I sigh that I cannot take on me immortality without going into the grave?

and shall I now repine, that to this feeble and common frame Nature did not give the faculties and durable nerves of a giant?

"How long a man should live he ought not to determine: death is an affair which rests alone with God; therefore if the toothless infant falls lifeless from its mother's breast, the parent should not dare to speak of injustice; or if the mortal, in the bloom of life, sinks into a sleep, and never thereafter awake, let neither his widow nor his children over his grave exclaim against the decree of that great Power, who cannot act unwisely.

"Think, Leopold, as I do; and when I am gone, your too gentle and susceptible heart will be nobly fortified; you will look tenderly and with a degree of calmness on my tomb; your hand will be chilled by the stone, but your breast will still glow with love for him who rests beneath your feet. Philosophy lies not in apathy, nor true affection in excessive grief. He who knows the full force of the passions, yet checks them before they engender a tempest, has the best claim to the title of a philosopher. Reason will allow us to feel cutely and very sensibly; he who feels more, generally spends all his sympathies in an early season, and scarcely leaves a mild regret for the future.

"I have often spoken of the manner in which I wished you to bear yourself when I shall be incapable of advising; and you know I had recommended you to spend your days in rural quiet; to farm some lands in the village in which you have passed so many happy days; to associate with the respectable; to encourage and support the poor; to think no man too mean for your notice, provided he is accredited for honesty; and, finally, dear Leopold, to take some gentle maiden whom the follies of the world have not tainted, and on her bosom, and in the society of herself, and of the children she should bring you, to participate the delights of love, and the sweets of contentment.

"Thus have I advised, and you have approved; but, for some few nights past, pain keeping me awake, I have thought differently on this subject. You have talents, my boy, you have genius, an honourable mind, a virtuous heart; and your ready acquiescence to whatever I have proposed, convinces me that, having passed your word to abide by my directions, you would be loth to retract when I am for ever deprived of the power of either applauding or disapproving of the means you feel inclined to adopt.

"Affection towards me may alone have made you happy in the monotonous life you have hitherto passed; but when we are separated, to wander no more in the forest, no more to converse with each other, no more to exchange the name of father and of son, then perhaps you may wish to seek for other friends, and in the world to view those things, and to observe the fluctuating occurrences, of which, at present, you have little more than read. It is natural that your inclination should thus direct you; and I now think it proper that you should go into society. But entertain no fallacious hopes: if you have a fault deserving of correction, it is that of a too warm, a too poetical imagination;— this, however, will be cured in an early season, for you will see the manifest imperfectibility of human nature, the prevalence of vice, the extent of oppression, and the absurdities and errors of many national as well as individual customs.

"Now, as I would save you from all vexation and regret, I release you from your engagement, leaving you the free master of your person, and of the little property which will come to you; but, at the same time offering another plan in the place of that which I think it just and proper to withdraw.

"You know Mr. Krotztien, at Vienna—at least you saw him once in this house; and from his conversation I will leave you to infer whether I may not presume to say that he is my friend. He is a man of fortune and of power, has access to the Cabinet, considerable influence with the Court and Ministry, and is esteemed, as you must have heard, a very able and discriminating statesman. Twenty years ago I was assured that his understanding was not more noble than his heart was good, or his disposition excellent; since that period I have seen little of him, and what he is now I will not attempt to determine. I dare not affirm that he is upright and worthy because at a far distant time I knew him to be so. With this paper, however, you will find a letter addressed to him, which I would have you personally deliver; and you must conclude, from this information, that you are the principal subject of it.

"I have commended you to his protection: if he is willing to allow it, you will receive it with respect; but if he is uncourteous, let the small independence which you will possess, teach you to meet the repulse with an unbroken spirit. Should you be encouraged, and placed by him in an honourable office, your advantages will be many and agreeable; on the contrary, should you miss the smile of the courtier, hasten back to this peaceful hamlet, and take on you that character which your poor old friend first wished you to assume."

The paper also recommended an early delivery of the letter, and contained some directions concerning the best manner of collecting, and afterwards of applying his property, together with many tender and affecting passages, relating to the separation that was about to take place between them.

Leopold sat musing over the letter of his friend a long time; it gave a new turn to his thoughts, and he determined on obeying the commands, or rather complying with the wishes of the Rector. He doubted not but that the letter which he was to take to Vienna, was written in a proper style; that it contained not a single servile phrase, and believed that he who was to present it, and to whom it immediately related, could not be embarrassed by its contents, whatever they might be.

"It is probable," he said, "that I shall move in a sphere which I have never thought of entering. My dear friend has always over-rated my abilities, yet I think I have the power of being useful in many situations which are not of the common order. If I meet with a patron, what an excellent chance I shall have of trying the gifts of Nature! I can be arduous in what is noble, and indefatigable in what is honest; at least so I venture in my present state of ignorance to determine. Ha!—My father!—A man of rank—probably connected with the Court, and with the

Ministers—I may see him, may hear him speak—may, in the course of employment, be deputed to converse with him!—Why did I refuse to hear his name?—I will write to Count Stendal."

He paused long and deeply.

"No, I will never, never know him!" he exclaimed.

The door was opened, but he noticed it not. Gertrude came up to him, but he did not perceive her;—she spoke—he however did not hear her.

"No, I will never, never know him!" he repeated, still more vehemently.

"Sir—Mr. Leopold—did you speak to me?"

"Gertrude!—No. I was saying—indeed I saw you not."

"Have you made your breakfast, Sir? Shall I take away the things?"

"Yes, if you please, Gertrude, if you please."

"Good lack! Why you have neither drank nor eaten! Every thing remains untouched, and the fire is gone out! Bless me, child, how you alarm me! Forsake your bed, neglect your food, and look so pale and strangely! I fear you are going the ways of my master. I nursed you in your infancy—ah, God! these withered hands may yet place the pall over your coffin!"

"My good friend, you distress me; you afflict yourself without cause."

"Your illness and your melancholy are the cause: I have felt sorrow in seeing a flower which had bloomed a long season, thrown on the earth; but if the bud that is now opening should perish——"

"It will not, Gertrude; it will survive the present storm, and you will hereafter see it smile and prosper."

"Well, that is as you should speak, that is as you should look too. I had once a son, Mr. Leopold, who arrived at the age of man; but he was wild and untender, and never half so kind to me as you have been. He is, however, dead, and God, I hope, has admitted his soul into paradise: still he was never so good to me as you have been!"

Gertrude pressed his hand tenderly, and he hesitated not in yielding to the impulse that directed his breast to meet the affectionate woman. A fine lady might have spoken more gracefully, but every possible elegance must have been less forcible than the simplicity of the matron, with whom Leopold retired to another room, in order to take that refreshment which he had before neglected.

In obedience to the directions of his benefactor, he immediately began to employ himself in the arrangement of his affairs; and in the course of a fortnight, with the assistance of a lawyer, he had converted the devised property into money, which he transmitted to the Bank at Vienna. Of his intentions he made no one person acquainted; for if they failed, his design was to return at the commencement of the Spring, if not sooner, and to seek for happiness and peace in scenes which were congenial to him. That it was highly probable he should do so, he informed the surprised Gertrude, whose concern for his proposed departure was distressing to herself, and also to him; and who, on the evening he bade her farewel, kissed a cheek which she was persuaded she should never see thereafter.

The following morning he began his journey. He was risen soon after the appearance of daylight, and his necessaries had been forwarded to the next post-town, to which, being only a league or two distant, he intended to walk. The air was keen, but healthful. Wrapping his coat around him, and putting himself into a quick motion, he soon acquired a comfortable warmth, and reached the brow of a hill which led to the highway, and on which he stopped, and turned towards the paths he had left behind him.

The whole hamlet lay before his eye, which could have numbered every well-known house and hut; he saw the mansion that he had just quitted, the cottage to which poor Gertrude was about to retire, and the church in which the prayers for the dead had passed over the body of his mother and of his friend; he looked still more minutely, and even distinguished the grave in which they both reposed:—a deep sigh followed his long gaze.

"Farewel, dear and precious objects, farewel! Pure and innocent you are, and in purity and innocence I trust I leave you.
Adieu!"

He then climbed a stile that separated the pasture and the
open road; and as he went forward, the word "Adieu!" frequently
passed from him, and his eye was neither dry nor joyous. Those
who are habituated to city crowds, and have been bred in them,
cannot feel any of the regrets of Leopold; but those who have
been more nearly allied to Nature, and have alternately mused in
her bowers, and frolicked on her lawns, may have felt emotions
similar to those which were in his heart.

The morning after his arrival at Vienna he took the letter of
the Rector from one of his boxes, intending to deliver it to the
person to whom it was addressed after he had eaten his breakfast.
Whilst he looked at it, he began to feel some embarrassment;
but his confidence soon returned, and all was quiet again within
his breast.

About noon he was at the door of Mr. Krotztien, but, on
enquiring for him, he learned that that gentleman was out of
town, and that he would not return for a fortnight. This was a
disappointment to Leopold; but telling the servant he would call
again on his master's return, he walked about the city, which was
entirely new to him, and which, till he could obtain an interview
with Mr. Krotztien, he wished to examine minutely.

The expence and inconvenience of living at an inn he soon
discovered, and he immediately hired two small apartments in
a house that stood in the suburbs, which he preferred to the
narrow, noisy, and dirty streets of the town. In noticing the buildings of Vienna, inspecting the various occupations of those who
resided there, observing the characters that in quick succession
met his eye, and partaking some few of the more general amuse-
ments, the time passed away till he found Mr. Krotztien was
returned from the country. A most splendid carriage and retinue
went from the door just as Leopold arrived there; and he found,
on enquiry, that it belonged to the former friend of the Rector,

who was then going to Court, and who could not be spoken to by any person during the remainder of the day. The gold and silver trappings were not regarded by him as favourable to his purpose; the glittering lace of the lacquies seemed to repulse his plain insignificance, and he walked away with no strong hopes in his heart.

At the time mentioned by the porter as that in which his master was to be seen, Leopold presented himself again; and, after an impatient delay, was conducted to Mr. Krotztien, to whom he advanced with respect, and with some slight confusion.

"Your name, Sir," said the senator, "sounds not familiarly to me: your business, please to communicate it."

"I was commanded, Sir," replied Leopold, "I was commanded, Sir, by the Rector of N——, to deliver this letter to you."

He presented it, bowed, and retired a few paces.

"The Rector of N——?—Oh, I remember. He is well, I hope?"

"Yes, Sir," said Leopold emphatically, "he is *well*."

"How, is he dead? Your dress, your manner—is he dead?"

"I mourn to say it, Sir; he is dead!"

"I am very sorry for it," said Mr. Krotztien.

These words conveyed a direct untruth to the ears of Leopold; they formed a common sentence, were spoken in a common tone of voice, and seemed to have been produced by habit rather than feeling. He was requested to take a seat. The statesman broke the seal, and was so little discomposed, that he previously examined the armorial impression; it is true that he took a sufficient time in reading it, but from the first line to the last his features neither contracted nor relaxed; and the reperusal of a manifesto, which he had dictated to his secretary, would have created an equal degree of interest.

"This letter, Mr. Warndorf," he said, putting it aside carelessly, "has created a great deal of concern, a great deal I assure you. I formerly knew the writer very well; he was a very good sort of man."

"He was a very excellent man!" cried Leopold with energy.

"True, a very excellent man, I am willing to confess. As a divine, he was—he was——"

"Learned and pious; and such a servant to God as the master must have approved."

"A remark similar to your own, young gentleman, I was going to make; and I am assured that in his private character, as it is called, he never failed to—to——"

"He never failed, Sir, to display, on every proper occasion, the qualities of honesty, of friendship, of affection, and of benevolence."

"I can believe it; and the manner in which you speak of him evinces your gratitude: it is a commendable trait in your character, young man; for he tells me in this letter that you are merely his adopted son."

Convinced that the word "merely" stood not in the epistle of his dear deceased benefactor, Leopold, though he felt the indelicacy of the introduction of it, answered—

"I was such as you mention."

"He also tells me," said Mr. Krotztien, "that you have been well educated, that he thinks you would appear to advantage in some public employment, and that you would not dishonour your patron, provided one could be found for you. He had great confidence: pray what can you say to all this?"

"Simply thus, Sir," replied Leopold, with a rising spirit, "that his confidence was generous, noble, and shall never be abused. That I hope I shall never dishonour my employer, however honourable he himself may be."

"Indeed," said Mr. Krotztien, "you have a very ready understanding, quick comprehension—very energetic I protest. It is, no doubt, unnecessary to inform you that my old friend, the Rector, has strongly recommended you to me; and I do assure you that it would give me more than a common pleasure to be of any essential service to you."

"Sir, I sincerely thank you."

"But you come to me in a most unlucky season; for the influence which I once possessed is considerably diminished. Some political circumstances, some division in sentiment—you comprehend?—I am inexpressibly concerned that you should apply to me in such an inopportune moment. It was only yesterday that I entered the names of two young men of family, but of reduced fortune, on my list; and it may be a long time before my means will come up to my wishes, even in regard to them."—

"Untutored as I am," thought Leopold, "I am capable of reading this modern volume."—

"It appears then, Sir," he cried, "that I cannot reasonably form any expectations of success. I am obliged to you for your candour, and shall console myself with the moderate independence which I can yet enjoy in a limited society."

"Independence!—Indeed—I am very glad of it. But be not too hasty in your conclusions, for I again declare myself your willing friend. There are many fluctuations in these things, but no regular tides. You positively shall stand my third chance, and I will pass your name among my very best friends."

His warmth seemed to increase, but so did not Leopold's belief in him: he desired the young man to call on him in the course of three or four days, and condescended to walk to the door with him when he retired.

"Were I assured," said Leopold to himself on his return home, "that this being corresponded with the generality of statesmen, I should no longer wonder at the oppressions heaped on nations, or at the frequency of wars and massacres; for I could almost fancy that Cunning actually begat him upon the bosom of Apathy. When he spoke of the man whom he called his friend, how cold, how insensible! A Laplander* would have looked more feelingly, and expressed himself more warmly. This man is changed, my dear benefactor, if he ever did possess those qualities which you spoke of. I will try, but not depend on, his friendship."

Leopold, on his entrance, had thrown himself into a chair, without shutting the door of his apartment; and he rose for the purpose of doing it, when a person, who came from a room above, passed hastily by, but so close to him as to brush against his hand. Without designing it, he threw his eyes upon the face of the stranger, and saw in it youth, female loveliness, and dejection; and though his view were so transient, he perceived the blush of innocent confusion spreading upon her cheeks. In the afternoon of the same day he again met the young stranger on the staircase; he looked earnestly at her, but perceiving that she was embarrassed by his notice, he accommodated her in passing, and respectfully took off his hat—a mark of politeness which she returned with a sweetness that went to his heart.

Her face was nearly half concealed; still much loveliness was visible. In one hand she carried a bottle, and in the other a small loaf of bread; and she went up the stairs as if she were afraid of disturbing some person who was either ill or sleeping. So Leopold thought, and her extreme caution made her appear still more amiable. She employed his mind much during the day, and on his return at night he enquired of the servant whether the young lady he had met belonged to her mistress's family. The girl informed him that the person of whom he spoke was a new lodger, who was living on the floor above with her mother, and that they had not been there above a week, but long enough to make her mistress repent of taking them in, as the sickness of the elder, and their manner of living, proved that their circumstances were very low and mean.

"Let your mistress fear nothing," cried Leopold; "let her treat the mother and daughter with respect; I will be responsible for whatever debt they may contract."

"Do you know them, Sir?" said the girl; "have you seen them?"

"I have seen only the daughter, whose loveliness——"

"Ah ha!" cried the servant, "I guess at it. The young lady, Sir, is indeed very beautiful, but I would lay my life you will never succeed in your designs. I am convinced, by her goodness, and by what I overheard this morning, that you will not."

"I have no designs," cried Leopold, "only such as an honest man should have. But what did you overhear this morning?"

"A melancholy sigh from her apartment, so long and deep, that it seemed to roll through my soul."

"You felt as you ought," said Leopold, affected; "go on."

"I stopped.——'Support us, God of Heaven! forsake us not, I implore thee. If death should chill this bosom, let me die on it before it shall be wholly cold!'—These words followed the moan that I had heard. I looked through the key-hole; the daughter had thrown herself, and was locked in the arms of her mother!"

Leopold turned from the girl, and by pretending to want something, he sent her out of the room. His emotions could no longer be checked; and had he not affected to cough, he must have sobbed aloud. This sensibility may be deemed unfitting a man; but Nature, not Leopold, was amenable for the fault, if such any one shall presume to call it.

On the two following days he saw nothing of the interesting young creature, and he forbore to ask any further questions either of his landlady or her servant. On the third morning he thought it proper to wait upon Mr. Krotztien, and he accordingly went to his house at the same hour that he had visited him before. It was with no great concern that he heard the statesman was then going out, though there were other men waiting in the hall, whose business, he conceived, to be similar to his own, who received the intelligence with impatience and chagrin.

Mr. Krotztien was then coming from the anti-room, and was passing the hall while Leopold took the answer of the servant. The man of power smiled, and bowed, as he walked along—

"Your most obedient, gentlemen; I am glad to see you—particular engagement—some other time if you will be pleased to call—good morning to you!"

This jargon was indiscriminately directed. Some of those who had before been frowning, were actually flattered by this mock condescension; but Leopold laughed behind his hat at their credulity, and his former opinion seemed more strongly corroborated.

"Can any man be so spiritless, so degraded," he cried, after he had left the portico, "as to continue, for any great length of time, this servile attendance? Can he be blind to the contempt that is directed towards him? Even the servants of the despiser draw up their lips at him. I have been told that many necessitous beings will miserably feed on hope, in great men's dwellings, from an early state of manhood till age creeps upon them. Would I do so? Rather let an acre of waste be allotted to me, together with a spade, a hoe, and some few necessary implements—I would build a hovel with clay and furze, would plant my ground with roots, live upon the produce, and at morning and at night sing the wild song of independence before I would bend before or sue to these dignified scoffers!"

At some little distance from his home he met his charming inmate;—he felt much inclined to accost her, but, on looking at her face, which she turned towards the ground, he saw that her pale cheeks were moistened with tears. She perceived, and recollected him;—drawing her hat still more over her eyes, and hastening forward, she entered the house, and ran up the stairs before he could reach the door without rudely quickening his pace. The statesman and his own disappointments were instantly forgotten, and he went into his apartment with a depressed spirit. His dinner, which was brought up to him, he neglected; and his wine he could neither commend nor disapprove, for he did not taste it. Perhaps the unhappy strangers above might be wanting what he could not with pleasure partake of; his fowl would be proper food for the sick woman, and his liquor would perhaps invigorate her feeble body.

"I will send them up; I will take them myself," cried Leopold, raising the dish from the table.

How often are the best and most noble motives of man checked and repulsed by ridiculous customs!

"What am I about to do?" he continued; "to make myself conspicuous by being charitable, and perhaps to act rudely when I wished to act kindly. I perceive the younger of these strangers to be very unhappy. I pity her; but I ought not to tell her so, lest it should increase her misery. The girl says they appear to be well bred. There is a genuine and independent spirit which poverty can never curb; it reigns not indeed in every breast, but in the mother of this young creature it may be yet unsubdued. No, I cannot proceed in this business with the little knowledge that I possess of the characters of these women."

To avoid singularity, he afterwards ate a part of his fowl, and drank some of the wine; still he wished these refreshments could have been enjoyed by those whose wants were greater than his own.—Sudden and immediate love had been allowed as possible; and many may suppose that Leopold had been inspired with that passion: such, however, was not the case; his feelings were all kindred to pity, and he was prompted only by humanity. He had seen but little of the stranger's face; he was convinced, however, that she had a considerable share of beauty: and so every person had allowed whose eyes ever met the countenance of Augusta Marilli.

Isabella and her daughter were really in a state of wretchedness: having voluntarily made themselves almost beggars, they consoled each other with the hope of being supported by their own ingenuity and industry. The greater share of necessary talents was in Augusta, the mind of her mother having been averse to what are termed female accomplishments:—in embroidery she had great taste and delicacy, and by employing herself strictly in that art, she happily thought she should be able to support herself and her mother. She worked, and offered her performances for sale; but she soon found that she had estimated her own abilities too highly, that her employment was the same which a thousand young women scantily supported themselves by, and that a very small emolument was to be gained by the means which she used for the subsistence of herself and her dear parent.

The concern of Isabella was far from being equal to that of her daughter; she smiled at every disappointment, and even seemed inclined to mirth when their meal was scanty: but Augusta knew the nature of her mother's feelings, and was nearly distracted when she beheld her strange conduct. A sigh never passed from the breast of Altenburg's mistress, a tear never rose in her eye when Augusta was present, but the vacancy of her looks, the frequent and long stare, and her inconsistent answers, were infinitely more alarming than any expression of grief or of sorrow.

On the day that Leopold had seen Augusta in tears, she had been on an unsuccessful errand; and though she was grieved to do it, she was obliged to confess her disappointment to her mother, who had two or three days previous to that felt an indisposition, which she could not conceal.

"I will allow no tears, Augusta," she cried; "all the miseries of human life could not draw one from my eye at this time. I have no longer any feelings; my heart is apathy all over; neither joy nor sorrow can in any wise affect it. I can almost believe in the metamorphic power; for the spire of yonder church has as many sensibilities as I have—nay, *that* will shake when the storm rages, but I am a huge rock of adamant, which the universal crush alone can destroy, or put into any state of motion."

Many speeches similar to this she had of late been in the habit of making, but towards the evening, she talked still more alarmingly: all the night she muttered away; in the morning she could not leave her bed, and as the day advanced, her disorder seemed to increase. The anguish of Augusta became insupportable; she had nothing comfortable to give her mother, no money to procure any thing that was necessary. Half frantic, she drew the curtains of the bed, snatched up her cloak, and ran out of the house, in order to sell it. With a part of the money which she obtained for it, she bought a bottle of wine; but, in her hurry she broke it just as she was entering the room. Still she preserved a glass full, and put it to the lips of Isabella, who drank it without taking any notice of the person who gave it to her.

"My mother! dear mother!" cried the daughter, "how are you now?"

"Ask that of the damned," cried Isabella, "and they will give you my answer.—Oh, I am—Come, we will go together."

She was rising from her bed: Augusta, unable any longer to conquer her terror, started from her, and ran shrieking out of the room. She knew not whither she went, and in a minute she was lying almost breathless on the bosom of Leopold. She could not speak, but she clung to him, and directed her finger towards the door. Her screams had brought up the servant of the house, and her looks impressed those who saw them with an idea of her insanity. Breaking from the arms of Leopold, she took hold of the girl's hand, and was drawing her to her mother's chamber; but the servant shewing extreme reluctance to follow, Augusta entreated Leopold to go up with her.

He apprehended that the woman above had committed an act of suicide; but on entering the room, he discovered her lying quietly in bed, with her eyes fixed on the ceiling. Augusta threw herself on her knees, and kissed the cheek of her mother. Isabella regarded her not, neither did she seem to hear the words which were addressed to her. Leopold was now assured of her situation, and with a brotherly affection he enquired of Augusta what had brought these miseries on herself and her parent.

"The cruelty of man, the violation of oaths; poverty, want, and despair!" exclaimed the daughter.

"Good God!" cried Leopold; "yet do not distract yourself;— the insanity of your mother has been of no long date I presume?"

"Strange she has been for many days; but it was only this morning that——Oh my mother!"

"Dear girl, you will destroy yourself. Your mother may soon be well again; perhaps to-morrow her reason may return. Some proper food, some nourishing cordials——"

"And where are they to be got? The beggars in the streets are Kings and Princes compared to us."

Leopold ran out of the room; he however returned in a

moment: his hands trembled, tears were rolling from his eyes, and he brought with him some wine and biscuits, and placed them on a table.

"From a stranger, a man whom I know not," said Augusta, "this generosity—Oh no—it must not be. God bless you, Sir, but I cannot accept these things."

"You must, you shall," cried Leopold; "it is even a duty in you to take them. What induces me to give them?—Humanity! If you reject them, you cannot know what humanity is; for what I now offer you, may be the means of saving your mother's life: should she perish for the want of them, you must be culpable and sinful."

"Give them to me!—God Almighty reward you! My mother has called man a polished savage; I find he may be an angel!— Drink, my unhappy parent, drink—drink—Oh, I shall die before her!"

"Miserable creature," cried Leopold, "exert yourself, rely on Providence, and you and your mother will yet be happy."

"Never! never!" exclaimed Augusta in despair.

"Does he say so?" cried Isabella, starting; "but tell the secret murderer that he has opened a passage for the blood of an inno- cent heart, and he will cry—"never never!"

Augusta, in her terror, again seized the hand of Leopold, but seeing her mother apparently composed, she once more drew near to the bed. Leopold withdrew, but previously whispered the servant, who had followed them, to stay in the chamber till he returned. He met the mistress of the house below; and assur- ing her that he would satisfy her demand on the unfortunate women, he requested her to procure a nurse as soon as possible, and also to recommend him to a Doctor of reputation. In less than an hour he came back with a man of acknowledged skill; and having stepped to the surprised and grateful Augusta to acquaint her with the intended visit, he went down again, and almost immediately after introduced the Doctor.

Augusta received him, and replied to his enquiries with emotion;—he went up to his patient, took hold of her hand, and spoke to her; but there was much spirit and incoherence in her answers, which again served to terrify her daughter, who turned her sad eyes upon the Doctor, and whispered to him her fears. He however strove to quiet her by telling her that the derangement was owing to a fever, which he hoped would soon leave her, and at the same time take with it the strange images of the mind; and as to her vehemence and resistance, he held them to be more favourable than tameness and melancholy. Poor Augusta had much sorrow in her heart, and she turned towards Leopold, who had been a quiet, but not unaffected, observer of the scene. The Doctor departed, and afterwards sent some draughts for his patient, which were administered by the nurse that had been provided; and Leopold having ordered some other refreshments to Augusta's chamber, retired to his own room, having previously entreated her not to neglect herself in her extreme care for her mother.

He was conscious that he had acted rightly in this melancholy concern: much curiosity had he still to satisfy; but, anxious as he was to know more of the strangers, he could not, at a time like that, advance any questions to the poor afflicted girl, who mourned so seriously for her mother. The youth and beauty of the one impressed scarcely more than the piercing eyes and the expressive countenance of the other; and at first he could hardly believe Isabella to be old enough for the mother of a girl of seventeen. In both of them he discovered a considerable share of beauty. The mental derangement of Isabella distorted not her face, but only gave a greater strength to her fine and noble features; an uncommon lustre frequently beamed from her eyes, and the fever had thrown a high colour upon her smooth brown cheek. The complexion of Augusta was much fairer; and, wanting the bloom of health, and the smile of happiness, she seemed, like the first flower of the year, to claim, and also to deserve much cherishing.

When Leopold again went to the chamber, he saw the mother

sleeping; the daughter was sitting near to her, with looks more composed, and with her hands clasped, as if her last thoughts had been devotional. It was a picture highly delightful to the eye of Leopold, who gazed alternately on the forlorn strangers. Fearing that he might make some noise, he silently withdrew to the door; but Augusta rose, and walking lightly across the chamber, stopped him on the landing-place of the stairs.

"Friend," she cried, "worthy friend! my mother sleeps, sleeps sweetly! The fever is high, but the Doctor gives me hope, the nurse gives me hope; and, if she recover, dear stranger, all the blessings of my heart will be too few for you!"

Her face was placed very near to Leopold's, one of her hands inclosed his own, and the other was innocently laid upon his shoulder:—there was no artifice in this—it was the look, the attitude of Nature; and such the heart of Leopold willingly allowed them. The one returned to the bedside of her mother, the other to his own apartment.

"What loveliness!" cried Leopold, "what innocence! I can believe that she is artless, and that there are some marks of honesty in my face, which have caused her to think generously of me. For what I have done, I am rewarded; one of those looks would repay me for a thousand better services."

The Doctor visited Isabella again in the evening; the fever was still high, and while he was standing over her, she awoke with a shriek: still he had not any serious fears for her safety. He ordered some other medicines to be given to her; and before Leopold went to bed, he found that she was again composed, and slumbering. The next day, however, her flesh was almost scorched, and her brain was become more seriously affected: the Doctor then looked on her with considerable gravity. Augusta scarcely retained her senses; and Leopold feared that Death was within a short march of the half subdued mortal. Five days more she continued in this state; on the sixth the fever abated; on the seventh—she knew and spoke reasonably to her daughter.

"Speak to me again, my dear mother!" cried the joyful girl.

"Augusta! My precious child!"

"God, I thank thee! God, I praise thee! God, I will ever adore thee!"

Isabella was again going to talk to her daughter, but was overpowered by faintness, when Augusta brought her some wine, and put it to her lips.

"Whence comes this?" said Isabella; "how long have I been ill?"

"Nine days, dear mother!"

"So long, and yet not famished!—I remember our—ha! has the Baron—you could not accept of his—"

"I have not seen him, have received nothing from him; but I have met a friend, a stranger, a good and excellent man! Under heaven I believe there is no one better. You must see him, mother."

"I must thank him for his *charity*."

"You must not; it will drive him from you. He calls himself an agent of Providence, and will not take what is alone due to the Power under which he acts."

"Is there such a man in this inhuman world?" said Isabella; "if there be—Ah, I am still faint! Raise me, Augusta. Oh, how happy again to meet the bosom of my child!"

Her mind now dwelt chiefly on the information of her daughter.—Saved by a stranger, a young and handsome man!—Her disposition had once been generous, liberal, and unsuspecting; but since the desertion of Altenburg, of him in whom she had for many years confided, it had become doubtful and misanthropic. She looked on Augusta, her innocent, her beautiful child—

"Dare he?" she cried, "dare he?"

"What, who, mother?" cried Augusta, fearful of her senses being again wandering.

"Oh nothing, my girl, nothing. Let me see this friend to-morrow; I am the benefitted object, and my gratitude must——I am not strong enough to-day, but let me see him to-morrow."

Augusta had not a single suspicion of her own, and she did

not catch at those of her mother, whose emotions she believed arose from an uncurbed spirit; and she doubted not but that the modesty and unpresuming manners of their friend would quell this internal disturbance. She saw Leopold in the evening in his own apartment; there was a joyous smile upon her face, an expression in her eyes, and a lightness in her steps, which made her appear an exquisite creature. The imagination of Leopold, which perhaps too often resembled that of a bard, recurred to a sweet description he had somewhere read of a sylph, or wood nymph; and he thought the present reality more delightful than the past vision.

The intelligence of Augusta was given with an unaffected pathos, and her voice might truly have been called musical: the ear of him who listened to her was charmed, and if her beauties had not increased, at least he thought they had most enchantingly.

"You will take the acknowledgments of my mother to-morrow," she cried; "you will find her capable of discoursing reasonably with you. She will survive, wholly recover; then what have we to fear? Think not ill of us, Sir, if our names should be concealed from you; if we were to tell you them, that could neither make your generosity more kind, nor our esteem more strong and sincere. Prosperity was lately with us, but she is gone, and I would forget her."

"Oh that I could recal her to you!" cried Leopold, warmly; "Oh that I could lead you again into her arms!"

He unconsciously took her hand, pressed it, and gazed upon her face, which was instantly blushing. He felt the impropriety of his conduct, loosened his hold, and placed himself in a chair.

"To-morrow then, Sir," said the confused Augusta, "to-morrow my mother may expect—you will—I shall see you?"

"Yes," replied Leopold, "yes, I shall see you."

She left the room, and for some minutes after her disappearance his eyes did not turn from the door.

"From whence are these sensations derived?" he asked himself. "I have compassionated thousands of mortals, of different sexes,

ages, and complexions; have stretched my services for them to
the length of my capacity, and seen many of them afterwards
smiling, and heard others attributing their happiness to me. But
my present feelings are new—they are delightful! Augusta has
certainly been the inspirer of them, and Augusta must certainly
be beloved."

On the morrow he went up to the chamber of the sick woman,
and was introduced to her. Isabella started, and in silence gazed
strongly on him; recalling her thoughts, however, which had
apparently for a moment been wandering, she put forth her
hand, and expressed her sense of his kindness and humanity. It
was a noble gratitude she gave him, and such an one as did not
confuse him to accept; and his reply was that of a fellow-being,
who was conscious of his duties—not that of a benefactor, who
was proud of his deeds. His manner reached the heart of Isabella, and she was no longer humiliated; he appeared to her such
a man as she had wished, but not expected to find; she pressed
his hand between her's, and raising it to her lips, he felt a tear
drop upon it.

Leopold, fearing that the emotions of Isabella might endanger
her weak frame, soon after retired, having previously requested
that he might be admitted again; which Isabella, to the pleasure
of Augusta, readily assented to.

In the evening, and till then many a delicious thought had
been in his mind, Leopold gently knocked at the door of their
apartment, and put a basket into the hand of Augusta.

"How is your mother to-night?" he enquired; "is she better?"

"Oh much better, Sir," replied Augusta cheerfully.

"And yourself, young lady, I hope you are well?"

"Yes, I thank you, well and happy!"

"God be praised! His blessings on you both! Good night—I
will not now intrude—I cannot—good night, good night!"

He went quickly down the stairs, and she carried to her
mother the basket, which contained some nourishing provision
and excellent wine. Isabella turned from it, and her spirit was

rising; but Augusta found a slip of paper, on which the donor had written a few emphatic words, which altered the tide of her mother's feelings.

"I will not wound this excellent man," she cried, "for I never before saw such true benevolence. I shall, I think, soon regain my strength, and till then I will not refuse his bounty. He is good and excellent——"

"And so very handsome!" cried Augusta, artlessly; "do you not think so, mother?"

"Yes," answered Isabella, with a deep sigh, and she pressed her hand on her forehead.

"What, do you not think him handsome?" said Augusta, not satisfied with the tone of the reply.

"Yes," Isabella repeated, and she laid her face on the pillow. Augusta was not pleased with this accordant monosyllable; but thinking that her mother wished to sleep, she gently drew the curtain, and went to a distant part of the room.

For several successive days Leopold was in the chamber; and when Isabella received him in her chair, he expressed such a lively and unaffected pleasure, that her astonishment and admiration increased.

Better able to hold conversation, she now discovered that, with a fine person, he possessed an excellent understanding; which was an opinion similar to one he had formed of her. His manner was free, but affectionate; and it was evident that the corruptions of the world, though he was not ignorant of their existence, had not yet reached him. The feelings he caused to rise within her breast, were nearly those of a mother; his respect and delicacy were alike directed towards her and her daughter; his eyes never assumed the smallest freedom, his tongue never expressed an improper word, and one evening he ingenuously confessed to them his name and situation. Though, at the same time, he protested he had not a wish to draw from her confidence, yet Isabella was pained that she could not be equally explicit; but the world had been busy with her appellation and concerns, had spoken injuriously of her—even Leopold, stranger as he was, might have heard some of its remarks and aspersions, and though she contemned the malice that had pursued her, she was yet too weak to speak on a theme which required composure and energy. Augusta saw the distress of her mother, but in a few minutes she smiled it away; her disturbance had also been noticed by Leopold, who suspecting that he had acted wrong, strove to atone, by speaking on some general subjects.

The day following this meeting, Leopold went again to the Minister, who condescended to see him; he had however to listen to a tale which, he was assured, had been often told, and to attend to some common promises and regrets, in which he was convinced there was little or no sincerity. He withdrew in disgust, and for a while his temper was much disturbed; but as he went homeward, his mind reverted to his former agricultural plan, and hope presenting a fair vision to his eyes in a female form, he met Isabella with a happy countenance, and happier it became when he saw the improvement of her interesting face. Augusta was not in the room; but soon afterwards she entered precipitately, and running up to her mother, incautiously exclaimed—

"Good heaven! we are discovered. I have seen Grotz, and he is coming up the stairs."

"I will die before he shall enter!" said Isabella, rising from her chair; "I will perish before I bear another insult!"

"Who shall dare to insult you?" cried Leopold; "suffer me to interpose, and to chastise the intruder."

"Oh, no, no!" said Isabella; "he is an old man, a good man; but his employer——Age has made him thoughtless, and he may tell—Pray, Sir, retire—yet stay—Augusta, go you and desire— no, I will see him myself."

"You must not, dear mother!" said Augusta, "your spirits——"

"Are roused, and capable of bearing me through any scene!" cried Isabella, with an enlarged voice, and with a dignity which astonished Leopold. "Will you allow me, Sir," she added, "the use of your apartment for a few minutes?"

"Most readily: let me assist you down the stairs."

"I thank you, but do not need assistance. I hear them coming."

"My arm, mother," said the trembling Augusta—

"Is not wanted, my girl; I can walk without it. I wonder while I feel my own powers, for I could—they come; remain where you are."

She shut the door, descended the first flight of stairs, and at the bottom met the steward, and also a person whom she had never before seen. She entered Leopold's apartment, and cast her eyes, full of disdain, upon Grotz; but the old man sunk upon the floor, and sobbed as violently as ever he had done in his childhood. Isabella had prepared herself to chastise him for his insolence; but when she saw how much he was affected, and read in his old face the legible characters of love and grief, she was subdued, and offered her hand to assist him in rising. He fixed his lips upon it.

"Oh this hand!" he cried, "Oh that sad and altered face! Ah God! Madam, I wish I had not seen you!"

"Grotz," replied Isabella, "Grotz, I have been ill; I thank you for your concern; but you must leave me—instantly too."

"I will go, Madam; I have long been seeking for you, but I will go. I have no business, and my affection I see offends you."

"Nay, nay, you mistake, good old man; I ever respected you."

"God bless you for it, lady; but I will retire; this gentleman must, however, speak with you."

"Stay, Grotz:—of this gentleman I know nothing; of the Baron I will *hear* nothing."

"Madam," replied the stranger, "I do not know the Baron, have never seen, spoken to, or received any directions from him. I believe I find in you Signora Isabella Marilli?"

"That is my name," she answered, restraining her wonder.

"You were formerly of Venice, Madam?"

"These questions, to what do they tend?—But—yes, I was formerly of Venice."

"Soon after you left Italy, your father died?"

"So I have been informed," said Isabella, sighing.

"Your elder brother survived him only eight years?"

"I have long known the circumstance, but never mourned for him—I loved him not."

"About a twelvemonth ago your younger brother fell in a duel."

"Indeed!—My younger!—Poor Antonio, I can still weep for thee!"

"You had only one sister, I believe? Her days ended in a Convent."

"She gone too—I hope she is with God!"

"And your mother, Madam—"

"Hold, hold," cried Isabella. She paused, and wept. "My mother, there you touched me tenderly—she is dead?"

"She died about two months after the fall of Signor Antonio: I prepared her will some few days before her dissolution, and she commanded me to present it to you. My search has been long and difficult, but I now give you the paper, which I wish you to peruse."

"What!" exclaimed Isabella, almost franticly, "to read the curses of her who bore me?—Let me go—I shall make my brain mad if I listen to you."

"Stay, Madam," said the Notary, "you misconceive. Your mother's fortune, owing to the extravagance of her eldest son, was not very large; but such as it was, she bequeathed it in tender terms to you, her daughter Isabella."

"To me! to me!—Support me, God!—I knew not that I *could* feel thus."

"And this paper," said the stranger, "was written by her not many hours before she expired."

He presented it to Isabella; she took it hastily, and threw her eyes distractedly upon the writing.——

"I am dying, but I shall die in peace with you! I have cursed you—Bless you! bless you!" ——

It contained no more. Isabella uttered a loud shrill scream, and fell senseless on the floor. Augusta and Leopold were with her in an instant; the former was filled with terror, the latter with amazement; and the old steward, who had thrown himself beside Isabella, was violently affected. Augusta, however, entreated him, and also the stranger, to retire before the senses of her mother returned, lest her relapse might be more dangerous; and with this desire they complied, previously informing the surprised and agitated girl that they would come again on the morrow.

Isabella soon after opened her eyes upon her daughter, and sobbed upon her bosom, when Leopold instantly withdrew, and the cause of this new affliction was explained to Augusta, who, dearly as she loved her mother, and pitied her sorrows, felt an inward satisfaction which she did not dare express. Isabella many times read the few words of her departed mother, and she was not much composed when Grotz and the Notary called on her the following day; but before she spoke to the latter, she took the former aside, and commanded him not to apprize Baron Altenburg of her circumstances, or place of residence; when she learned of the steward that his Lord was gone to England.

She started, but immediately turned to the Notary, who was very explanatory in the affairs which he had hinted at on the preceding day: he informed her of the sum that she might expect, and also named six weeks as the period within which she would be in the possession of it. After this they had only two more meetings; the Notary then left Vienna, but the affectionate Grotz entreated that he might sometimes call on and see his Lady and Augusta; which was not denied by either of them.

Isabella still continued pale and unhappy; but at the end of a week, perceiving that Augusta watched her anxiously, she was more guarded in her looks and actions, and strove to converse with composure.

Leopold had not congratulated her on what many would have called her good fortune; but he had, in delicate terms, expressed his satisfaction on the change of her circumstances, and entreated her to let his purse become a joint supply till the Notary made his promised remittances; to which she had thankfully and unreservedly consented.

Though the space allotted by her heart to Leopold had never been a narrow one, still she had always closely observed his conduct; and though she was convinced that her first hasty suspicions were unjust, yet she now, with some concern, perceived that friendship for one object had engendered love for another. He seemed to be always upon his guard, always cautious in speaking to, or looking at the unsuspecting Augusta; but Isabella's discrimination was strong, and she often drew just inferences when conversing with apparent indifference, and deeply scrutinized what she scarcely seemed to look on. Leopold's affection was evident to her, but she loved him herself, and did not doubt his honour; still she was pained by her own assurances, as the acquaintance might probably end in unhappiness and regret. She knew little of him, but she was convinced of his understanding being good, and his heart excellent; he had told her some things relating to himself, and his circumstances, without being altogether explicit; nor had she wished him to be so, as she could not repose in him an equal confidence.

Leopold still spent much of his time with them, nor could Isabella oppose it: he sometimes played on the flute, sometimes sung to them, and he often brought home some interesting book, and read to them on an evening;—but his eyes frequently wandered from the page, and fixed on Augusta; and though he turned them again on the volume when he came to the gathered period, yet Isabella was not unmindful of the circumstance; on which she silently commented.

Whenever Leopold was alone, he found himself uneasy; he was too romantic to think his love improper, though it was fixed on the daughter of a stranger, whose name and character were alike unknown to him, and of whom many men would have had no small number of suspicions. He believed his happiness depended on Augusta. Sometimes he despaired of ever attaining the object, and sometimes he indulged strong hopes of possessing the first woman he had ever loved. The felicities of rural life, and of calm independence, would at the same time enter his mind; and in the village in which he was born, he thought of finding, with his Augusta, all the joys which were supposed to pertain to Arcadia.*

The Notary had not been unmindful of his promise; for the fortune of Isabella's mother, which had previously been gathered in, was punctually remitted to her at Vienna, and she found that it would yield an annual competence for herself and her daughter. The loan that she received from Leopold she returned; but she did not offer to pay him for those services in which his humanity and benevolence had been so distinguishable.

Augusta felt the advantages of this unexpected independence, and so did Isabella, but the happiness of the latter was not much increased: she evidently struggled hard to subdue the grief, of which she spoke not; and though the natural vigour of her soul and mind would frequently discover itself, yet sometimes she felt a dejection, which she could neither banish nor conceal. Altenburg and England, were words which she would often repeat when she was alone; but she never suffered them to reach the ear of her daughter, and she had strictly commanded Grotz not to apprize Augusta of the Baron's journey.

The winter season had commenced with rigour, and Leopold often claimed a place at the fire-side of his female friends. He had paid his last disgusting visit to the oily statesman, had renounced every thought depending on Courts and Ministers, and his mind again turned towards his native village, in which perhaps Augusta might make his happiness complete. This hope, however, was sometimes checked by his fears, one of which was the disapprobation of her mother—and another, the want of affection in herself; that she possessed an innocent and tender heart he was assured, but her manners were nearly those of a sister, and he could not flatter himself that her heart had ever felt any stronger emotions than those arising from gratitude.

The painfulness of uncertainty, at least, he was determined to remove; and one evening when he was alone with Isabella, he confessed to her the love which he bore for her daughter, stated some plans which he had formed in case an union with her was practicable, and entreated the mother to speak to him on the subject before the return of Augusta. Isabella was not surprised, but she was somewhat concerned, and she also appeared confused, and remained silent; the apprehensive Leopold, however, urged her to speak, and she at length declared that she saw no probability of his ever being united to her daughter.

"But we must ever be friends," she continued, taking his hand; "I must become insensible indeed when I do not esteem you. Yet how romantic is your attachment! Your acquaintance with us has been short; your knowledge of us scarcely amounts to any thing. We may, for aught you know to the contrary, be Princesses in disguise, or proclaimed criminals, hiding ourselves from the pursuit of justice."

"My life," cried Leopold, "even my life would I pledge on your worth and honour!"

"Beware!" said Isabella, in a changed tone, "beware of those whom you would so unguardedly trust. The world is full of evil: the spirits which are said to inhabit a region beneath us, are no less wicked than many of ourselves. Millions of us, of men and of women I speak, merely by stepping into hell would become very devils. The name is local—the matter is not so. But this relates not. I love you, Leopold; indeed I wish you happy."

"Give me Augusta then—let me call her wife, and you mother!"

"Hold, Warndorf; you have partly made yourself known to me, and I trust you. But, admitting that Augusta were to love you, there are certain notions in the world, opinions, prejudices: Poverty is contemned—so is Vice, if she be ill-cloathed; with a robe of purple, however, crowds will make lanes for her to pass, and men will elbow one another for her accommodation. Then illegitimacy! Oh fie on he or she who is illegitimate! There your cause is lost!"

Leopold started from his seat, and threw from him the hand of Isabella, which he had been holding for some time past.

"Madam," he cried, "though you at first spoke satirically, your allusion has not failed to strike me. I know not how you have discovered what I foolishly concealed, but am assured that the means were dishonourable. Yes, I am illegitimate; and by the soul of my dear mother, which is in heaven—by God, who commanded his angels to bring her before him, I would——"

"Leopold," exclaimed Isabella, starting forward, and throwing herself upon his neck, "Leopold, what have I said—what have I done? Friend, by the God whom you now called on, I swear I knew not what you have confessed!—Augusta, she—I meant no other—she is illegitimate!"

Leopold was struck with shame and astonishment; neither he nor Isabella could for several minutes utter another word; her face was laid upon his breast, and his own had fallen on her shoulder.

"Pardon me," at length said the one of them, and "forgive me," the other. They heard Augusta on the stairs, when Leopold started from Isabella, and left the room by another door before she entered it.

The next day he contrived a private interview with Isabella; he extenuated his past fault by laying every part of his history before her; and she, in confidence, gave him the outlines of her own, concealing only the name of him whom she was compelled to speak of in ungentle terms.

Again Leopold fondly mentioned Augusta; and Isabella, after some deliberation, assured him that if the happiness of him and of her daughter should thereafter seem to depend on an union between them, she would not withhold her consent from it.

"You preserved my life," she cried; "perhaps both I and Augusta had perished without your assistance; and I shall never forget you. But there are no proofs of my girl's loving you, and I have plans which——hark! she comes.—Pray retire for a while, for I wish her not to see you at this time."

Leopold pressed her hand, and went to his room, where, his surprise having subsided, he indulged the hopes of love, and fondly thought of becoming the happy husband of a woman who was really his sister.

Isabella strove to examine the heart of her daughter without discovering her design: this she did by enquiries made with seeming indifference, and by remarks which led towards the person, the understanding, and the different qualifications of Leopold. To every thing said in his praise Augusta readily assented; her own observations were tender and simple, sometimes affectionate, and they generally conveyed an idea not very remote from that which is formed of love.

Isabella smiled on her unsuspecting girl, who seemed not willing to turn from the subject;—her consent had been passed conditionally to Leopold; his success was in the highest degree probable, and for a few days she amused herself with reflecting on the virtues of her child and her lover, and also on the tranquil hours which she might thereafter enjoy with them. These thoughts however pleased but for a little while; a succession of new images broke into her mind; she became visibly dejected, and one evening, to the astonishment of Leopold and Augusta, declared her intention of going to England.

"To England, mother!" exclaimed Augusta; "if you are serious, to what purpose would you go thither?"

"By travelling," replied Isabella, "my health may be amended, and my mind diverted. Italy I never intend to see again; France is familiar to me; of Germany I am weary; England I have never seen, therefore I mean to go thither."

Augusta could not speak, but Leopold said—

"The season, Madam, is unfavourable to a voyage; you doubtless will not go till the spring?"

"I shall perhaps depart next week," she replied; "the season does not alarm me; I have been accustomed to storms, and no longer dread them. What is the tempest of the elements when compared with the tempest of the soul? I shall have so much fortitude, that in supplying Augusta with it, I shall not find my loss."

Though the last words were spoken with a smile, her daughter's features could relax but little; Leopold was also much agitated and perplexed, but there was then no opportunity for him to speak to Isabella, as he wished.

When they next met, she anticipated him, by saying—

"Augusta is in the next room, and I was wishing that you would come to me. I saw your surprise last night, when I told you of my design—a design which I am impatient to execute. We shall part, Warndorf;—how long I may be absent, I know not; but on my return to Germany I shall expect that you will be the first friend to greet me."

"You remember your promise?" said Leopold.

"Having made one," replied Isabella, "I do not easily forget it. My Augusta esteems you; perhaps I should not err, if I were to say that she loves you."

"Love me!—Oh heaven!—Love me! And would you part us?"

"Your separation will not be a long one. On our return, if her sentiments shall be in your favour, and she inclines to it, I protest she shall become your wife."

"Madam—mother—you must not divide us; I must go with you; nay I conjure you, do not forbid it. Love me! Dear Madam, I never felt such joys as those you now bestow! I must go with you to England. If you deny me, I shall not have a moment of happiness till your return. You know not what it is to be separated from that object which is most dear to you!"

"Oh! Oh, yes I do!" cried Isabella, throwing her eyes on the floor.

"Then I entreat you," said Leopold, "to grant my request. I will be your son and protector! You know not the language of the country; I do perfectly: you will therefore find me useful, as well as affectionate. Will you, will you permit me to—"

"Hush!" cried Isabella, "Augusta is coming."

"But shall I accompany you?"

"We will talk of it hereafter."

"Nay, now, now—before my beloved Augusta enters. A single word will decide it—no or yes?"

"Yes," said Isabella, "yes, Warndorf."

Augusta then entered, and noticing the extraordinary animation of Leopold, smilingly enquired the cause of it, when her mother informed her it had been agreed that he should accompany them to England, and the intelligence was received by her with evident pleasure. Leopold, whose anxiety had previously been strong, was delighted by the acquiescence of Isabella, and still more by the opinion that she had given him of Augusta's sentiments. He suspected that the former had other motives for her journey than those which she had acknowledged, and the eyes of the latter, he thought, seemed to throw some doubts on them; he rejoiced, however, that he was to be their companion, for, independent of his love, he had a wish to see the country to which they were going, the language of which he had been taught by a polished native, who resided several years, and died in his native village; and to its literature he was fervently attached.

Within a fortnight following the intimation of Isabella, they all embarked; and after a rough but quick voyage, arrived perfectly safe in England, and proceeded almost immediately to the capital. It had been agreed that they should still occupy one house; and Leopold soon busied himself in looking for suitable apartments: conveniency was to be attended to, and also the plan of economy regarded; he inspected several lodgings, but fixed on none. He, however, met with some which he much approved, and which he proposed to engage, if the mistress of the house could prevail on one of her inmates to resign a little room which would be altogether necessary. The next day he was informed that the apartment had been readily given up, and on the following the foreigners left the hotel, and took possession of the private house.

The weather becoming more temperate, the first week was spent by them in viewing many parts of the town, with which the young travellers were much pleased; but Isabella, who had, while in Germany, declared that curiosity alone would carry her to England, viewed the many objects with more indifference, and, in the absence of her mind, she frequently disregarded the remarks which were directed towards her. Augusta saw this conduct with concern, but was silent on it: Leopold also noticed, and ventured to ask the cause of it. Isabella, however, endeavoured to persuade him that her mind was free from every serious vexation, and carried him from the subject by entering with spirit into another.

It was at this time when Leopold begged that he might be allowed to declare to Augusta his affection, which he had never spoken of to her; but Isabella desired him to delay it for a day or two, and till she had in some manner prepared her beloved daughter to hear him. A few hours after she took Augusta to her chamber, and throwing her arms around her neck—

"Dear daughter!" she cried, "to you I can no longer be an hypocrite. I have marked your surprise and pain when you have witnessed many of my actions, and your silence on them evinces your love and tenderness. You are my friend as well as my child, and I have no other on earth."

"Dear mother," said Augusta, "you forget Warndorf."

"Oh no—I hold him in my heart and memory! But I am going to make a discovery that will perhaps astonish you. I am not come hither in pursuit of either health or pleasure; no, I came in pursuit of Altenburg."

"Of my father!—of my dear—"

"Hold!" cried Isabella, "beware of what you say; recollect yourself, and be virtuous."

"Oh, I beg your pardon—I forgot.—But my father—the Baron, is he in England?"

"He is: his wife also is here; and I believe they do not intend soon to return. What do you think of my following him after all his cruelties?"

"That even those cruelties have not been able to destroy your affection—that you still love him."

"Love him—Oh Altenburg!—Love him? Aye, and I could kill him too!"

"You terrify me!" cried Augusta. "Kill my father! For God's sake do not talk thus!"

"Nay, Augusta, the fault lies in you, for it is you that lead me to talk wildly; but fear me not—doubt not the propriety of my actions. I cannot account for the affections of my heart; Altenburg, however, sometimes seems to me better than an angel, and sometimes worse than a devil. In one hour I could throw myself upon his breast, with all the tenderness I bore for him before you were born; and, in the next, I could almost twist a bow-string around his neck, and darken his face with agonies. I must see him—if possible talk to him—"

"Where—how—in what manner, mother? Let me go with you!—Were the world mine, I would give it to kiss his cheek!"

"Do you love him so truly?" cried Isabella, hiding her face; "Oh, daughter! daughter!"

They wept several minutes in the arms of each other; Isabella, however, first threw aside her weakness, and told Augusta that she had something to say which related to Leopold.

"And what of him?" said Augusta, in a manner which shewed that she was considerably interested.

"He loves you, my girl!"

Her eyes fell from the face of her mother.

"He loves you, Augusta," continued Isabella, "he has confessed it to me; entreated me to allow him to speak to you of his attachment, and I have given him my permission."

"I shall never dare to look at him again, mother! I never can see him more!"

"What!" cried Isabella, "can you be abashed by an honourable love? I would not on such an occasion make a woman's diffidence a criterion of her genuine modesty. Warndorf is an excellent young man, handsome in countenance, good in disposition, and noble in principles. Without his aid I had perhaps now been reposing with the dead; you probably had pined in grief. And can you not love the man who rescued your mother and yourself from so dreadful a situation as that in which he found us?"

"I do love him, dear mother—love him as if her were your son and my brother."

"Could you not love him if he were to propose himself as your husband, Augusta? You know my respect for sincerity, my dislike to affectation; therefore answer my question without hesitation or confusion."

"Warndorf," replied Augusta, "is, I believe, worthy of the good opinion of every person; he has long had mine, and I could love him in the character to which you have alluded."

"Then may I hereafter," cried Isabella, "see you his wife? But no more of this at present. When you next meet him, do not be discomposed; and if he speaks to you as a lover, fall not into embarrassment. There is ever a delicacy in his speech and manners which must win all hearts; and I do not think that he has the *power* to act dishonourably."

"But my father—let us talk again of him."

"Not another word," said Isabella, rising; and in a few minutes she left the room.

Augusta remained in astonishment; the discoveries that had been made to her interested her greatly, but that which related to her father surprised her even more than the love of Leopold. What the views of her mother were, she knew not; many serious apprehensions took possession of her mind, and the well-known impetuosity of Isabella made her tremble.

The declared affection of Leopold, and the wishes of her mother, agitated her, however, scarcely less than the former subject; she had confessed she had long regarded him with tenderness, but the thought of marriage had never intruded, and all her feelings, she believed, came from no other source than that of gratitude. The acknowledgment she had given to her parent now threw a blush upon her face; and though she had been charged not to discover any timidity when Leopold should meet and speak to her of his wishes, yet the idea of seeing him, in spite of a strong remark her mother had made, occasioned her to feel a considerable degree of confusion.

When she next saw him, however, she soon found her confidence return; for Isabella, having delighted him by repeating a part of the last conversation, charged him not to take up the subject with precipitancy; no allusion therefore escaped him, and his conduct was not less pleasing to the mother than to the daughter.

At this time Leopold became, in some manner, acquainted with a gentleman of the name of Asterley; the person who lodged in the house, and who had so readily resigned his apartment. Warndorf, having been informed by the occupier that the room had been very genteelly given up, thought his personal thanks would not be improper, and accordingly gave them to the obliging stranger, whom he found a young, agreeable, and handsome man. They afterwards met several times, and at length an intimacy was formed between them; the person and manners of the Englishman were highly pleasing to Leopold, who, in the course of a few days, introduced him to his female friends.

The ages of Warndorf and Asterley were nearly equal; the form and countenance of the one were not inferior to those of the other, and in conversation both possessed the art of pleasing. Isabella and Augusta found him an agreeable companion; their dialogues were carried on in the French language, and Asterley alternately appeared to them the creature of sensibility and vivacity. In wit he was superior to Leopold—in sentiment they perfectly coincided: that tincture of romance which appeared in Warndorf, was frequently discoverable in Asterley; and though the eyes of the Englishman often threw from them the happiest smiles, yet there were times when his pensiveness was not to be removed by the endeavours of his companions.

Every day since the arrival of the foreigners in England, Leopold had aimed at instructing them in the language of the country. Isabella was the more arduous scholar of the two; and though concerns of greater weight would often press on her mind, yet her efforts and natural powers enabled her, in the course of six weeks, to make some considerable progress. But before that time had passed, Leopold offered his fairer pupil a sweeter lesson, for he spoke of his love to Augusta, and addressed her with so much gentleness and sincerity, that he drew from her a reply which he listened to with admiration and joy.

"We shall be happy!" he exclaimed, "dear girl, we shall be happy! The similarity of our fortunes and of our past circumstances, will serve to make us more precious to each other. Your mother shall be our only parent; we will look up to, will acknowledge no other. Sweet Augusta, I have at this moment too many joys in my heart; they overflow—Oh let me pour some of them into your own beloved bosom."

"Dear Leopold!" cried Augusta, "dear Warndorf!"

"God shall ever be praised by me," he said, "for sending me to the assistance of you and of your mother, whose sorrows will speedily be lost in the happiness of her children. On our return to Germany, we will retire to the village in which I was born. It is a charming place, Augusta; the hills are so pleasant and healthful, the valleys so fruitful, and, in the spring, the forest is delightful! You will almost wish the flowers that grow in it were not so numerous, as you will break the stems of many of them when you are wandering among the shades with your Leopold. The honest villagers will praise the beauty of Warndorf's wife; their partners will extol her goodness; and the little children will be taught to bless her name. Oh how delightful are these anticipations!"

Augusta was prevented from replying by the entrance of her mother, to whom both she and Leopold ran, and throwing themselves at her feet, she sunk on her knees, and, while she clasped them in one embrace—

"I call on God, my son!" she exclaimed; "I call on God, dear daughter, to bless you!"

After this declaration had been made, Augusta became less timid, and she no longer dreaded the approaches of her lover; but thinking on the Baron still continued to pain her, and she was also much concerned and grieved by the situation of her mother; whom she entreated to return to Germany, but from whom she received an answer by no means satisfactory, or favourable to her wishes.

Leopold, a stranger to the name of Augusta's father, and equally so to the object of Isabella's journey, endeavoured to console the lovely girl whenever he saw her distressed; his tenderness often succeeded in soothing her, and he led her to hope that it would not be long before they should go back to their own country in peace and in happiness.

Mr. Asterley still continued to claim their friendship, and to spend many evenings in their society:—when his mind was free, he was a most engaging companion; spleen must have been murdered by his anecdotes; his knowledge of society was extensive, and his remarks on public characters were judicious and frequently humorous. But there was a strange inequality in his spirits; one day he would be the laughing son of joy, but in the next he would appear with the clouds of sorrow hanging over him; and Leopold, in the presence of Isabella and Augusta, once ventured to enquire the cause of it.

"I am conscious that your remarks have been just," replied Asterley, "for there are times when the air seems scarcely lighter than my body, and there are times when its substance is like that of the earth, and only fit to be commingled with it. The cause must be traced in my mind: if I am happy, I can seldom be reflective; if sad, I either am, or recently have been ruminating on many of the occurrences which have befallen me, and also left behind them an indelible impression. The great author,* of whom we were talking yesterday, has said that "a man used to vicissitudes, is not easily dejected." I can judge no other mind by my own, but all *my dejection* is occasioned by the vicissitudes through which I have passed. Will you attend to me for a little while? If so, you shall hear, and judge me."

They all bowed, and Asterley proceeded.

"I will describe to you the original images of my memory. This is the first picture of life I can recollect. An ill-clothed woman, not arrived at the middle age, with dark sorrowful eyes, and wan cheeks; a tottering garret, in a narrow street, dark and melancholy; a bed in which sleep was scarcely to be obtained, but by the most abject and insensible; a chair, a rotten table, and a grate, often black and cold when December was howling—I remember nothing so well as what I have now described. The forlorn object I speak of was my mother; the room, the wretched place in which she lived.

"I pretend to know of no events which preceded my fifth year, and at that time my mother seldom left her garret during the day; when evening approached, however, she went into the streets, took me with her, and begged for charity. She lived by these means till I was eight years old, and at that early period I began to be mindful of the horrors of our situation, and also to enquire the cause of it. I saw that my mother was, in many respects, different to other beggars: I never heard an execration pass from her mouth; when she received a pittance from the humane, she was silent; when she was pushed and spurned, she would sigh deeply, and often in a low voice say—"God protect me!"

"Cold and hungry we frequently went to our bed; but indiscriminate donations sometimes provided us a coarse plentiful meal. My mother would not allow me to play with the ragged bantlings of the alleys, and if I used an improper word, which I had taken from the mouths of the dissolute, she always severely chid me, though there were moments in which her love and tenderness melted my young heart. She could read, and I suspected that she had once been what I then simply termed a fine lady; for she one night held a long conversation with a gentleman in the street, which she afterwards told me was French.

"She had an old Bible in the room, by which she learned me to read; afterwards I picked up some pens and waste paper in the Inns of Court* and other places, and I was soon taught to write; she wrote a fine hand herself; I imitated it, and within eight months I really thought myself an uncommon scholar. I loved to lounge at the booksellers' windows, and to peruse the title-pages; I turned over the old wares of the stalls, till I was driven away by the cruel epithet of a young thief; and whenever I saw a stranger seeking for any place by a written direction, I offered my assistance with a secret pride, and blessed my poor mother, who was pining at home. I forgot that every charity-school boy was as well taught as myself, and thought it hard that I should be obliged to prowl the streets like a hungry cur, and that no one would offer me an honest employment, because I was covered only with rags. I asked the reason of my mother, but it made her sigh deeply; and when I enquired who my father was, and how long he had been dead, I perceived that she was agonized, and therefore desisted.

"She still continued her nightly supplicatory rambles, and I always followed her at a little distance. More than once we were taken to a watch-house,* and cast among thieves and prostitutes. A woman may be thrown into situations when she should not blush even at obscenity. My mother was often compelled to hear the most disgraceful language; the abandoned women cursed her for her silence, and the rascals became more foul in their words; but she would look at them without speaking, draw me to a corner of the room, and sometimes on the wooden seat we have slept in each other's arms.

"At length she fell sick, and I was almost killed by grief; for she would never acknowledge to what parish she belonged, and I could scarcely find a morsel of bread, or a little beer, to keep her in existence. When I entreated charity, I was called an idle young rogue, a villain; and if I spoke of my sick parent, the name of liar was heaped upon me by thousands.

"My mother must not die!" So I thought; I bought a link,* assured her that I would bring something home to comfort her, and then hastened to the Piazzas of Covent Garden, and obtained eighteen pence by lighting different people to their carriages. Good God! how joyfully did I return to the garret!

"The next night I was again the busiest at the play-house door, and was commissioned by a young gentleman and an elegantly dressed prostitute, to procure a coach. I obtained one, but with difficulty; I then walked obsequiously before my employers, opened the door of the carriage, threw down the steps, and held out my hat for a recompence. A shilling was thrown into it—"If you will give me another, Sir," I said, "you will enable me to afford more comfort to my poor sick mother."—The girl laughed. "Poh! nonsense! you lie, sirrah!"* cried the gentleman. I held the link up to my face—"May God Almighty," I cried, "take the life of myself, and also of my mother, before this flame shall go out, if I do not speak truth!"—The girl laughed still louder, and the coachman curled his cord around my leg; but the gentleman looked at me with surprise, and put another piece of money into my hat.

"It did not feel like a shilling. I ran to the door of a coffee-house, and held the donation up to a lamp—it was a guinea! I sent forth an exclamation of joy, threw my link into the kennel,* ran home almost breathless, and without speaking, put my treasure into the hand of my mother.

"What have you done?" she cried, "robbed, stolen this money?—Unhappy boy, you will be hanged!"

"I told my story to her; she knew that I had never uttered a lie, and on that night I heard her speak a prayer, which would not have discredited a priest before a congregation. On the following day I purchased a few comfortable things for her, and she soon recovered.

"Reserving half a crown, I purchased a few old books, and some pens and paper, and every day endeavoured, and with success, to improve myself in reading and writing. Our means of life were dreadfully precarious; but every mite that came to our hands, was spent in the best manner: I still hoped that some person would take compassion on me, and as I was now thirteen years old, I thought it might not be long before I should be more serviceable to my mother.

"The two little circumstances that I am going to relate to you, will at least discover the different species of gratitude. I was one morning strolling near the Horse Guards, and at the time of parade; a smart little fifer attracted my eye, and drawing several lines of comparison between him and myself, the most favourable of which all inclined to his side, I had resolved on being in the Army, and went marching with the big idea in my mind, as far as the Serpentine River in Hyde Park.* Just as I arrived at the bank, I heard a woman scream, and saw a child fall into the water;—no person except a female servant was near; the shriek pierced my heart, and the little girl had disappeared. Such garments as mine were soon laid aside, and I stripped even to my skin in less than a minute. I was an excellent swimmer, strong and fearless; the place in which the child had sunk being fortunately shallow, I brought her out without difficulty, and carried her towards the maid, who affectedly ran away because I was naked. The lady (I afterwards learned she was of quality), however, received the poor little thing, who soon recovered; and, taking out her purse, to the preserver of her daughter's life she gave half a crown! I did not often act or feel like a beggar: the parsimony and ingratitude of this woman surprised me; I received her money, threw it into the river, and smiling in her face, walked away.*

"This was to me a day of adventures—it stamped me a knight-errant; for near Kensington I saw another lady in apparent agony, which I found was occasioned by a large mastiff having got a favourite little spaniel in its paws, at a small distance from the spot on which she stood. Taking up a large stone, I aimed it at the head of the enemy brute, and struck him, upon which he abandoned the victim, and flew towards me; I however resolutely threw myself upon his neck, which I squeezed till I almost strangled him, but afterwards releasing him, he ran away howling.

"I have never thought of the conduct of this woman without a strong propensity to laughter; she shook my hand, called me a gallant, an heroic fellow, declared that the bravery of the action charmed her, and used many other strange and extrava-

gant phrases, of which, poor as I was, I knew the signification.
The former woman had given me half a crown for saving the life
of her child; the latter presented me with a guinea for rescuing
a dog, and bade me carry the maimed little animal to her house.
This lady was of a singular character, romantic, and an author-
ess; she wished to know my story; I related it, and in a manner
with which she declared she was charmed. She sent my mother
some clothes, desired me to call on her again, and within a fortnight she prevailed on a gentleman of the law to take me into his
office.

"The joy of my mother almost deprived her of reason, and my
own was nearly as powerful: the proud thoughts which penury
could never repress, were again growing active; and having in a
great degree risen, I hoped soon to rise still higher. I could now
support myself and my dear parent in a decent manner; society
no longer regarded me as an outcast, and I passed the four years
following my advancement with respectability. Mrs. Bolton, my
patroness, still noticed, and lent me books; and my mother gave
me some instructions in the French language. She had grown,
in her appearance, a fine and respectable woman; melancholy,
however, preyed strongly upon her, and in looking on and pitying her, it became one of the features of my mind.

"I often pressed her to tell me her history, but she always
entreated me to be silent on that subject; and sobbing on my
breast, she sometimes declared that she dared not speak of it.
I was nearly nineteen when I buried her. A few days before her
death she explained the mystery!—Dear mother, I shall never
forget you! Never let my mind dwell on your fault, after having
so many proofs of your love and tenderness. She told me, while
she lay death-stricken in my arms, that she had, at the age of
two-and-twenty, and contrary to her inclinations, been married
to Mr. Asterley (a name I had never heard before), a gentleman of considerable property, and of handsome person, but of
no good morals. Indifference came soon after the nuptials; and,
at the time I was born, it was notorious that he associated with

another woman. My mother heard of it; it struck deep into her heart, and she looked on him with aversion.

"Eighteen months after I was born, my mother brought forth another male child; but the love of her husband was gone, and he did not even attempt to screen his attachments. He became gross, unfeeling, and cruel; and at length she—she groaned when she confessed it to me—committed adultery with a man of rank, who had recounted all the base actions of her husband to her.

"Her criminality, shocking to herself, was detected; but before my father was acquainted with it, she fled, and secretly carried me away with her. Her own crime swallowed up all the vices of her husband, and from that time she never saw either him or her betrayer. She took with her a casket which her father had given to her before her marriage; for the jewels it contained she procured two hundred pounds, and on this money she subsisted till within a few weeks of the period to which I have at first alluded.

"This narrative astonished me;—dying, she entreated me to forgive and bless her. I did so a thousand times; and, at her desire, I brought the minister of the parish to pray to her, before whom, and two other persons, she made an affidavit of my name, birth, and legitimacy: she expired a few hours afterwards.

"My grief was strong, and it was a considerable time before I could subdue it. Had not my mother carried me away, I might have been educated handsomely, and, perhaps, have enjoyed wealth and respect: but then I should have been separated from her; and when I thought on what she had been to me, I was satisfied with that part of her conduct.

"The error which I have alluded to, and which was a worm in her conscience, I could not condemn her for; the brutal conduct of her husband took away half of the offence, and I had not an atom of pity to bestow on him.

"Soon after I had put the body of my mother in the earth, I made some enquiries concerning my family; when I found that my father had been dead several years, and that his supposed only son was then in possession of his estates. My brother was at

that time in the country; and I travelled upwards of an hundred
and fifty miles to see him: but I did not make myself known, as
I discovered that he was as corrupt as his father, without possessing any of his abilities. I returned disgusted to London, and
consulted with an eminent barrister on my title to my paternal
estate; but he seemed to view the circumstances suspiciously, and
was so discouraging, that I thought no more of putting in my
claim.

"I had never been partial to the law; the gentleman to whom
Mrs. Bolton had recommended me, was lately dead, and she herself gone to Italy, in consequence of which I was again visited by
necessity. I am sick when I think of the mischances I afterwards
met with, and of the many mortifications I suffered. I affirm,
without being influenced by any common prejudice, that men
in the law, taken generally, are the most arrogant, unfeeling, and
illiberal people in the world; and my solicitations to them were
few and reluctant.

"Possessing some powers of imagination, I commenced
author; but I had too much modesty for the trade, and wanting
breath to puff with, as well as confidence to seek for a patron, I
burnt my pen, and sighed over my manuscript.

"I had always loved the drama, and flattered myself that I
had talents adapted to the stage; and one morning I introduced
myself to a new-made manager in Soho, from whom I received
a peremptory rejection, which however was politely dressed and
given out.

"I shall not describe the particular manner in which I spent
the next eighteen months that followed my poor mother's death:
but I shall never more say of him whose body is staked in the
highway, 'this man deserved the contempt of his fellows, and
also the displeasure of his God.'* Poverty often raises the mind
above, or sinks it below the standard of reason: even melancholy
is a species of insanity, and despair is more nearly allied to it:
I have felt the influence of them both, and I often wonder at
my preservation. But I learned that my brother, owing to excess

and intemperance, had actually fallen into the state which I have attempted to describe, and that, in consequence of it, he was confined in a private madhouse.

"About this time I was strongly advised to prosecute my claim to my father's estate; and I found a gentleman who not only offered to become my solicitor, but also to supply me with money till my right should be decided in a court of equity.

"It will not be long before I shall be either rich, or a most forlorn beggar; the document of my mother, and the credibility of the witnesses, are much relied on; and the hopes of the attorney are nearly certainties. But my energies have grown sluggish, and are unwilling to be revived: I am like a plant that has been long neglected in a dry season, and the showers which are looked for, will perhaps fall too late."

Asterley's friends had listened to his narrative with considerable interest: Leopold pressed his hand, and bade him shake off the melancholy fiend; the fine eyes of Isabella beamed with a strong compassion, and Augusta sighed, while she unaffectedly exclaimed—"Poor Asterley!"

The weather being generally very severe, they were compelled to stay much at home; but when a fine morning presented itself, they were all anxious to be abroad.

Asterley, on some occasions, was very pleasant and diverting; still in his other mood, he was painful not only to himself, but also to his observers. Leopold and Augusta often, in private, talked of their intended union, for it was a subject dear to them both; and they anticipated the joys they should find on their return to Germany. One circumstance, however, created much concern in Augusta, and an equal surprise in Leopold; this was a custom which Isabella had of late adopted of going out alone, and of being absent sometimes two or three hours, without satisfactorily accounting for it. Augusta indeed was partly in her confidence, and guessed her motives; but Leopold could only wonder at them, without expressing a curiosity which he knew would be offensive.

About this time he was somewhat perplexed by not receiving an expected remittance from Vienna; the money he had brought over with him was nearly expended; and though Isabella had a supply, he did not wish her to know of his deficiency.

Taking up a newspaper one morning, he saw an advertisement, by a German gentleman, for a private teacher of the English language: a very liberal premium was offered to any man of ability; and Leopold finding himself well qualified for the office, wished to engage in it, if it were to be done without depriving him of much liberty. He copied the address of the advertiser, and soon after went to the house referred to, without apprizing Augusta of his intention; neither did he speak of it to Asterley, and Isabella had gone out soon after breakfast.

He found that the initials had been used by Baron Altenburg, to whom he told the servant he wished to speak. While standing in the hall, to his astonishment, some person pronounced his name; and on turning his head, he saw a man advancing, who almost immediately took hold of his arm.

"Warndorf!" cried the stranger, "this is not generous; I have never been accustomed to have a spy attending on me, nor shall I soon forgive you for becoming such."

"Amazement!" exclaimed Leopold; "you overpower me with surprise. Good God! what am I to think of this?"

"Did you not know me then?" cried Isabella; "did you not come in search of me?"

"Neither, by heaven!" he replied; "and I dare scarcely trust my senses now. What am I to think of this?"

"Any thing—nothing—think not of it at all. Do you know the Baron? have you business with him? Are you acquainted with his being the father of Augusta?"

"He!—The father of—No, upon my honour I knew it not: but I have business with him."

"Then, if you love my daughter, if you value my eternal quiet—Hush! the servants are coming. You know what I mean—Remember!"

She broke from him, and left the hall, when a servant came to conduct him to the Baron. Surprise had so strongly seized him, that he could not shake it off: Isabella appeared in a suspicious light; he thought that she and the Baron had renewed their acquaintance, and a hundred mysteries were in a moment revealed. He knew not but that she might have even mentioned his name to Altenburg, and for this reason he determined on concealing it; he therefore introduced himself under a fictitious one, and explained his business as well as in a state of agitation he possibly could.

The person and manners of Baron Altenburg interested him, in spite of prejudice; and having in some degree recovered from the shock which his own first direct lie had given to him, the conversation, on his part, was no longer laboured. He found that other applications had been previously made, but was flattered when Altenburg decided in his favour, though he came without recommendation: Leopold respectfully accepted the proposals, and was requested to call again on the following day.

"It is late in life with me," said the Baron, as they were separating, "to think of the study of languages; and, though I am desirous of acquiring that of the English, my residence in this country will not perhaps exceed a year. But to remove some weights from my mind, to expel from it some images which too often intrude, are the motives which——You will call on me to-morrow," he added, with a sigh that seemed to steal into the breast of Leopold, who, filled with wonder, hastened home, and there he found Isabella in her female attire.

His blood mounted into his cheeks when he looked at her, and his eyes, falling from her face, were placed upon Augusta, from whom he could scarcely conceal his confusion. Though Isabella had sunk in his esteem, his sentiments for her daughter were still the same; and though he believed the one to be the slave of a passion which was clandestinely gratified, yet he was assured that the other actually possessed all the innocence in which she appeared. These thoughts flew through his mind, and finding himself incapable of conversing with calmness, he took a book from his pocket, and seemed to peruse it, when Isabella sent Augusta to her chamber, to look for something which she knew could not easily be found.

"The subject of the volume, Sir?" said Isabella, as soon as her daughter was gone.

"Madam!" cried Leopold, looking up to her. She had thrown herself back in her chair, the lower part of her face rested on her hand, her bosom had swelled with pride, and her eyes were fixed with an eagle's strength upon his face. He saw the keenness of these silent reproaches, and the book fell from his hand.

"I read your thoughts, philosopher!" she cried; "your mind and soul are open to me. Virtuous censurer! liberal Warndorf!"

"Oh! for heaven's sake, Madam!"

"Sir, you have tried to probe me deeply: you touched, but did not wound me. You saw me in a strange situation this morning, and your imagination grew foul upon it; cleanse it, young man, cleanse it, and be wholesome."

"I have not deserved this," cried Leopold; "Augusta's mother—"

"Altenburg's—chuse a word, Sir, and place it; I doubt not but that the epithet will be delicately selected. Augusta's mother!— Augusta's mother would think herself too noble to call Warndorf her son, while he retains his gross opinions. I would stake my soul that you think me base and criminal: I confessed to you this morning what Baron Altenburg has been to me; and you suppose that neither his desertion nor his marriage prevented a renewal of our former intimacy?"

"Let the consequence be what it will," cried Leopold, "I will not make myself a liar. Your charge is just—I have thought of you as you suppose. Our strange meeting—your disguise and confession—You told me to think any thing, and now despise me for my thoughts; if they are wrong, on my knees—dear mother, forgive me."

"Oh Warndorf! Warndorf!"

"It is enough, I have your pardon!"

"You have, you have. Ah! Leopold, you never loved like me: you know not what it is to dote upon an object which you wish to hate. Altenburg threw me from his heart; I cannot banish him from mine. He fled from me; I have followed him hither; I have discoursed with him, and in a feigned character, excited his pity. I have pressed his hands, and am the happier for it. His wife I have conversed with: before I saw her, I thought I should have detested her; but she appears to me an excellent creature. Augusta knows not of my stratagem; my habit is always carefully locked up, and when I go out, I am wrapped in a cloak, which conceals my person even to the feet. I go to the Baron's in a coach, which, with the covering I leave in it, waits for me in an adjoining street. I am convinced that I am not suspected; but I will not, Warndorf, much longer indulge myself in this folly: we will go back to Germany soon. Your hand, Leopold—there, there, our quarrel is forgotten."

Leopold kissed the pledge of her amity, and had just time enough to relate the cause of their extraordinary meeting in the morning, before Augusta came to them. By the paleness of her cheeks, and the quickness of her eyes, it was evident that she had noticed the secret disagreement before she left the room; but the smiles of Leopold, and the kindness of Isabella banished her concern; and Asterley soon after joining them, they spent the remainder of the day together not unpleasantly.

The young Englishman had received some favourable news from his solicitor, and was in excellent spirits till they were about to separate at night, when he became silent, reserved, and dejected.

The chamber of Leopold was divided from that of Asterley only by a slight partition, and he had found that for many preceding nights, his friend retired late to his bed, and that it was become a habit with him to pace his chamber, and very often to repeat "Poor Asterley! poor Asterley!" Leopold doubted not but that he was in those moments ruminating on his family misfortunes; and though he sincerely pitied the complainer, he was silent on the subject, for he knew that expressions of compassion more frequently opened than closed a wound.

Leopold was not very serene when he was preparing to go to Baron Altenburg on the following day; and he was sorry that he had been induced, by surprise and apprehension, to give in a fictitious name, under which it was now become necessary to pass. He was somewhat repugnant to accept of the employment offered to him by the father of his Augusta; and thinking that Isabella might be averse to it, he demanded her sentiments, resolving if she did not approve of it, immediately to abandon the undertaking.

"I would not advise you to decline it," she replied; "go to the Baron, and think not of us while you are with him. I shall not see him many times more, and perhaps I may learn of you to—But we will soon return to our country, Warndorf: should you, however, meet with me again at Altenburg's, be guarded, and express no surprise.

Leopold then, still more agitated than tranquil, went to the house of Christiana's aunt, and was conducted to the library, where he found the Baron, who received him in a manner which was highly pleasing, and which, on the instant, removed his embarrassment. In the dialogue that ensued, the elegance and nerve of Altenburg's sentiments and observations were felt and acknowledged by his young tutor: gravity generally accompanied his remarks, and his countenance was frequently serious; but a ray of vivacity sometimes broke into his mind, and the smiles it produced made his face truly worthy of admiration.

Augusta had one day, in confidence, read to him some parts of her father's letters, and had many times, when her mother was not present, spoken affectionately of him. Leopold, therefore, was now inclined to view him as a man of error, rather than of guilt; and the plea which he had made to the mother and daughter, of his having been dictated by necessity, really seemed to have some strength. The conversation was both literary and political; the Baron spoke of many authors who were the favourites of Leopold, and quoted, with great taste and propriety; and he was so pleased with the young stranger, that he invited him to dine there on the following day.

This early mark of respect was highly flattering to Leopold, whose pride had previously been rather above his occupation; and on his return home, he held some conversation with the anxious Isabella, in which, though he regretted the division between her and Altenburg, he could not forbear becoming, in some degree, the encomiast* of the latter.

"Yes," replied Isabella, "he has powers to captivate; he wins the heart without seeming to aim at it; but when he has made the conquest, his defects become palpable. His understanding, I am persuaded, you do not over-rate; his person——Ah! Warndorf, I am becoming garrulous, and will give myself a timely check. Altenburg to me ought not to be any thing. I am only the mother of his child—nothing more, nothing more!"

Her manner of speaking the last words greatly affected Leopold, and with pain he saw her leave the room, with her arms laid across her bosom, and her eyes fixed upon the floor. But he hoped that the period was not far distant when her mind would be tranquillized. It was his design to persuade her not to renew her strange and hazardous visits, to leave England in the course of a month, and previous to their voyage, to give him in marriage his sweet Augusta, who was no less anxious than himself to return to Germany.

She and Leopold afterwards had several conversations on the subject; thinking that, of the two, he had more influence over her mother, she entreated him to urge their departure on every occasion, as she was in continual apprehension of the happening of some disagreeable events.

"But why, why, dear Augusta," he said to her one day, "are you silent on the circumstance that I wish to take place before we leave England?"

"Not because I love you less, dear Warndorf, than I have ever done; not because I think less tenderly of you; be assured it is not. Indeed I cannot account for it; only let us return to our country—only let us draw my poor mother from hence, and I shall go over the seas the happy wife of Warndorf!"

Such a declaration as this was a powerful stimulus; and in the afternoon of the same day he put his arguments to Isabella; and, after many struggles on her side, she assured him that in the course of six weeks she would leave England, and that, some few days before her departure, she would attend him and her daughter at the altar.

"Nay, no thanks, Warndorf," she cried, perceiving he was about to speak, "for I shall be happy to see you the husband of my girl, happy in calling you my son. I often thank God in private that Augusta has no brother; had I given Altenburg a boy, and the passions of the mother had been hereditary, I think the heart of his father would not at this time have been sensible of either pain or pleasure. In my mind I have been a murderess! Before I left Vienna, the fiend Revenge was always torturing my brain, presenting to my eye dreadful spectacles, and urging me to diabolical acts. This, I believe, was the cause of my illness and derangement, for I had thought on blood, and been scared by phantoms. This confession—you must neither hate nor despise me for it. I was not wicked, I was not culpable—I was mad, and therefore no fault can be attached to me. In Germany, however, with you, Warndorf, and with your wife, all may yet be well. But I do not promise you that I will not take up my disguise again. Can I return without seeing Altenburg once more? No, Leopold, I must have another gaze before I depart. You will continue to attend him, but I charge you to be private, and never mention either me or Augusta to him. I love him still; I begin to respect his peace, and I should now be loth to disturb the tranquillity of her, to blast whom, in the hours of frenzy, I have even wished for

the means of sorcery. No! happy be they both—happy Altenburg, and happy his wife!"

Leopold mourned that a better fate had not attended this
woman; and he resolved in every after hour, by the kindest
attention, love, and respect, to endeavour to alleviate her pain
and concern. Every day he attended the Baron, as a tutor, and
received from him so many marks of kindness and esteem, that,
situated as he was in regard to Isabella and Augusta, still he
could not but look with respect on him who had deserted them.

Leopold saw that he was not perfectly happy; but the tenderness with which he always spoke of the gentle Christiana, and
the love that shone in his eyes when he looked at her, destroyed
every idea of his being still attached to Isabella. The person and
manners of the Baroness also delighted Leopold; and he did not
wonder that they had removed the hatred of Augusta's mother;
for he held it impossible that any person could view her without
interest, or converse with her, and feel no pleasure.

She was calculated to charm him, because, in a great degree,
she resembled Augusta. An eye that was never dull, but which
was not always joyful; a heart that could feel deeply, and a tongue
that constantly spoke with unaffected tenderness, were the prop-
erties of Altenburg's wife, as well as of his daughter; both were
excellent in their minds, and lovely in their persons; and he was
concerned that the singular merits of the one should unfortunately have been the means of depriving the other, who was
equally deserving, of a large portion of happiness.

Altenburg was not very inquisitive as to the concerns or fortune of Leopold; but after they had been known to each other a
month, he offered a note to his instructor, as a part of his salary.
It was for a sum equal to that which had at first been proposed
for six months' attendance; Leopold, however, having previously
determined on accepting no reward, declined the bill, by saying
he would take it at some future time. The kindness of the action,
and the accompanying delicacy, did not pass the memory of
Leopold, who found that Altenburg could indeed "win the heart

without seeming to aim at it;" which was a remark that had been recently made to him by Isabella.

About a fortnight after the arrangement had been made for their journey, the cause of Asterley was decided in his favour, and prosperity was to reward his past sufferings. Though the extravagance of his father had been great, and his lunatic brother had been equally depraved and inconsiderate, yet, when the encumbrances which were on the estate, were discharged, an ample fortune would be remaining for the new possessor.

As soon as he could disengage himself from the lawyers, he ran to his lodgings, and scarcely sensible of what he said, imparted his success to Leopold, to Isabella, and to her daughter, all of whom heartily rejoiced on the occasion, and were warm in their congratulations.

They requested him to give them his company for the remainder of the day, and nothing could have sounded more agreeably to him; he became one of the happiest creatures then in existence; no being under heaven was more felicitous, and his words and looks animated all the party. But as the evening advanced, his spirits decreased; on parting, he languidly wished them all a good night, and his voice from his chamber afterwards conveyed the sound of "Poor Asterley," to the ears of the surprised Leopold.

The clock struck one, and he was still waking and walking; and he did not go to bed till another hour had elapsed, though the morning was exceedingly cold, and the hail rattling against his window.

Leopold was astonished by what he heard; and the melancholy of Asterley seemed so unseasonable, that he began to think the young Englishman had omitted some distressing occurrences in his narrative, on which he was then ruminating, as he had done at several preceding seasons.

The next day, however, he met Leopold with a placid, and Isabella and Augusta with a smiling countenance, which increased, and not in a small degree, the surprise of him whom his plaints had so recently reached.

The stipulated time for Isabella's departure was arrived within three weeks; Augusta was to become the wife of Leopold in the course of a fortnight, and the principal thing that remained to be previously done by him was, to apprize the Baron of his intention to return to Germany. In what particular manner he should do this, he had not however determined; and had not the exchange of situation been such as it was, the leaving of Altenburg would have caused much regret. His motive for withdrawing himself, he could not fully explain; and the unwillingness that he felt to speak his purpose, made him delay it from time to time, and he meant not to declare his intention till a day or two before he should become the husband of Augusta.

As the period of his marriage drew nigh, Leopold was more joyful; every moment in which he and Augusta were alone, he was starting some new scheme of happiness, which she smilingly listened to, and generally approved. But both of them were frequently concerned to see the extraordinary change in Asterley, who, though now removed from want to affluence, retained none of his former good spirits, but seemed to be under the influence of melancholy. The quick smile no longer darted from his fine eyes; the hue of health was vanishing, his tongue became languid, and his words were almost entirely confined to necessary and laconic replies.

Neither Leopold nor Augusta could conjecture the cause of this extraordinary change; but Isabella had watched him secretly, and though she was silent on the subject, her conclusions afterwards proved to be just.

Leopold one morning went out, and previously bade his friends not to expect him till the evening; but in the course of two hours he returned, and informed them that he should spend the remainder of the day at home. He went up to his chamber almost immediately on some occasion; in a few minutes, however, he returned, and going up to Augusta, he smiled, while he whispered something to her.

"Indeed, Warndorf," she replied, "I have not got it, neither

do I know any thing concerning it. Perhaps my mother does.—
Leopold," she continued, turning to Isabella, "has missed a
miniature; have you taken it out of his room?"

"No," answered Isabella, "I have not been there this morning."

"This is extraordinary!" cried Leopold; "I had the picture
in my hand just before I left the room, and afterwards put it
into the drawer, from which place I find it has been removed. I
thought one of you had taken it away in sport, and am alarmed
by your declarations. Pray ring the bell; I must make immediate
enquiries of the servant, and of her mistress."

Asterley, who was present, rose hastily from his chair, and
placed his hand upon Isabella's as it was touching the wire. His
blood mounted into his cheeks, his whole frame was agitated,
and with a faltering voice he begged Leopold to follow him to
another apartment, on which they both withdrew.

A suspicion had rushed into the mind of the latter, and he
looked sternly at his English acquaintance, whose distress
became almost insupportable, and for a while imposed silence
on his tongue.

"Speak, Sir," said Leopold, "why have you brought me hither?"

"Oh Warndorf! what will you think of me?"

"That still remains to be known: but if you have purloined the
picture, I will—"

"Do any thing to me," cried Asterley, "use me as you please;
hate me, despise me, *kill* me if it will satisfy you. I never yet was
a liar; see, here is the picture of Augusta! I took advantage of
your absence this morning, entered your room clandestinely and
removed your treasure."

"And how could you presume—for what purpose did you take
the miniature—in what manner intend to dispose of it?"

"You shall be answered fully, Warndorf. There are some hearts
that would pity—your's, I see, abhors me. I have long envied you
the possession of the picture; when you went out this morning,
I sent for an artist to copy it; and had you not returned till the
evening, he would have made the outlines of his work, and the

original would have been replaced. I can say no more in my jus-
tification: if you plunge a weapon into my breast, or if you give
me up to the law as a robber, I have had, and for ever shall have
the image of Augusta at my heart."

"Asterley! do you love her?"

"Love her! neither sight nor life are more precious to me than
Augusta!"

"What, when you know that within a few days she is to
become my wife? Presumptuous! How could you dare to love
her?"

"You might as reasonably ask yourself—'How could I dare
to love her?' Like you, I have powers of sight, of perception,
and of feeling; if my eye is lured by a beautiful object, does that
constitute presumption? and if my heart adores a woman, still
disdaining all that may interrupt her happiness, am I to be considered as a criminal? My affection for Augusta will never be
subdued; but I knew that she was to be your wife, and no thought
of supplanting you, or of disturbing her tranquillity, ever was in
my mind:—no, I swear it! I suffered, but did not complain; and,
finding the little alliance there was betwixt reason and passion, I
had resolved, on the morning of your marriage, to take an eternal
farewel of her, and in some far distant place to mourn in secret
that Warndorf's love was prior to Asterley's."

"Friend," cried Leopold, affected, "give me your pardon, and
in exchange take mine. I have been mistaken: I rely on your
honour—let us therefore go back to the women."

"Never!" replied Asterley; "my eye shall never more be turned
on her; I have confessed my passion for her even to her lover,
and at this moment both she and her mother must be filled with
a thousand strange suspicions. God bless you, Warndorf! may
you and your wife be eternally happy! I shall never more press
your hand—never more hear the voice of Augusta; yet, when far
divided, I shall think that she sometimes speaks of me, and sometimes, sanctioned by her husband, exclaims—"Poor Asterley!"

"Good heaven!" exclaimed Leopold, struck by the force of the last often repeated words, "stay, friend—I entreat you to hear me!"

"It is too late, Warndorf; all my past vicissitudes seem nothing when compared with this. Adieu!—I must unburthen my heart, or it will sink irrecoverably."

He then released himself from the hold of Leopold, and almost in a minute he had left the house.

Pained and astonished, Leopold returned to his female friends, to whom he unreservedly repeated the conversation and confession of Asterley. The concern, but not the surprise of Isabella was great; Augusta, however, was divided between pity and wonder, nor did she affectedly attempt to conceal her true feelings.

It was evident that the young Englishman did not intend to see any of them again; for on the following day he sent a letter to the woman of the house, charging her to take care of what things he had left behind him, and informing her that he should retain her lodgings for two months longer, but not reside any part of the time in them.

Though Leopold was on the eve of the most happy events, he could not banish the recollection of the sorrows of Asterley, who appeared to be fated to endure almost all the miseries known to human life, without participating any of the felicities which sometimes pertain to it. He and Isabella had several conversations on the subject, in which they spoke with equal feeling; but Augusta was embarrassed whenever the circumstance was named to her, and though she esteemed and pitied the man, she wished, if possible, wholly to withdraw her mind from him.

The day appointed for the marriage of Leopold and Augusta was drawing very nigh, and they were making some arrangements for their departure for Germany; it was now become absolutely necessary to apprize Baron Altenburg of his intention, and he prepared himself so to do, though the task seemed to him unpleasant and embarrassing.

On the morning he intended to open his designs, he walked

slowly and thoughtfully towards the Baron's residence, and just as he came in sight of it, Isabella, in her disguise, took hold of his arm, and silently led him to a coach that she had, as usual, retained.

He did not wonder that she had been able to impose on Altenburg, as he could at first scarcely believe her to be the mother of Augusta; for independent of her male attire, she wore a large black covering on one of her eyes, and also hair very different in colour to her own. When they were both placed in the vehicle, Isabella threw herself on the neck of Leopold. For a few minutes she attempted to suppress her emotions, but they obstinately forced their way, and she sobbed loudly, while her tears fell fast from her eyes. Leopold only pressed her tenderly in his arms, giving her time to recover, and to speak without being urged; and within a few minutes she raised her head from his shoulder, and looked in his face.

"Warndorf!" she cried, "I entreat you not to censure this weakness, and I would not have you think meanly of me for the sorrow into which I have been led. My eyes must be closed by death, and afterwards opened by immortality, before I shall see Altenburg again. We shall meet no more on earth; the idol of my soul, the father of my child is, from this hour, separated from me eternally! Eternally, Oh no—I will believe that one of the joys of the next world will be to dwell with him in friendship, in love, and in harmony. My soul will prepare for its pilgrimage of joy, Warndorf, while you and Augusta shall be weeping for the apparent pangs of my body."

"Banish these melancholy thoughts," cried Leopold; "you will yet be happy with your children."

"Happy!—Yes, yes, it may be so. The virtues of you and my girl will effect all that can possibly be done for me. I find myself, however, so much changed of late, I cannot but consider that event, which must ever be as common as life, as fast approaching. I once had health, an ardent spirit, a vigorous mind, and a well-fortified heart; some of them have fled, the others have been subdued. Well, well, I shall not resist the inevitable decrees of ——"

"For Heaven's sake, dear mother," cried Leopold, "for Heaven's sake talk not thus despondingly! Will you inform me in what character you have lately passed with the Baron?"

"As the brother of an unfortunate Italian Nobleman, with whom he was several years since intimately acquainted. To forward my project, I have dissimulated, and spoken many untruths. Altenburg has, like an angel, pitied my feigned distresses; has given me money for my supposed necessities, which I shall return to him the day before our departure; and has often endeavoured to persuade me to give him more of my company: but this request I always refused with a plea which seemed to him sufficient. Part of my face only I allowed him to see, attributing my covering of the other part to the loss of one of my eyes by an accident. And even in those moments, when I fondly viewed him as my once faithful Altenburg, as the father of my precious child, I did not forget my false accents. He believes that I am returning to Italy; he and his wife have given me their good wishes, and the late objects of my hate are become the objects of my love. Oh Altenburg! I thought it would be easy to despise thee; but my affection for thee will go even to the brink of my grave!"

The coach stopped, and Isabella seemed to recal her powers; she endeavoured to assume a composed countenance to meet her daughter with, and while she was returning to Augusta, Leopold, affected by what he had seen and heard, again went towards the Baron's; but having witnessed the distresses of Isabella, he was too much discomposed to mention his intentions; and after an interesting discourse with Altenburg, he withdrew.

On the following day, however, he entered into the subject, and spoke of his determination to leave England in the course of the ensuing week.

"I fear," he continued, "that your Lordship will be displeased with me for forming an engagement with you; but at the time I made it, I neither foresaw, nor soon expected, an important event, which is now likely to happen; an event which must be productive of the greatest happiness to me—I hope of felicities which will end but with my life."

"Marriage, my young friend?" said Altenburg; smiling, "your fervour and animation, your voice and countenance, all lead me to conclude that it is so. Am I not right?"

"You are, my Lord. In the course of two days I shall be made the husband of a lovely and excellent woman!"

"May you be truly happy!" cried Altenburg, pressing him with hands which had once as tenderly pressed poor Josephine. "Is the object of your choice of England or of Germany?"

"Of Germany," replied Leopold, "to which country she is impatient to return. As soon as our nuptials are celebrated, therefore, we shall embark, and probably never see England again."

"I will go with you to the altar; my wife shall attend on your bride, and the marriage feast shall be eaten in this house. I esteem you much, and I wish to be your friend, for you have long since found your way to my heart."

"Your Lordship is good—condescending—I am much obliged—But, after I am married, I cannot possibly see you again; we must never thereafter meet, neither in England nor in Germany. Look not displeased, my Lord; I shall ever think of you with a mutual esteem—I would say with affection, did I not fear you would consider the word as too free. But we must never meet—I regret that circumstances forbid it; I mourn that I must necessarily be deprived of the pleasure of seeing and conversing with a man whom I so truly respect, and for whose happiness I shall ever wish."

"My happiness!—Ah! that is never to be recalled!—Well, my mysterious tutor, you force me to think well of you; perhaps we may correspond—is that prohibited?"

"And will you, my Lord, will you indeed condescend to write to me? I shall be happy, very happy in such notice; for it is what I wished to propose, and nothing but the fear of being thought presumptuous, checked the request which I was anxious to make."

"Your hand then," said Altenburg; "I can be your friend, without prying into your secrets, and *will* be such as long as you desire it."

"For ever, for ever, my Lord!"

"With all my heart, provided without intercourse it be possible. I will write to you from England, and also from Vienna on my return thither, which will be soon after my Christiana's delivery. From your intimation, I conclude that you intend to dwell in retirement, otherwise I should be desirous of seeing you in some capacity which may be within the reach of myself, or of my friends. I will not take your adieu to-day; but to-morrow, as you wish, we will separate. This ring, present it in my name to your wife, and tell her that he who sends it, wishes her always to wear it with happiness."

They soon after separated: Leopold was glad to depart, as he began to be affected by the generosity and tenderness of the Baron, who was not only surprised but also concerned by what he had listened to; for Leopold had grown in his favour, and was viewed by him with no common regard.

Mysterious as some part of Leopold's conversation had seemed, Altenburg was not however prejudiced by it; for he could place no doubt on the honour or integrity of his young friend, whose intended seclusion he imputed to the influence of that romantic spirit, in the blaze of which reason would sometimes disappear.

While Altenburg was speaking to Christiana of the loss he was going to sustain, Leopold was telling Isabella and Augusta of his late conversation, which was listened to by them with many different emotions. The ring was received with ecstacy.

"It is the gift of my father," cried Augusta, "of him, to whose breast I have a thousand times been clasped—of him whom I have a thousand times kissed! See, mother, what he sends! It shall remain here for ever; it shall remain as a precious pledge even when my shroud shall be put on me!"

Leopold participated her joy, and her language was such as

he delighted to hear. Isabella also smiled while the arms of her daughter enfolded her; but her smiles were sickly, and shewed that they originated not in true pleasure.

The time came when Leopold was to bid a last adieu to the Baron, to whom he did not go till the evening, when he left Isabella and his Augusta busy in preparing the simple bridal dress for the morrow. Altenburg received him with true kindness, and Christiana expressed her regret that he was so soon to depart;— after staying with him about half an hour, and bidding him a kind farewel, she retired from the room, and left him with her Lord.

"I am as much concerned as the Baroness can be," said Altenburg, "that you should fly from us just as you had established yourself in our favour; but wherever you go, I wish you happy, successful, and content. You offered yourself as my tutor; I wished to make you my friend. I have received some advantages from your superior talents; our agreement was a narrow one; this note will speak what I wish to do better than my tongue."

"My Lord," replied Leopold, "I have been amply repaid by your notice, and nothing more can I accept. I have a sufficiency for myself, and also for the woman who will to-morrow become my wife; more I do not wish for. You will therefore excuse me if I decline your gift. Can I be of any service to you in Germany, my Lord? Have you any packets which you may think proper to entrust with me?"

"Yes, and I would propose two or three things: the first of which is, a travelling companion. There is an Italian gentleman who has lately made himself known to me; I have been affected by a recital of his misfortunes, and more so by a repetition of some particular events which were within his knowledge. I have felt his sorrows, and he has, undesignedly, made me more severely feel my own. I learn that he is returning to Italy, and that some warm hopes induce him first to go to Vienna. I think you will find him sensible and interesting; and if you can make acquaintance with a melancholy man, I wish you to be a companion to him to Germany."

"I—I agree to it," said Leopold, colouring; "a letter of introduction from your Lordship will—will be—"

"You shall have it, and indeed it is already written; I will also
trouble you with these letters to my steward at Vienna, and this
small packet I could wish you to deliver personally to Count
Stendal."

"To Count Stendal! With pleasure. I should have sought for
him myself, without any commission from you, for there is no
other man on earth whom I am so anxious to see."

"You astonish me!" cried Altenburg. "Why did you never tell
me that you knew my excellent friend? for I love the Count as
if he were my brother. Since I first saw you, I have mentioned
your name in letters to him, and to one of them have received an
answer; but it contained nothing concerning you which bespoke
any personal knowledge. You surprise me greatly!"

"Without explaining my motives," replied Leopold, "I confess
that I first gave your Lordship a fictitious name; yet I am no
criminal, and have nothing to blush at. I never saw Count Stendal but once, and even then he almost rent my heart asunder.
Had you named to him Leopold Warndorf, of ——"

"Oh God of heaven!" exclaimed Altenburg; "are you, are you
Leopold Warndorf, the child of Josephine?"

"I am—she was my mother.—You, *you* know Josephine?"

"Son—son—son!"

"Of Josephine I know. What ails you? Why this emotion?
These tears—your eyes—are your senses gone? Speak to me—if
you have any reason, speak to me!"

"Cast me to the earth, and stab me!—No, no; come to my
heart, and bless your father! Do you not know me to be such?
My blood is gushing from me; put your hand here, and staunch
it."

"Trifle not with me—you cannot be my father—proofs,
proofs!"

"You are my child, and for God's sake do not disown me!
Forget the wrongs of your mother, who is in heaven. You tor-

tured me when you refused to listen to Stendal. This mysterious meeting! You move not, you come not to me—There, I hold you now! I will not take my arms from your neck till you have blessed your father!"

"Away, away!" cried Leopold, almost with a shriek; "do you consider me as the brother of Augusta?"

"Of Augusta! What do you know of Augusta? Yes, yes, you are both my beloved children!"

"Then I accept your offer. You shall go with me to the altar to-morrow, and your wife shall attend my bride thither. You shall sanction the union of me and my sister; the priest shall do an act which is forbidden by God, on which you shall calmly look; and though the words be fair and holy, and the deed damnable, you, *you* shall smile, and say, Amen!"

"You rave—what do you mean?"

"The marriage feast shall be eaten in your house, and we will lie under the roof of our father; for in any other place the devils, who sicken at all earthly joys, would in the dark hours abandon their native hell, and scream in our ears—"Incest! incest!""

"My brain catches at your madness! Son—Warndorf—recollect yourself, and speak to me calmly."

"You are my father—you are the father of Augusta—Isabella and the Italian are one. Something of this I knew before, but not enough—not enough to save me from distraction. I and your daughter met by accident. Of what I am to her she is still ignorant; I knew it not till this moment.—Aye, tremble, and look pale. My flesh and limbs are quivering! I love Augusta as dearly as one object can ever love another. To-morrow we were to have been married—were? and shall we not still? Must I resign her?—must I give her up? Never, never! All this ruin and misery your crimes have effected. I will not believe myself your son—I will keep her ignorant of what may be true, and will yet marry her. I may be an object of Heaven's punishment, but she never can; and in the next world—God!—my father will not allow us the hope of being happy even there!"

Altenburg fell speechless and almost insensible on the floor; the voice of Leopold, who rushed out of the room, alarming the servants, immediate assistance was given to the fainting Baron; and his son went rapidly through the streets, which were now dark, with scarcely reason enough to find the house that he had lately left.

He passed by the servant who admitted him, and running up the stairs, he sought and burst into the apartment where Isabella and Augusta were still sitting. He caught the hand of the former, and pressed it to his lips.

"Mother, farewel!" he cried; "a long, an eternal farewel to you, dear mother!"

Isabella was terrified by his words and by his countenance, and she strove to hold him; but he put her hands from him, and, with visible agony and distraction, strained Augusta to his breast.

"This is my last embrace," he cried, "this is my last kiss; these are the last moments my eyes will rest on you. Beloved Augusta! blessed sister! burn your bridal ornaments, for I could as well and as happily gaze on your burial clothes. Fate has sent a searching dart at me, and I am the most accursed being in the world. Bless you! bless you!"

"Oh, for God's sake stay, dear Leopold!" cried Augusta.

"Away, dear girl, come not near me. I am agonized, distracted. Oh this Baron—this Baron! Take your arms from me: if you recal my love, you may perhaps make me act with dissimulation, which would afterwards doom me to purgatory. Adieu!—Another kiss! There—the world must be consumed before we meet again!"

He instantly disappeared, and Augusta, shrieking, cast herself into the arms of her affrighted mother, who was scarcely strong enough to support her. Their imaginations were equally disturbed; and though Augusta could no longer see Warndorf, she almost raved for his return. Neither of them on that night took any rest; they watched vainly for the re-appearance of Leopold; three days however passed over, and he came not to them, but on the fourth, and after many strange suspicions had pained their minds, they received from him the letter which is transcribed beneath.

"Before me lies the far extended ocean; the vessel in which I shall within an hour embark, I see surrounded by the agitated waters; and the wind, though it points not against us, is growing in its fury. Friends of my soul! were the hazard an hundred times as great, and if the waves were to aim at touching the heavens, still I would be gone. I must fly from you. At a distance I must strive to erase from my heart the images set up in it by an unhappy love; and by some means, which are yet unknown to me, endeavour to suppress a passion which I bear for my sister.

"Augusta, I have made a strange discovery. Oh that I had ever remained ignorant of what has been revealed, then we might have been happy indeed! It is only common reasoning to say that there can be no criminality in us, if we neither feel the consciousness of guilt ourselves, nor raise it in the minds of others. We had been blessed and virtuous without the interposition which has lately distracted me. You are the daughter of Baron Altenburg, and—I am his son. This discovery of my father was not made till the day previous to that on which I was to have married my sister. Fate was a most ingenious foe to us, and I have cursed her in every hour since the commencement of her machinations.

"Oh, what hopes have I indulged! What beautiful pictures have been sketched and tinted by my imagination!—Away all that is pleasant, all that is delightful! Anguish now is my companion. Augusta, as a bride, should have warmed my heart; but to despair I am indissolubly united. I would talk of our father, whom I sometimes pity, and sometimes execrate. My tongue, however, can scarcely speak his name, and the sinews of my arm contract when I attempt to write it. Altenburg! thou hast been a cruel scourge to me, and to all those whom I most love and reverence; yet, as a stranger, I esteemed and respected thee; as a son,—Oh! I shall grow wild if I dwell on a topic like this!

"Hasten, dear friends, from England, and I entreat that neither of you will attempt to see the Baron any more. I must not, for a considerable time, appear before you again—I feel I must not; Philosophy forbids it—but if my mind can be soothed, and my heart new modelled by her precepts, I will return when I am confident of my own strength—return to Isabella and to Augusta, and be to the one of them a dutiful son, to the other an affectionate brother.

"I conjure you to depart from England immediately. I wish you to retire to my native village, and in the evenings of summer, Augusta may muse among the shades of the forest which was once dear to Leopold, and to which, in some twilight hour, he may come back with the calm steps and resignation of a pilgrim. If such a moment ever shall be, speed it, Eternal Father, and let the present agonies of my soul subside, and be forgotten! Oh! my reasonings and my feelings are strangely at variance, and my feigned resolution is mocked by my tears!

"Be stronger than Leopold, Augusta, and sooth the agitated spirits of your mother, whose pangs, I know, will be as severe as your own. Adieu, sweet girl! dear sister!—Adieu beloved mother! My only hope is that we shall meet hereafter in domestic peace. I will write to you, Augusta, again in the course of a month, and shall address you at the place I have mentioned, to which, once more, I entreat you to hasten. You shall know where I am wandering; you shall judge of the state of my heart; and when you shall think, by the characters of my letters, that I may with prudence be recalled, only say to me—'Return, dear brother; the heart of your sister is full of wishes to be near to you!'—Say only this, and I will fly from whatever solitude I may then be concealed in, to meet the bosom of my precious sister.

"Leopold Warndorf."

It is a fashion with some writers, particularly of that class which is often, by dulness and affected wisdom, sneeringly called storymongers,* to take leave of their readers most abruptly; and there are others among them who, for different purposes relating merely to themselves, will carry a tale beyond the interest which may have been at first excited, and cause their wounded snakes to crawl languidly and offensively in the paths from which the tired imagination is anxious to depart. Both of these modes are pretty general; and if the author of the preceding sheets should, in some circles, be thought to close the following ones rather too precipitately, he trusts that among his readers there will not be wanting those who will deem his plan more judicious than if his story had been lengthened by a yesty* volume.

It was not designed that Melpomone* should direct the concluding scene of this little drama, though she is the best beloved muse of the writer. Having said this, anticipation stretches no further; but it is entreated by him who must consequently be most interested, that the perusal may be continued through the few subsequent pages.

Isabella and her daughter were astonished and agonized by the letter of Leopold; the passions of the former burst forth with their accustomed violence, and the first attack that grief made on the latter had nearly proved fatal to her. The circumstances which then came to their knowledge, almost seemed to exceed credibility; still they could not doubt the truth of them. Isabella would not again dare to trust herself with the Baron; and her unhappy child urged her to attend Leopold's request, and also to sail by the first vessel; to which, without a scruple, she consented.

Their voyage was quick; during the time they were on the water, the arms of the one were scarcely an hour from the neck of the other; and the bosom of Isabella caught many a tear which she could neither banish nor reprove.

With all possible speed they went forward according to Leopold's directions. When they arrived at the place of their destination, they found a small neat residence provided for them, and also a letter from their beloved friend, who had arrived with an expedition equal to their own, and departed from thence as soon as he had prepared for their accommodation.

His epistle was tender and affecting, but it boasted not of a fortitude even equal to that which he had written to them in England; nature spoke in it oftener than philosophy, which caused the sighs of Isabella, and the tears of Augusta to be more frequent and oppressive. The latter carried it in her bosom, and many times, breaking from her mother, would she retire to the particular spots which Leopold had, with a pleasing remembrance, mentioned to her, where she would uninterruptedly weep over the sorrows of herself and of her unhappy brother.

The rigours of winter had been succeeded by a most lovely spring, and the various treasures of a still later season were beginning to shew themselves in every sunny day. They continued to hear from Leopold very frequently, but there was for a considerable time, a strange irregularity in his letters; afterwards, however, reason and prudence grew stronger within him, and in autumn he sent his sister a full narrative of his wanderings, which was generally written with apparent calmness, and almost entirely divested of those characters which had before so greatly alarmed Augusta, to whom his growing philosophy was a necessary lesson.

She became more happy and composed, and was anxious to recal her beloved brother in the manner his first letter had intimated; but her mother, though not less desirous than herself of seeing him, opposed it for the present, as she had more seriously reflected on the qualities of the alien's soul, than ever her daughter had done.

They had now been seven months in Germany, and another having followed, the despoiler of Nature's beauties began, in a voice of hoarseness, to announce his determined approach.

Isabella's health was somewhat impaired, and Augusta noticed it with great concern; she was, however, desired to check her apprehensions, and her mother, whose disorder arose in the mind, spoke of it with seeming indifference.

One evening they returned from walking in the forest, which was strewed with the fallen leaves; and as they entered their house, the servant delivered a note to Augusta, which hastily opening, she found to contain the following words.

=====

"Tremble not, dear girl, when I tell you that I am but a little distance from you. Separation is no longer necessary, for I would live with you as a friend and relation. Without your permission I will not approach; but send it, and in the course of an hour Leopold and Augusta shall meet."

=====

"Mother!" she cried, in a manner which at once spoke both joy and pain, "mother!"

"Let him come to us instantly," said Isabella; "my excellent, my beloved Warndorf!"

Augusta ran to a table, and quickly wrote—"Return, dear brother, the heart of your sister is full of wishes to be near to you!"—With this the messenger departed. Isabella was agitated, and the breath of Augusta was nearly gone. They scarcely spoke to each other afterwards, and their eyes were fixed upon the door, which was in less than the time that had been mentioned, opened by the expected Leopold, who rushed forward, and enfolded them both in his arms.

Neither of the young people could command any words, and even the firmer Isabella was, for a considerable time, necessarily silent; at length, however, she interposed between her children and their sensibilities, and welcomed Leopold with a smile, which she wished to see spread upon his own pale face. His countenance confessed to her that he had suffered much; but she found that his mind had not excluded the rays of reason, and that the conquest over his once strong passions had been a noble one. He did not speak directly of his disappointments, nor did he allude to his father, the principal author of them; still he had wishes in his heart which he dared not to reveal, and which, he was assured, must be banished from thence before happiness could again take its station in his bosom, or the hue of health be discoverable on his cheek. The look of regret which he first cast on Augusta was indeed forcible; but he seemed to reprove himself for it, and also to be afterwards guided by the best instincts of affection and of kindred.

After the first half hour was passed, he much surprised his friends, by telling them that he had an acquaintance waiting for him at a little distance.

Retiring for a while, he returned, and, to the astonishment of Isabella and Augusta, he was accompanied by Asterley, by whom they were informed that he and Leopold had lately by chance met at Hamburgh. This singular event he did not further account for; and a deep blush was on his face, while he acknowledged thus much to Augusta, who, amid all her pleasures, felt an embarrassment from which she could have wished to be freed.

Asterley had given her true information. From the mistress of the house that he had so abruptly left, he learned some of the particulars which have been related. When his astonishment had decreased, his love grew still stronger on the intelligence; the sorrows of his friend, and his own secret hopes alternately pained and pleased him; and knowing the case of Leopold to be unalterable, he indulged an expectation which was a restorative to his languid spirits.

He was sorry that he had not been earlier apprized of that extraordinary event, as he did not return to his lodgings for upwards of five months; but the world containing no other object so dear to him as Augusta, he resolved to seek her immediately in Germany, and in some proper season to express to her those sentiments which the impetuosity and resentment of Leopold had, on a former occasion, drawn from him. He was an adventurer, whose heart was often cheered by hope, and often saddened by apprehension. He embarked for Hamburgh; but owing to the necessity of putting back again, and to the shifting of the wind after he had a second time left the harbour, the voyage was long almost beyond example.

The meeting between him and Leopold, which happened the third day after he had disembarked, was regarded by both of them as somewhat extraordinary; and from his altered friend, who had been nearly a fortnight at Hamburgh, Asterley found that he had not been misinformed, and also that Leopold would no longer oppose him as a lover, but willingly take him by the hand, and give him the name of brother. Leopold was now very desirous of his recal;—still sore with those wounds which had been made by the rod of affliction, he entreated the young Englishman not to speak too often of the past occurrences: they travelled together from Hamburgh to the residence of Isabella, and the unexpected meeting has been already described.

They again formed a family, as they had done in England. The winter lingered, and spring succeeded; and while the forest was still blooming with flowers, and the cheeks of Leopold were again collecting their former tints, Asterley took Augusta as a bride to the altar. Isabella smiled upon the union, and the surpliced priest was not more devout than Leopold. He seemed, all the time they were in the house of holiness, to be imploring the blessings of the Power to whose service it was dedicated; and when the ceremony was over, he pressed the hand of the husband, and kissed the cheek of the bride, saying—"God bless thee, brother! God bless thee, sister!"

* * * * *

Poetical justice certainly does not demand the sacrifice which is going to be made; but as the happiness of two persons must ever be preferred to that of one, and supposing truth is intended to apply to some particular parts of this narrative, the original design will be executed.

How melancholy would it be to believe that Virtue meets all her rewards on this side of the grave! It is known, and often seen, that her garments are poor, even to beggary; that she is pained by hunger, and shrivelled by cold; and that, if she could deck herself with the gems of the East, the heart which she carries within her bosom, must sometimes be a mere receptacle of pains and miseries. The mind, to be perfectly content, must travel beyond the limitations of human life; the chief consolation lies in the thereafter; and whatever it is, he who expects least must, comparing the coming with the past, look for things vast and infinite.

Thou, Christiana, hast discovered them, for on thy fair and innocent breast there is a weight which will not be removed till all thy beauties shall have been mingled with the dust.

The Baroness died in England, and the child which she bore perished soon after its mother. Altenburg stood despairingly by the side of her bed; but when he saw her departing, he cried— "Wife! Christiana! look at me again!—Live, live, dear wife, and be happy!"—She made a last effort, and threw one of her arms, the other being lifeless, around his neck; no dying saint ever smiled more heavenly. She touched him with her lips, and faintly articulating—"I am happy!" she sunk gently down, and never rose again!

Altenburg seemed still desirous of persuading himself that she was not dead. He pressed her wrist, he laid his hand near her heart, but he did not touch a single active nerve. He put his mouth to her lips, from which no breath issued, and he gazed on her eyes, in which he read a strange and full confirmation that they would never open again. It was a shriek rather than a groan that then passed from him; he sunk, giddy and insensible, by the side of the corpse, from which the attendants soon removed him; and it was a considerable time before the sense of his misery again returned to torture him. Mrs. Gardiner could afford him but little consolation; she was herself too much afflicted to discourse on fortitude and resignation, for she had loved her niece with the tenderest affection, and now mourned her dissolution with the deepest regret.

Christiana, it seemed, had entertained some manner of presentiment of her fate; and though she was unwilling to alarm her beloved husband, she had, on the day preceding her death, requested that her remains, in case she was destined to fall so early, might be conveyed to Germany, and deposited in the vault that had been erected for her parents. Altenburg afterwards executed this melancholy business: his adieu to Mrs. Gardiner bespoke his agony; he hung over the shell that contained the body till his arrival at his own country; and having laid the corpse in the cold family recess, he fled from society and loquacious pity!

Six months, apparently lengthened to years by melancholy, he passed without hailing a single friend; in the beginning of the seventh, however, his respected Stendal was near his heart; and as the Count, his wife, and his family remained some considerable time with him, they served greatly to amend the dissonance of his mind. But after they parted, his spirits were again depressed, and the energies seemed to have flown beyond recal.

Christiana had been dead a twelvemonth, and he still thought of her loss with extreme sorrow; other objects, however, now began to be equally dear to his memory. Many painful ideas had often dwelt upon Isabella and his children—ideas which it was almost madness to harbour, and difficult to banish; and he wished it possible that a re-union between him and the dear companion of many of his happier years could be effected. But he feared that his transgressions and sins had been too many: Isabella could never love him again—Augusta could never forgive him—and his conduct towards his son had perhaps driven him to commit some act of desperation.

Such were his apprehensions, and they long deterred his purpose; at length, however, he enquired for Isabella, of whom he could learn nothing: it then remained for him to seek for his son. The village was the only place to which he could direct himself, and on repairing thither, to his surprise, he discovered that it contained all those for whom he was seeking.

It was early day when he arrived at the hamlet; and before noon, as he was sitting at the window of the inn, he saw his son go by, rosy, beautiful, and blooming. "Warndorf!" he cried. He started up, he threw out his arms, and attempted to follow; but his limbs grew weak, he panted, his heart beat violently, and he sunk down again, blinded by the quick flood of his tears.

In less than half an hour he also saw Augusta treading the path that Leopold had left behind; she was smiling on the handsome Asterley, who bore in his arms a cherub, fair and sweet as its mother had been in her infancy. Altenburg's eyes followed them into a meadow at some little distance, where they were soon joined by Warndorf. They all sat down on a green bank; the child was passed from the arms of one of them to another; Asterley tossed it in the air, and Leopold playfully wove a wreath of wild flowers, and twined it around the laughing sprite, who soon after clung to the milky breast of its mother.

"These are my children," cried Altenburg, "and yet I must not embrace them; these are my children, yet they would all disown and execrate their father!"

He was nearly choked and blinded by his passions; but he looked again on the happy group; he felt a growing resolution; he left the house, and stealing softly behind the hedge, soon arrived near the spot where they were still sitting. They all were smiling on the child, who laughed while he banqueted, and put forth one of his snowy arms to his father and uncle, while he exultingly retained the yielding nipple between his rosy lips.

The heart of Altenburg was bursting. He forced the fence, rushed forward with rapidity, and at the time he threw his head into the lap of his daughter, he also seized the hand of his son, and drew it to his breast.—"Now," he cried, "now for the final curse, or healing blessing! Daughter, is it love, or everlasting hate? Son, you must now either free my heart from misery or deprive it of every buoyant hope for ever! Speak, speak, dear children!"

Neither of them *could* speak—Augusta gave the babe to Asterley; a strange broken sound issued from her mouth, and she threw herself on the neck of her father. The countenance of Leopold grew pale; he rose, staggering, from the ground, his arms mingled with those of his sister, and the faces of both were hidden in the breast of Altenburg.

There was a pause of several minutes, broken only by their sobs. When the father raised his head, one of his children kissed him with love and rapture; and when he stretched forth his hand, the other pressed it fervently, and shed filial tears upon it. All was forgiven, resentment was not named—love, eternal love, was vowed by the parent and by his offspring.

The discovery was, within a few hours, made by Augusta to her mother, whose fortitude had scarcely ever, on any occasion, been so much affected; her passions rose not with violence; she wept while she said that a re-union could never take place, and mournfully begged that she might not be urged to it. Augusta was kneeling before, and pleading to her, when Leopold entered, and having carried his sister out of the room, he returned with Altenburg, and placed the weeping Isabella in his arms.

"Mother!" he cried, "I have sworn to bury all enmity, and to live with my father as kindred should live, loving and beloved. The completion of our happiness depends on you alone; you can harmonize every thing that has sounded like discord; do it, therefore—do it, dear mother, and God's blessings will thereafter shine over our heads like summer clouds."

He then left them; but in the course of an hour, and accompanied by his sister and by her husband, he returned; when he found that a tender reconciliation had been effected, and that the Church was to sanction the renewed loves of Altenburg and Isabella.

Their embraces were repeated.—Altenburg, in the name of

God, blessed his daughter, her Asterley, and their infant; he kissed, with delightful emotions, the cheek of his beloved Isabella, and in the arms of Leopold, and while his eyes were fixed on the beautiful face of his son, he murmured—"Oh my dear boy, this pleasure, though late, is delightful! From this hour I will neither yield thee to, nor be separated from thee by any power except that to which we all must yield!"

FINIS.

NOTES

3   *Kemble, Siddons, Jordan*: John Philip Kemble (1757-1823) and his sister Sarah Siddons (1755-1831) were considered two of the greatest performers of their age. Siddons was an expert at playing Shakespeare's tragic heroines whereas her brother John Philip excelled in Shakespeare's male protagonists. Dorothy Jordan (1761-1816), actress, who even as a woman of 40 years of age convincingly played young romantic heroines, which may explain Summersett's hopes of her one day playing the part of Augusta. It appears that the character of the Marquis would become Altenburg; Victoria would become Isabella; Antoinette would become Augusta.

3   *a new Play . . . what I had then written and designed*: Summersett is referring to Kotzebue's play *Das Kind der Liebe* (1780), which translates into English literally as *Child of Love*. The play was adapted into English by Elizabeth Inchbald (1753-1821) as *Lovers' Vows* (1798). First performed at Covent Garden theatre in October 1798, it was, as Summersett suggests, a great success.

4   *Monthly Reviewers*: *The Monthly Review* (1749-1845) was the first periodical in England to offer reviews although Summersett may be referring to periodical reviews in a more general fashion. His previous novel *Mad Man of the Mountain* (1799) had not fared well in *The Anti-Jacobin Review* (1800).

4   Peregrine Pickle . . . Humphry Clinker: *Peregrine Pickle* (1751) and *Humphry Clinker* (1771) are novels by Tobias Smollett (1721-1771).

4   *Hamlet . . . very like a whale*: Here, Summersett likens the eighteenth-century critics to the court flatterer Polonius from Shakespeare's play *Hamlet*. Just as Polonius agrees with Hamlet's deliberate misconstructions of the shape of a cloud, Summersett suggests his critics will search for meaning and allusions that are far removed or unintended on his part. Furthermore, Summersett suggests that such criticisms are always inconsistent and contradictory.

11   *Venus . . . Minerva*: Venus is the Roman goddess of love, sex, and fertility. Minerva is the Roman goddess of wisdom. The tutor is more interested in Italian women (possibly prostitutes) than in gaining wisdom from study.

11   *Epicurus*: Greek philosopher (341 B.C.–270 B.C.), whose ideas about

pleasure, happiness, and tranquillity could be misunderstood and channelled into a purely hedonistic lifestyle.

26 *Schiller and Kotzebue*: Both men were admired by Summersett. Friedrich Schiller (1759-1805) was a German poet and dramatist. Schiller's plays are melodramatic in content. August von Kotzebue (1761-1819) was a German dramatist, writing over 200 plays. Like Summersett, Kotzebue's works were also charged with immorality by his opponents. Many of Kotzebue's plays are also of a melodramatic nature.

46 *the doctrine . . . himself visible*: The theory that man, out of self-love, attempts to ignore all of his faults since he cannot bear them being pointed out to him, was first propounded by Blaise Pascal (1623-1662) and recorded in the posthumously published *Pensées* (1669).

55 A very angry early nineteenth-century reader has written in the left-hand margin "False" and indicated with a line the offending passage in the novel. This is in the first edition copy housed in the British Library.

60 *Apollo . . . Adonis*: Apollo: In Greek mythology, the god of prophecy and poetry. Adonis: In Greek mythology, a strikingly beautiful young man.

65 *Bacchanals*: Followers of Bacchus, Greek god of wine; drunken revelry.

72 *toilet*: Typically a table or space where a woman would apply cosmetics and dress herself.

74 *Mercury*: Mercury is the Roman god of eloquence, communication and commerce.

75 *lancet*: A surgical instrument used for bleeding. Altenburg's self-prescription follows the contemporary medical belief that a man should bleed himself to remove ill humours.

83 *unities*: The unities of place, time, and action. Rules for drama outlined by Aristotle in his *Poetics*.

86 *Astræus*: In Greek mythology, god of the dusk.

87 *Channel into France*: As Shakespeare does in *King Henry V, King Henry VI, Part I* and *King John*. With regard to enchantment, Summersett is probably thinking of Shakespeare's late plays such as *Cymbeline, The Winter's Tale* or *Pericles*. All three plays require the swift passage of several years for their dramatic resolutions to take place. *Cymbeline* also features the heroine Innogen embarking on a voyage to Milford Haven.

107 *Laplander*: A native of the Arctic Circle. Summersett seems to suggest that a cold body invariably leads to a coldness of sentiment. David Hume in his essay *An Enquiry concerning*

Human Understanding (1748) had also mentioned a Laplander possessing "no notion of the relish of wine" as an example of an individual who has never experienced a certain sensation because the opportunity has not risen, ultimately lacking knowledge of that feeling.

126 *Arcadia*: A mountainous region in Ancient Greece idolised for its pastoral solace and peacefulness.

137 Dr. Johnson [Summersett's note]. Samuel Johnson (1709-1784), the great eighteenth-century author. The quotation comes from Johnson's *Rasselas* (1759), which charts man's illusory quest for happiness.

138 *Inns of Court*: Four separate buildings of the four legal societies in London training young men, in theory, for the legal profession. The four buildings consisted of the Inner Temple, the Middle Temple, Gray's Inn and Lincoln's Inn. Asterley has evidently begged the resident students of one of the Inns for these goods.

139 *Watch-house*: A house used to receive and detain any disorderly or suspicious people brought in by the watch.

139 *Link*: a torch for lighting people along the streets, often the occupation of young boys.

140 *Sirrah*: A term of contempt.

140 *Kennel*: The gutter in the street.

141 *Serpentine River in Hyde Park*: This river, in London, was created in 1730 at the behest of Queen Caroline.

141 *half a crown*: Equivalent to two and a half shillings (30 pennies). This is a very small amount for Asterley to receive for saving the life of a child whose mother is evidently financially well-off, hence his disgust at her stinginess.

144 In other words, Asterley contemplated suicide. As an act of self-murder, a person who committed suicide would be buried at the crossroads rather than in a parish churchyard.

151 *Encomiast*: One who praises or flatters.

169 *Storymongers*: A particular type of writer who exploits current literary vogues for quick financial profit, often at the expense of crafting a coherent or complete story for the reader. Narrative events may be concluded fairly swiftly, if at all. Summersett appears to be attempting to distance himself from such charges.

169 *Yesty*: Swelling; light and superficial. The *OED* cites Shakespeare's usage in *Hamlet* (V.ii.152) from the 1623 folio.

169 *Melpomone*: Melpomene is the muse of tragedy in Greek mythology.

9781941147061